THE HUNTERS

Staunton walked out into the field. He stopped about twenty yards in, squatted down on his haunches and stared back at the ditch where the girl's body had been found.

Then he was motionless for a while, absorbing the details of the place, picturing it in darkness, the girl, her screams muffled by the murderer's hand, being dragged along the inside of the hedge, struggling madly in the last moments of of her life.

He picked up a clod of dry earth, broke it in his hand and let the soil trickle through his fingers. He spoke out loud, aiming his words at his unknown quarry. 'I'm going to get you, you bastard,' he said.

The Hunters

Peter Hill

CORONET BOOKS
Hodder and Stoughton

Copyright © 1976 by Peter Hill

First published in Great Britain 1976
by Peter Davies Limited

Coronet Edition 1977

---

*The characters and situations in this book are
entirely imaginary and bear no relation to any real
person or actual happening*

This book is sold subject to the condition that
it shall not, by way of trade or otherwise, be
lent, re-sold, hired out or otherwise circulated
without the publisher's prior consent in any
form of binding or cover other than that in
which this is published and without a similar
condition including this condition being
imposed on the subsequent purchaser.

Printed and bound in Great Britain for
Hodder and Stoughton Paperbacks,
a division of Hodder and Stoughton Ltd.,
Mill Road, Dunton Green, Sevenoaks, Kent
(Editorial Office: 47 Bedford Square, London, WC1 3DP)
by Hazell Watson & Viney Ltd,
Aylesbury, Bucks

ISBN 0 340 21976 9

For George, who tutored and encouraged
For Pamela and Lena, who tolerated and believed

ONE

The pain smashed through his half-open eyes and ricocheted round his skull. The intense agony was made worse by the total inability of his brain to suggest a reason for this vicious and unexpected attack.

Easing himself gently back into a prone position, he tried to relax the muscles pulled string-bag tight by his panic reaction to the assault on his nervous system.

The pain slowly subsided, leaving a background of throbbing drums. It enabled him to make a serious attempt to rationalize the events of the last few seconds.

He identified the symptoms in what was, in the circumstances, a commendably short time. There was no doubt he had a hangover and from the shattering effect of his attempt to hoist himself into a sitting position, it seemed it was a hangover of monumental proportions. He relaxed further, eyes tight shut, relieved that so simple and likely an explanation existed. The drums faded into the distance to be replaced by a feeling of gentle nausea and when this too had abated, he ventured to investigate further.

Blinking to clear his vision, he panned his eyes left and right without moving his body. He learnt from his mistakes.

The bedroom was dimly illuminated by a pale shaft of early morning sunlight which filtered apologetically between the partly drawn curtains. His restricted field of vision revealed only the light blue ceiling, in the centre of which hung an ornate tasselled lampshade, looking too heavy by far for the slender links by which it was suspended.

His attention was caught for a moment by a spider, busily engaged in the construction of an interlacing pattern between the tassels on the shade, working methodically towards the creation of a minute masterpiece. He watched absorbed but incapable of speculation or aesthetic appreciation.

The noise which had first woken him had continued unabated, and now, dragging himself away from the contemplation of the spider's industry, he was able to identify the direction of its source.

Rolling carefully on to his left side, he took in the garish opulence of the bedroom furniture and finally concentrated his attention on the alarm clock, shuddering in its clamorous efforts to attract attention.

He slid his right hand out of the covers, let it hover for a moment, then dropped it on to the clock which thereupon subsided with a final, muffled buzz. His arm, for want of further orders, dangled limply down beside the bed, his fingers just touching the thick pile rug.

He stared uncomprehending at the jumble of female impedimenta that littered the dressing table facing him across the room. His surroundings stirred feelings of familiarity but clearly this was not his own flat. It did not seem to matter very much.

He executed a slow body roll to take in the rest of the room and should not have been as shocked as he was when this movement brought him hard up against his bedmate.

Leo came wide awake then and risked a recurrence of the pain in his head as he screwed himself upright to see who it was he had finished up with this time.

She was lying on her side facing away from him, her long dark hair covering her face, one arm thrown up across her chin as if in defence. She smelled of alcohol, hair lacquer, sweat and stale perfume. Her body, where it touched his thighs, was hot and damp. He felt the stir in his stomach, the start of an erection.

The voice in his head, his moralizing, critical and insistent alter-ego, broke through the alcohol barrier that had held it at bay and screamed at him.

'For Christ's sake, Leo, you can't feel randy.'

The patent untruth of this observation produced a flicker of a smile on Leo's face. The voice prodded him out of vain contemplation of his sexual capacity.

'Who is she? . . . find out who she is, you idiot . . . she may give you something you can't get rid of.'

At this sobering thought Leo moved away from her a little. She was breathing deeply and rhythmically, one broad limp breast exposed, the nipple dark brown and heavily wrinkled. Moisture twinkled dully on the hair under her arm which did not quite cover a large mole.

Recognition brought him relief from fear of disease. Paula Delaney owned and ran Paula's Place, an almost straight drinking club off Charing Cross Road. Paula was all right. Paula was clean. The voice in his head nagged him.

'One of these days you won't be so lucky. One of these days you're going to get stoned out of your mind and finish up in bed with some old crow who'll give you a right dose.'

Leo recognized the truth of this but felt on balance that at that moment he could have done without the moralizing. The voice was determined not to let him off the hook.

'So what about work, Leo? . . . Work!'

He turned away from Paula and stared at the clock ticking complacently to itself beside the bed. Half past eight it said. At least he would be in the office by ten, even if he were in no state to do anything when he got there.

He pushed back the covers and swung his legs over the side of the bed. After pausing for a moment to gain the courage to test out his legs, he eased himself uncertainly to his feet and walked stiff-legged to the bathroom door. He pushed it open and leant against the lintel as he felt for the cord of the electric light, pulling it down with unintended violence. The retaining screws gave a fraction under protest. The voice stated the obvious.

'You're going to pull the bloody thing down one day . . . it's the booze . . . affects the co-ordination see.'

Leo did see; he was, after all, familiar with the condition. He negotiated the narrow strip of carpet and sat on the edge of the bath staring at the sink.

The note, propped up behind the hot tap, stared back at him. He leant forward and picked it up with a hand showing a fair degree of shake.

The writing was large lettered, oval and rather untidy, more like the work of an eager schoolgirl than a mature woman. 'Good morning, Leo darling,' it said, 'you'll find the shaving gear on the table. The toothbrush is new, I just took the plastic cover off for you. There's aspirin if you want. Don't wake me, I've took a couple of sleepies, love, Paula.' A line of hasty crosses terminated with a P.S. 'You're still a good lay.'

A clever girl was Paula. She knew Leo well enough to accept that he would remember little of the previous night's events and men in general well enough to feel intuitively that they often needed the kind of reassurance the postscript contained.

Leo grinned to himself as he screwed the note into a ball and lobbed it in the direction of a flowered plastic bin. It missed. He gripped the sink and levered himself to his feet.

His face, or was it his? confronted him in the mirror. Thick blond hair matted with sweat, lined forehead, wide blue eyes with white full stops of mucus in the corners, a short straight nose with a fresh crop of blackheads round the base, full lips and a rounded chin now covered with a fair but heavy beard. It was not by any standards a pleasant sight and was more than his carping alter-ego could bear.

'Jesus, what a revolting sight. Where's the beautiful blond Adonis that started out last night for a few quiet beers? You're not yet thirty and you look fifty. You'll have to get off the booze Leo, it's making an old man of you. That and your adolescent attempt to lay every female you can in the shortest possible time. So what are you trying to prove?'

The question remained unanswered. Leo completed his toilet with mechanical deliberation, then gentled himself back into the bedroom where he found his clothes folded in a neat pile on a chair. He dressed slowly, taking care not to lower his head or move suddenly. He automatically checked his wallet, then moved round the bed to look at Paula.

Her face still wore yesterday's mask but, relaxed in sleep, it had taken on an air of innocence, a vulnerability that never showed in her waking hours. He pulled the bedclothes up round her neck, tucking her arm back into position beside her with careful gentleness. She slept on.

She was no longer any great beauty and all of ten years older than he. The grey light of morning played havoc with her defences and sleep had robbed her of the will and opportunity to fight against the onset of middle age.

Despite the intimacy they had enjoyed for the past two years Leo felt at that moment that he was an interloper, an unwilling voyeur and it engendered a twist of unease. The voice crept up on him unnoticed.

'Ugly, isn't she, Leo? A few more years and the fire will have gone out. All you'll get then is a night's kip and a couple of aspirins. Maybe that's all you really want . . . a bit of fuss . . . Mummy's boy.'

With an effort Leo put down the insurrection in his head and left the room. He put on his overcoat at the street door and stepped out into the morning, hunching his shoulders against a wind that was in truth inoffensively mild but which chilled him to the bone.

He wandered through the back streets, finally emerging in the Bayswater Road. He felt weak and light-headed, detached from the world around him, an observer, a non-participant. A lone taxi dribbled down the road towards him, the driver certain of a fare even before Leo raised his hand.

If the streets were strangely deserted for that time of day, the fact did not register with him. The voice in his head left him in peace and he lived for the duration of the journey in the strange, once-removed world of indifferent neutrality that is the least objectionable result of a surfeit of alcohol.

The taxi cut through the back streets of Victoria and pulled up at the rear entrance of New Scotland Yard. Leo paid the driver and turned to cross the front of the ramp that leads down to the underground garage. He tripped slightly on the kerb, adjusted himself and pushed his way through the heavy revolving doors that led into the reception foyer.

Fat John was studying a newspaper at his seat behind the reception desk. Fat John loved policemen. His gross body and limited intellect had denied him a cherished place as one of them so he had settled for a job as a civilian employee, a life with them but not part of them. It was his boast that he knew every face at the Yard and he took great interest in their careers, especially those he thought were going to the top. He selected budding senior officers with a flair and insight that in another man would have earned a fortune on the race track.

He had a particular soft spot for C.I.D. officers; they were, in his opinion, the élite. If asked to make a selection amongst them of the fastest rising star he would probably have plumped for Detective Inspector Leo Wyndsor even had he known that officer's present condition and the reasons for it.

As Leo entered the foyer Fat John flipped his newspaper under cover with practised ease and greeted him.

'Good morning, sir.'

Leo, unaware of Fat John's evaluation of his potential, grimaced in his direction and passed on towards the first bank of lifts. Fat John smiled patronizingly at his departing back as he retrieved his newspaper.

In the office on the fifth floor marked 'C.I. COMMUNICATIONS', Detective Inspector Ron Mount leafed in bored fashion through a year-old travel brochure. The long, green-topped desk at which he sat was immaculately tidy although three-quarters covered with telephones, reference and record books, roneo-ed instruction sheets, availability charts and message pads.

In one corner of the room a teleprinter clacked to itself behind a glass partition. In another, on a table, lay a pile of buff-coloured hard-backed books, mostly much handled and dog-eared. It could have been the communications office of any large industrial concern except that it was less opulent, less clean and had a pervading atmosphere of determined efficiency. This room was the heart of Scotland Yard's murder squad.

The only overt sign of this were the two large black pegboard sheets affixed to one wall, their white lettering standing out in relief. On one of them was indicated the whereabouts of the murder teams already operating, listing places as prosaic as Grimsby and as evocative as the Bahamas. On the other a list of numbers from one to twelve ran down one side, listing the order in which the teams in waiting would be called away. At the top of the list, coupled together, were the names 'Chief Superintendent R. Staunton' and 'Detective Inspector L. Wyndsor'. In the parlance of the murder squad they were 'number one'.

Ron Mount threw the brochure into a wastepaper basket and was enjoying a huge yawn as Leo Wyndsor walked into the room.

'Morning.' Leo's greeting was unintentionally curt. He walked across to the table and shuffled through the buff-coloured books.

Mount replied in like style but with an element of surprise in his voice. At forty-two Mount was balding and running to fat. He had no great regard for Leo Wyndsor and normally would have had little to say to him but now his curiosity was aroused. Why should Wyndsor have appeared in the office on a Sunday morning when he was supposed to be off duty?

Leo picked out the book marked '6 Squad' and flicked it open. He stared in disbelief at the legend at the top of the page, 'Sunday 7 August'. Could he really have been that drunk he couldn't tell one day from another?

'Yes,' said the voice in malicious delight. 'Yes, you bloody well could.'

Mount broke in on his thoughts. 'What're you doing here then?'

Leo turned to him and lied easily. 'Felt a bit edgy, thought I'd pop in . . . you know.'

Mount was incredulous. Leo Wyndsor exuded strength and self-confidence, gave no hint of the doubt and uncertainty that daily assailed him.

'Don't give me that crap,' said Mount.

'All right I won't.' Leo dropped the book back on the pile and walked out, leaving Ron Mount staring at his departing back.

Within half an hour Leo was entering his tiny bachelor flat. He went first to the telephone in his bedroom and dialled.

'At the third stroke,' the woman told him, 'it will be . . .' he cradled the receiver, satisfied. The voice in his head was not.

'Blew it last night, didn't you? If there'd been a call they'd never have found you, would they? You'd never have talked your way out of that one, clever dick!'

The open suitcase on the floor gaped at him as he stripped rapidly. It was full of newly laundered clothes, enough to last a month. As he had just been reminded, he had to be ready to leave in a matter of minutes when the call came.

He padded naked into the bathroom and flopped into the bath whilst the taps were still straining to fill it. Half an hour later, after a rough towelling, he was in bed and instantly asleep. It was 11.30 a.m.

The murderer was digging methodically, the spade an extension of his body as it rose and fell, turned, released its load and rose again. Sweat beaded his forehead, ran in rivulets down the side of his face and lost itself amongst the hairs of his broad chest.

He was a big man and the spade looked puny in his grasp. He worked automatically, with practised skill and economy of movement but none the less he was tiring. He knew it and it pleased him. He sought physical tiredness as the lover seeks the loved. It quietened the sexual urges of his muscled body, urges he was unable to control or satisfy.

He stopped work, leant on the spade, wiped the sweat from his brow with a tanned forearm and looked round his garden. It reflected the years of work he had put into it, neat rows of flowers in geometric patterns bordered immaculate lawns and slide rule paths, sturdy trellis supported floribunda and Peace, rock plants crawled in profusion and deceptive disarray, dahlias pushed proud heads up to the summer sun.

He derived no pleasure from the beauty around him. It represented so much work, so much tiredness.

Anne Partridge saw him as she hurried back to the Haywain, ready to start work behind the bar. She waved and smiled, he was a handsome man.

He watched her go, her haste pulling her light summer dress against her well-rounded body. It aroused no desire in him, the garden had done its work.

He started to dig again. He gave no thought to his victim. She lay where he had left her, ravished and torn, face up in a lonely ditch.

TWO

Chief Superintendent Robert Staunton did not like Sundays. What others regard as a well-earned day of rest was to him a bore, an unwanted excuse for idleness. He sat in an armchair staring morosely out of the french windows at the pocket handkerchief garden that huddled at the back of his small semi-detached.

Normally the garden pleased him, he fussed over it, encouraging the flowers, swearing at the weeds, watering, fertilizing and poisoning. He waged a constant and losing battle against an army of insect pests, decimating them on his few days off but during his frequent absences from home they re-grouped, bred in profusion and faced his next onslaught with apparent disdain. Now it irritated him, there was not a weed or bug in sight. It offered no further excuse to potter, to fill time.

Bob moved irritably in the chair in an attempt to find a position less aggravating to the haemorrhoids that had plagued him for years, but with little success. To him any illness was a sign of weakness, to be despised in himself even more than others.

His wife fluttered into the room, a frail pretty woman of fifty, two years younger than her husband. She knew this mood of his well. The waiting affected detectives in different ways, Bob was invariably morose and irritable.

She stood behind his chair, tickled the back of his bull neck gently for a moment, then moved away. She took a bottle of whisky from the sideboard and placed it with a glass beside him. She felt his boredom, his frustration, his anxiety. She loved this man.

'I hope they call you soon,' she said.

His hand moved slightly on the arm of the chair, she smiled and faded from the room to prepare his lunch as silently as she had come. The communication between them no longer relied solely on words.

Bob stood up, a short thickset figure with a shock of unruly iron grey hair. He poured himself a drink of healthy size and paced the small room as he sipped it.

It wasn't just the waiting this time, there was something else. He had twelve successful murder inquiries under his belt and was conscious he had come to be regarded as nigh on invincible. He felt it was right that he should be so thought of, he was after all the most experienced murder investigator in Britain; he had earned his reputation and enjoyed it, there was no false modesty in Bob Staunton.

As success had followed success however, the pressure had mounted. To the press, the public and even his fellow officers he was all but infallible, only Bob Staunton knew for sure just how fallible he was. He got through by dint of a wealth of experience, hard work and dogged attention to detail, he was no intuitive genius. He well knew that one day he would face the impossible investigation, no clues, no motive, no lines of inquiry, nowhere to start. He did not relish the prospect.

He finished his drink at a gulp and continued pacing. There was another worry, Leo Wyndsor. In the past he had been able to select himself the men he took with him, he chose officers he knew and trusted and who knew and admired him. With eight teams already away he had been paired with Wyndsor whether he liked it or not. He didn't.

Bob was prepared to grant that Wyndsor was good, he wouldn't be in the Department otherwise. He had the reputation of being lucky as well. You needed luck.

Unfortunately he was not particularly amenable to discipline and his attitude to senior officers had come close to insubordination. Bob wasn't sure he could get on with this young man who was not likely to afford him admiration and respect solely on past record, wasn't sure Wyndsor would be able to create the atmosphere in which he could work at his best.

He grunted to himself and poured another large drink, the first hadn't touched the sides. He dropped back into his armchair. This waiting made him morbidly introspective. Young Wyndsor would be licked into shape when the time came as many a cocky youngster had in the past. He picked up a detective novel and immersed himself in it. It was 12.30 p.m.

Deep in the Suffolk countryside Brian Cavell walked slowly along a hedgerow that bordered a field within sight of the river Orwell. He was a tall gangling lad of eighteen. A few adolescent spots still dotted his country face and the open-necked shirt revealed a tanned chest as yet devoid of hair. He looked awkward and ungainly but despite his heavy working boots he moved silently. His eyes roved the hedgerow ahead of him, his ears pricked for the telltale flutter that preceded the flight of his prey.

It had been a wasted afternoon, he had worked his way up from the river's edge without getting within range of a single one of the plump-breasted wood pigeons that normally abounded. He pressed on, determined not to go home empty-handed. He was unconscious of the brisk east coast wind that worried at his lank hair and fluttered the leaves of the thick hedgerow beside him.

By the time he reached the gate giving out on to the winding road that marked the border of his permitted territory, he was still no nearer filling the bag that was looped across his back. He stopped and shucked the old single-barrelled shotgun into a more comfortable position as he looked wistfully across the road. It was Joe Cracknell's land over there and Joe was notoriously short of temper with trespassers.

Brian swung over the gate and walked down the road heading back towards the river, still struggling with temptation. The gap in the fence invited him, he stopped and looked around, listening hard. He sifted out country sounds and isolated the distant hum of heavy lorries on the Ipswich to Felixstowe road, leading to and from the vast container docks at Felixstowe. With a bit of luck Joe Cracknell would be working in his vegetable garden, he usually did Sunday afternoons.

He turned quickly off the road, through the gap and along the inside of the hedgerow, doubly alert now, the spice of danger added to his quest. He had gone about ten yards when the sudden flash of sunlight at ground level caught his eye. He stopped and picked up the object from the grass in front of him, fingered the cheap shiny metal, then pulled it in two.

He recognized it now, his sister Rowena used these things to paint her eyebrows. He stuffed it in his pocket, a cheap enough present.

Rowena wasn't to know where he got it. He looked ahead and immediately saw the powder compact, the soggy pack of tissues, the lipstick, the black plastic handbag dirtied and gaping open.

His face screwed up in puzzlement as he walked slowly ahead, his quarry and Joe Cracknell's wrath forgotten.

He froze and the cherished shotgun fell unheeded at his side.

The body lay with arms and legs at unlikely angles, a discarded knitted doll, the face distended, flecked with the rubble of the hedgerow, the eyes stared blindly up at him, through him and away up to the powder blue sky. The shock emptied his brain but his legs moved, backing him away, turning, then picking up speed until he was running full pelt back to the village. It was 5 p.m.

Colonel Teddy Boulton was a worried man. He sat forward in his chair, head in hands, tweed jacketed elbows on his desk.

In front of him a cup of tea stood unheeded, getting colder by the minute. He puffed nervously at his pipe and stared into the middle distance. It was unusual indeed to find him in his office on a Sunday evening, but the circumstances had left him no choice on this day. A decision was called for, he had to make it and it could not be long delayed.

He had found life in the regular army much easier than the police force. You had clear rules, instant obedience, always a higher authority to refer to. As Chief Constable of the East Anglian Constabulary he had steered a middle course, avoiding contentious decisions and concerning himself mainly with the substantial administrative side of his work, leaving practical matters much to his senior officers.

It was a policy that had worked well, he had a contented and efficient force and was well thought of by those members of the public who came within his social ambit. Now he was within six months of retirement and after years of solid, comfortable and relatively uneventful success, the chicken had come home to roost.

Joy Louise Prentiss had disappeared. Initially she was dealt with as a missing person. After four days however, the matter had been brought to his notice and all the available evidence suggested that her disappearance had not been voluntary. He had placed his senior C.I.D. Officer, Detective Chief Superintendent Bruce Day, in charge of the case, with instructions to treat it 'as if it were murder'.

After a further two days no progress had been made and the press were yapping at his heels. He called a press conference and spoke for an hour during which time he said nothing. It had bought him time. He cherished the hope that the girl would turn up.

Now she had, and very obviously murdered.

He shifted his position in the chair, remembered the tea and took a sip. It was cold and had formed a skin which adhered to his moustache. He replaced the cup hastily and dabbed fastidiously with a handkerchief at his mouth.

The problem was simple but nonetheless difficult to resolve. Should he place his own man, Bruce Day, in charge of the murder inquiry or bring in Scotland Yard? If he took the latter course, Day would be upset at what he might well consider a slight on his ability and it might look as if Boulton was taking the easy way out. On the other hand the prospect of ending his career with an unsolved murder did not appeal. Day, although a capable officer, lacked experience of major inquiries and had already had the case in his hands for several days with nothing to show for his efforts.

He knocked out his pipe in the ashtray and dug at the deposit in the bowl with a penknife, scouring it absentmindedly and with rather more violence than was necessary. He tossed the problem back and forth as he re-stocked the pipe and lit it.

It belched out great gusts of smoke, signalling his decision. If he called in the Yard and they, the finest investigators in the world, failed, no blame remained with his force. If they succeeded some of the credit remained right here at home.

He reached for the telephone and put on his official voice.

'Get me Central Office, New Scotland Yard,' he said. It was 7.15 p.m.

Detective Inspector Mount was prone to profess at boring length to any who would listen his outrage at the salacious content of the popular Sunday press. Only the severe bulk of *The Sunday Times* was delivered to his house and that he scanned himself before the rest of his family were allowed to view its contents.

On occasions he would justify this censorship by quoting to them suitably edited examples of the offerings of the profane and pornographic gutter press and was usually gratified by the rapt attention afforded him. Under the circumstances it was regretfully necessary that he should now and then peruse such cheap filth in order to pass on to his family the benefits of his informed and considered opinion.

Thus it was that, when the telephone rang in the C.I. Communications room, Ron Mount was deep in an article exploring the social problems of a nymphomaniac lesbian and was interrupted just as that unfortunate lady was about to reveal how, at the age of fifteen, she was seduced by a fourteen-stone choir mistress.

He pushed the newspaper aside with a grunt of annoyance, picked up the phone and announced himself. The problems of the nymphomaniac lesbian faded from his mind and he sat up sharply as he listened to the Chief Constable of the East Anglian Constabulary.

He slipped out his pen with his free hand, pulled a scribbling pad across the desk and made curt notes. 'Ch. Cons. E.A. Constab. Rqst ass. Murder. Joy Louise PRENTISS. Age 20. Miss. 7 days. Fnd field Bacton Ford Sffk. Col. E. Boulton. Strangle-ligature.'

Before Colonel Boulton had finished his story, Mount was reaching for the notebook containing the home telephone numbers of the Department's senior C.I.D. Officers. Boulton was talking on now, his worries spilling out in the form of time-wasting verbosity. Mount politely cut him short.

'Thank you, sir, if you would confirm this by teleprinter immediately, I'll get things under way.'

He cradled the telephone and was already dialling the Commander C.I. by the time Boulton had realized that the conversation was at an end.

For the next few minutes Mount worked at top speed. He relayed the request and brief details of the inquiry to the Commander, leaving him to contact the Assistant Commissioner Crime for covering authority.

Whilst waiting for the Commander to ring him back with instructions to send for Staunton and Wyndsor, he checked the times of trains from London to Ipswich, collected cash for them from the Divisional Office safe and removed their names from the 'waiting' board replacing them on the 'operating' board beside the legend 'Suffolk – Murder of Joy Louise Prentiss'.

As he finished, the teleprinter started to chatter to itself in its glass cubicle in the corner. Mount walked across to it and watched as it typed up six copies of Boulton's request, now irrevocably committed to paper. The machine stuttered to a halt and he tore off the message, casting the carbon paper into a waste bin as he returned to his desk. He splayed the copies of the message in front of him and marked the top one 'A.C.C.' As he marked the second copy 'Commander C.I.' the telephone jangled at him.

To the Commander C.I. one more murder was no novelty, he was entertaining friends and had no time for idle chat. Having established that the request had now been confirmed by teleprinter he issued his instructions to call out Staunton and Wyndsor under the verbal authority of the A.C.C. This done he returned to his guests and dismissed the matter temporarily from his mind.

Mount took a few seconds to catch up with himself. Every telephone call he had made or received now had to be written out on a telephone message pad and filed in order. Copies of the teleprinter message had to be allocated to various senior officers for information and the last copy filed in C.I., later to be initialled by the Commander authorizing officers to be sent out of London.

These administrative matters attended to, Mount picked up the telephone yet again, this time to make the call that would bring relief to Chief Superintendent Staunton's itch for action.

Robert Staunton was slumped deep in his armchair, watching with mounting impatience as a television interviewer struggled to extract some small statement of a factual nature from an urbane politician determined not to say anything that was not capable of at least six interpretations.

'Idiot, bloody questions they ask.' His cockney accent gave sharp edge to the observation. In the chair opposite, his wife was industriously knitting baby clothes, a labour of love for a mounting brood of grandchildren. She answered mechanically, deep in a dream world of tiny toes and talcum powder.

'Yes, dear.'

'That bloody M.P. is walking all over that interviewer. Do better myself.'

'Yes, dear.'

On the screen, the interviewer gave up the ghost and with a sickly smile returned his viewers to the studio. A young man with obscenely perfect teeth promised that next they would see that ever-popular quiz game 'A Question of Truth' in which the resident team of three nuns faced a challenge on religious knowledge from students of the London School of Economics. The teeth seemed to think it was likely to be an excitingly balanced encounter.

Bob Staunton grunted his disgust and levered himself out of the armchair, intent on shutting the teeth out of his life for ever.

As he reached his feet the telephone rang and he changed direction, heading eagerly for the hall. His wife put aside her knitting and walked out behind him, leaving the nuns to answer their first question without an audience.

Bob barked into the phone. 'Staunton.'

'Inspector Mount, C.I. reserve, sir.'

'Yes?'

'Request for assistance from Chief Constable East Anglia Constabulary, sir. Girl of twenty been missing a week, found 5 o'clock today in a field. Strangled by ligature, no suspects. A.C.C. has given his authority.'

Mrs Staunton was already on her way up to the bedroom to prepare for her husband's departure, unhappy at the prospect of lonely weeks ahead but glad his waiting was over. Bob was deep in that other world of his in which she had no part.

'Car laid on?'

'I'll do that now, sir. Should be there in . . . about half an hour.'

Bob felt the excitement building up inside him but his voice was calm as befitted an old campaigner. 'Better ring young Wyndsor.'

'Will do, sir, see you here shortly.'

Bob's mind was already flickering ahead, recalling the little he knew of the County of Suffolk – Constable Country . . . strangulation by ligature, we've had those before. He pulled himself back to the present.

'Eh? . . . oh yes, right.' He replaced the telephone and skipped up the stairs as if he had suddenly shed a dozen years.

As he entered the bedroom his wife was already packing his suitcase. She smiled up at him.

'All ready,' she said. 'I've put in some cream for your bottom. . . .'

Bob cut her off, not wishing to indulge in an inventory of the more personal items she had packed for him. 'Right, I'll have a quick shave then, luv.'

He was gone for fifteen minutes and when he returned she had finished her task and was locking the case.

'Come on then, downstairs, good luck sherry,' he said.

It was a ritual they observed every time he went away, almost his only superstition.

He carried his suitcase downstairs, left it by the front door then joined his wife in the sitting room. She handed him a tiny drop of sherry in a miniature glass, they clinked and swallowed the liquid at a gulp.

'Good luck,' she said, 'I hope it goes well.' She replaced the glasses on the sideboard and went to him. He held her awkwardly in his arms. In the corner the teeth was announcing the result of the quiz. Nuns six, students nil.

'I see the nuns won then,' Bob said, but his mind was elsewhere.

In the C.I. Communication office Ron Mount was in no hurry now. Cars were on their way from the pool to collect both Bob Staunton and Leo Wyndsor. He had not yet telephoned Leo and was in no hurry to do so. He saw no reason for allowing Leo ample time to get ready, let him raise a sweat for a change.

He made out telephone messages of the Commander's call and his own to Bob Staunton, then as an afterthought, wrote out another anticipating his call to Leo. Since there was no other reasonable excuse for delay, he picked up the phone and dialled Leo's number.

At almost the very moment that Brian Cavell had found Joy Prentiss' body, Leo had woken from a deep and refreshing sleep. He got up and cooked himself a belated breakfast, faintly surprised at how hungry he was. The chore of washing up over, he wandered into the bathroom for a leisurely wash and shave.

The face that stared back at him now was related only in structure to the haggard horror that had faced him in Paula's flat that morning. He felt good, bloody good. The voice congratulated him.

'That's more like it, Leo. See what clean living does for you? Makes sense, doesn't it?'

For once the moralizing raised no counter of resentment in him. He combed his hair into place and splashed himself liberally with aftershave. The perfume drifted into his nostrils and added to his sense of well-being.

He picked up his pyjamas and padded back to his bedroom, leaving a trail of talcum powder across the fitted carpets. There was not a problem in the world except what clothes to wear and that required only that he decide where he was going that evening.

Maybe he would call Annette, she was teetotal and sex never had the debilitating effect on him that alcohol did. He dropped his pyjamas on the unmade bed and wandered aimlessly out into the living room where he put on a jazz record and flopped, still naked, into an armchair, letting the music flood over him.

The trouble with Annette was she talked so much. Even in bed, as if by talking about something else she could pretend to herself that she wasn't really doing it. He drifted into a reverie in which past exploits floated through his mind in delicious disarray. Maggie who worked for Qantas Airlines and had ridden him like an amazon queen ... Kate who always said no and was still saying no after it was all over.

The voice infiltrated itself. 'You could always have a quiet night at home – music, bring in some food, early bed.'

Oddly enough the idea was not totally unattractive. The matter was still not resolved when he was brought back to the present by the phone ringing in the bedroom.

Some sixth sense told him that this was it. He was already wondering where he was destined for as he picked up the phone.

Mount was not very forthcoming. 'The car will be round for you in ten minutes.'

'Where are we going, Mr Mount?' Leo's tone left no doubt that he wanted to know now.

'You're going moonraking, my son,' said Mount. 'Silly Suffolk. Twenty-year-old girl strangled. Missing for seven days, no suspects. Sounds like a tasty one.'

'Thank you for giving me ten minutes.' Leo banged down the phone and set about dressing in world record time. It was something at which he had plenty of practice, since facing suspicious husbands is difficult enough anyway without the practical and psychological disadvantage of being naked at the time.

When the car arrived he was waiting at the entrance to his block of flats, suitcase in hand, immaculately dressed and looking composed and confident. It was 8 p.m.

THREE

The 22.30 from Liverpool Street sped northwards from London, hesitated briefly at Colchester, an army town since the time of the Roman Legions, then pushed on into East Anglia.

Leo Wyndsor and Bob Staunton sat facing each other across an empty compartment. Staunton's eyes flickered up and rested on the bulkier of the two suitcases on the rack above Leo's head.

'That murder bag of yours straight, eh?' He stared hard at Leo as he put the question. He had decided to let this young man know just who was the boss right from the start.

Leo, uncertain as yet how to handle his senior officer, smiled politely back at him. 'Yes, sir, I put it together myself . . . it's all there.'

Bob grunted and shifted in his seat. 'It'll make a change if it is, mate. Last job I did we went to nick the bloke, nasty bastard he was, and we didn't have a handcuff between us.'

Leo pursed his lips and looked out of the window. 'I heard about that, sir,' he said. 'One of the other D.I.s raided your man's murder bag to keep his own straight.'

Staunton leaned forward and poked a finger in the general direction of Leo's chest. 'Right, and if I ever catch the git who did it I'll have his guts for garters.'

Leo gave a guilty start. Staunton's eyes seemed to bore through him, reaching into him for the truth.

'You did a pretty good job without the handcuffs, sir,' said Leo, trying to sound as if he were stating a fact rather than attempting weak conciliation. Staunton's grin held no humour.

'Yes, mate, I always do,' he said, 'and let's get it straight right from the start, so do you – or else.' The pointing finger came into play again, emphasizing where little emphasis was needed.

'When I say jump, you jump, if I want something done I want it done yesterday and I'll want to know where you are every minute of every day – you're gonna live in my pocket, son.'

'You won't have any complaint, sir,' said Leo defensively.

'Right, now how much did you draw from the imprest?'

'A hundred, sir.'

'Better let me have a fiver, I don't want to arrive skint.'

As Leo handed over the money the voice in his head giggled into life.

'He's got you taped, Leo. Hasn't he just. You won't talk your way round this chap. It's all work and no play this trip.'

Leo settled back into his seat and stared morosely out of the windows at the night-shrouded fields flashing past. He felt uneasy and resentful at Staunton's blunt words. It wasn't a good start. When he looked back a few moments later, Bob Staunton was fast asleep.

Detective Superintendent Bruce Day and Detective Sergeant Roger Cobbold were waiting when the train pulled in at Ipswich Station just before midnight. They were an ill-assorted pair, Day tall, slim and dapper, Cobbold short, plump, ruddy of face, his suit straining to contain his ample girth.

Bob Staunton bustled off the train, leaving Leo to struggle along behind him weighed down by his own suitcase and the murder bag. Five minutes later all four were driving through the centre of Ipswich with Cobbold at the wheel.

'Would you like me to bring you up to date, sir?' asked Day formally.

'No thanks, mate, we'll have a conference eight o'clock tomorrow morning, we can't solve nothing tonight, that's for sure. Have you got a place to set up an incident room? That's the first thing.'

Day, who was finding Staunton not quite what he had expected, answered rather stiffly.

'We've taken over the village hall provisionally, but I can arrange for you to have an office at Ipswich H.Q. if you would prefer.'

'It's not "you" it's "us", you're in this too, mate,' said Staunton positively, and then to Leo, 'Village hall all right, son?'

'Perfectly all right, sir.'

'Right, village hall it is then. Where're we staying?'

Sergeant Cobbold inclined his head back towards them without taking his eyes off the road.

'I did exactly what Inspector Wyndsor asked, sir.'

Staunton flashed a puzzled look at Leo. 'Oh yeah?' he said.

'He said you'd want to be staying at a pub, not an hotel, and as near the scene as possible like, so I've booked you two rooms at the Haywain. It's the only pub in the village, there's no other guests. Tom Stack'll look after you all, give you a key and that, so you can come an' go as you please.'

His comfortable Suffolk accent made it sound like an impending holiday.

'Are you quite sure that's what you want, sir?' asked Day. 'There are several very good hotels.'

'No thanks, mate,' said Staunton. 'The pub'll do me, I can't stand head waiters and the hours we keep don't suit hotels, besides you want to be on the spot, don't you?'

The car picked its way through the outskirts of the town and a few minutes later emerged on the A45 to Felixstowe. They passed a sprawling mass of industrial buildings on their right, the night hiding their uglier face. Day leaned back across his seat and pointed.

'Orwell Engineering, sir, that's where the dead girl worked. She was on her way home when it happened.'

They drove in silence for a couple more miles then turned right at a road sign pointing drunkenly to Bacton Ford.

The secondary road dipped and curved through trees and shrubs that screened the surrounding countryside and arched green arms above them. Cobbold drove fast, headlights full on, lining himself expertly for bends in the road that were invisible to the others.

Suddenly the trees cleared and there was a brief sight of silent, moonlit fields before they entered the village.

Bob and Leo stared out at the place that was to be their home for an unspecified period of time. The architecture varied from Tudor to Georgian, from Victorian to post-war but somehow a symmetry had been achieved, nothing looked out of place. It was as if a Methuselah among architects had designed the village as a whole but over a period of several hundred years. It was neat and tidy and the fact that few of the buildings had front doors giving on to the main street gave it a feeling of determined privacy.

'Pretty, ain't it?' said Staunton.

'We're only a few miles from Ipswich but it seems like the back of beyond,' said Leo, as the car pulled up outside the tiny village hall. Day nodded his head.

'They're a funny lot around here, keep to themselves, don't like strangers, as no doubt you'll find out.' Day sounded faintly bitter, it was clear his experience of the locals hadn't been encouraging.

Staunton levered his bulk out of the rear door of the car as Leo and Cobbold hauled the heavy murder bag out of the boot. 'You're not local yourself then?' he asked Day.

'No, I'm from Northampton, transferred here as Detective Superintendent a year ago. That's why I've got Sergeant Cobbold on the case, he was born and bred round here.'

Cobbold led the way into the small brick and tile building, making light of the heavy murder bag. The village hall was a single room with a tiny stage at the far end. On either side of the stage were two doors clearly leading to small rooms behind the stage. The main room was empty except for cheap folding chairs stacked round the side walls.

A single light illuminated the stage on which a plainclothes officer sat at a trestle table littered with papers, talking on a jury-rigged telephone. Behind him was a backdrop of an ill-painted woodland scene in which a number of slightly deformed animals capered round skeletal trees and unlikely looking undergrowth, clearly a hangover from last year's homespun pantomime.

Leo looked round and was unable to keep the dismay from his face. He had been hoping that he would find some kind of administrative system already in operation. One desk, one officer and one telephone wasn't even a start.

Bob Staunton read Leo's face accurately but ignored him and turned a broad smile on Superintendent Day.

'This'll do fine, you made a good start for us.'

Day relaxed a little. 'I'd been running the inquiry from my office, we only moved down here this evening so it's still a bit primitive I'm afraid.'

'No sweat,' said Staunton. 'Leo here'll have this place buzzing like a beehive in the morning, that's his job, you can forget all about it and get on helping me with the real work.'

Leo put on a bland smile, knowing Bob was simply putting Day at his ease, making him feel involved. You don't alienate the local officers, you are going to need them.

'Yes, sir, no problem,' he said, and then turning to Cobbold, 'if you could just drop the murder bag over there by the desk old chap, thanks.'

Staunton looked at his watch. 'Christ, it's half past twelve, time we went to bed. Give me a copy of the statements you've taken so far. I fancy a bedtime read.'

Day picked up a thick bundle of typed sheets from the desk and handed them over. 'Most of these were taken when she was just being treated as a missing person. I haven't seen the parents again since we found her body, I thought I'd better leave that for you.'

'Okay, fine,' said Staunton. 'We'll meet here at eight tomorrow morning. We'll have a conference and get things going, eh?'

'Very well, sir, Sergeant Cobbold will take you to the Haywain and introduce you to the landlord.'

'When's the P.M.?'

'The post-mortem has been arranged for eleven o'clock tomorrow morning and I ought to mention there's a press conference scheduled for ten.'

'What!'

Day was instantly on the defensive. 'I had no say in it, sir. The Chief Constable arranged it. He's had the press on his back ever since she disappeared, it's not been easy for him.'

Staunton rapidly recovered his composure. 'All right, mate, not your fault, I just don't want no one making arrangements for me I don't know about, that's all.' He punched Day lightly on the shoulder, 'Go and get yourself some kip, see you in the morning.' He looked round for Leo, 'Come on, son, let's have you.'

Cobbold drove them the few yards down the deserted main street and pulled up outside the tiny forecourt of the Haywain. The thatched roof of the old pub frowned down at them – a single light shone through the leaded window of what was obviously the main bar.

Tom Stack had the warmth and charm of the professional publican. He ushered them into the bar where Cobbold made the introductions and bid them good-night. They looked round the room and felt instantly at home.

It was dominated by a huge inglenook fireplace, an enormous stone and oak mouth, wide open in permanent welcome. The huge beams of the ceiling were a bare six foot above the floor, causing Leo to stoop slightly. A spray of fresh flowers sat bolt upright in a small silver vase on the oak table in the bay window.

The wood floor was worn away along the line of the solid oak bar where a million feet had scuffed and shuffled over as many pints of beer. You just knew that the heavy wooden handles of the old beer engines pumped up beer from real wooden casks in a cellar designed by men who really knew the temperature that beer needed to be at its best.

'Bloody lovely pub you've got here,' said Staunton in frank admiration.

'I really didn't think places like this existed any more,' said Leo. 'I can't believe it's not plastic.'

Tom Stack grinned, 'Nor did we till we found it and I promise you it really is three hundred years old and those horse brasses have really seen a horse. Have a drink?'

Staunton rubbed his hands. 'Wouldn't mind a quick Scotch,' he said, settling himself down on a bar stool.

Leo sat down alongside him, resigned to a late night and an early morning. Bob Staunton was renowned for drinking the night away and then leaping out of bed as fresh as a daisy after a couple hours' rest. A few days of that and Leo would have been dead on his feet. 'I'll have a half of mild,' he said.

Despite Leo's forebodings, half an hour later he was in bed in a room above the bar, just big enough to take his single bed, a wardrobe and a miniature chest of drawers. Having slept earlier in the day he was not tired and sat up preparing a list of the staff and equipment he would need to service the administration of the inquiry. The job really started the next morning.

He heard Bob Staunton banging about in his room next door, his heavy tread in the hall outside, then he appeared in his pyjamas at the door of Leo's room armed with a bottle of Black Label and two glasses.

'Time for a nightcap, mate, what you doing?'

'Just getting a few things ready for the morning,' said Leo, covering his surprise at Staunton's unexpected appearance.

Bob poured out two hefty drinks, handed one to Leo and sat himself on the edge of the bed. 'I've got a good feeling about this one, son,' he said. 'I think we're going to crack it.'

'I'll drink to that, sir,' said Leo.

'Tell you what you can do for me . . . take that press conference tomorrow morning. I can't be doing with the press before I got myself organized, you know what I mean? Just dish out a bit of spiel, keep them happy for me.'

'Right, sir, I'll give them some copy and stall them until the afternoon. Will you see them then?'

'Make it six in the evening.'

'Right, sir.'

'Look, I know you're going to be a bit busy tomorrow, but try and find time to knock me out an official press statement for them. We want them on our side but don't get in too deep, right?'

'I think I know what's needed, sir.'

'Tell them we'll buy a beer downstairs as soon as we get a chance.'

'Us buy *them* a beer?' said Leo, as surprised as he sounded.

'Just a manner of speaking,' said Bob grinning. 'I don't plan on actually paying.'

Leo grinned back, 'You had me worried for a minute then, sir,' he said.

Bob downed his drink and stood up, collecting the bottle with his spare hand. He scowled at Leo.

'I think you and me are goin' to get on okay,' he said, 'but get this, I want that office set up and running smooth as clockwork tomorrow.'

'It will be.'

'Night, son.' Bob Staunton and his bottle disappeared as rapidly as they had come.

Leo finished his drink, cleaned the papers off his bed, put out the light and settled down. After a few minutes the desultory noises in Staunton's room subsided and Leo drifted towards sleep to the quiet nagging of the voice in his head.

'You'll want three phones, no better make it four, one in Staunton's room – separate line. Now, three typists to start with, two checking statements, one on the index . . . if you get the crime squad they'll have their own transport so just one car . . . or maybe two . . .'

Not a mile away the murderer tossed and turned in troubled sleep, unaware that the hunt was on.

FOUR

Leo was woken just before seven the next morning by a noisy union meeting being conducted on his window sill. He lurched into a sitting position, leaned forward and tapped on the window. The starlings flew away to continue the discussion elsewhere.

He sat staring out of the window, entranced by the view that met his eyes. It was England's countryside at its soft, elegant, early-morning best. The rear garden of the Haywain had been lovingly tended. It was neat, tidy and laid out with precision into sections for flowers, vegetables and fruit. At the foot of the garden a wooden gate gave into a paddock of rough grass in a corner of which a pony was scratching itself with slow sensuous movements against the stump of an old tree.

Beyond the paddock, fields and hedgerows paraded into the distance and between a heavily wooded valley could just be seen the occasional twinkle of the river Orwell, the whole partially clothed in the remains of a morning mist. It was easy to recognize the timeless beauty that had captivated Constable many years before and which he had immortalized on canvas.

Leo dragged himself back to the present. Murder was always ugly but in this setting it was particularly obscene. The travelling alarm clock buzzed fitfully at him and he heard its companion in Staunton's room set up in competition.

He felt the stir of uneasy anticipation in his stomach. It was the same before every job, no better, no worse this time.

He appeared downstairs at seven-thirty immaculately groomed and dressed, briefcase in hand, to find breakfast laid out at table in the bay window of the main bar and Staunton already making heavy inroads into a large bowl of corn flakes.

He looked up as Leo entered and waved his spoon in the direction of the window, spraying the area round the table with milk as he did so.

'Bloody lovely, ain't it?' said Bob by way of greeting. Leo sat beside him.

'It certainly is,' he agreed.

'Get a good breakfast inside you, mate, start the day right.'

A few minutes later Tom Stack appeared with two plates laden to the sides with fried stuff. He seemed never to have heard about calories. Leo had just about got through it when Sergeant Cobbold appeared at the door. Bob Staunton greeted him in typical style.

'Morning, mate, ready for the off then?'

Cobbold was a little taken aback at the familiarity Bob displayed but grinned his consent.

'We've got a few minutes, give us a run through the village before we start, want to give my eyes a treat, get the smell of the place, right?'

'All right, sir, though there's not much of it to see to tell the truth,' said Cobbold, as if in apology.

He was right. Bacton Ford consisted of one hundred and four homes, three shops, one public house, one church and the village hall, all clustered round the main street with, perhaps symbolically, the church at one end and the public house at the other. The village hall and the shops being roughly in the centre of the village, facing on to an immaculately kept triangle of grass.

Within ten minutes they had travelled all the roads it offered and were back at the village hall, taking with them an impression of careful husbandry, almost fanatical neatness and quiet indifference to the world outside.

Detective Superintendent Day was waiting for them at the door and inside four plain clothes officers were milling around the stage area.

Staunton swept through the hall giving a wave and cheery greeting to the waiting officers. He led Day and Leo into the room to the left of the stage that he decided on the instant was to be his office. It was a small room, bare except for a stack of chairs and trestle tables against one wall, but the austerity was relieved by a large window that overlooked the village green.

They quickly set up a trestle table, took a chair apiece and went straight into the first conference of the inquiry. Bob Staunton took from his briefcase the bundle of statements Day had given him the night before and plonked them on the table.

'I've read that lot,' he said. 'Now, Bruce, tell me all about it.'

Superintendent Day sat back in his chair and ticked off the data in his mind as he brought them up to date, pleased at the rapt attention Bob and Leo gave him.

'Joy Louise Prentiss was twenty, she was employed as a canteen assistant at Orwell Engineering, you saw the place last night. She lived with her parents in a tied cottage about a mile outside the village. Edward Prentiss is a farm labourer working for a company called Anglia Farms. Mrs June Prentiss works as a cleaner at the Haywain. Joy was an only child. They're a hard-working, respectable family, who've lived here for generations. Joy had a boy friend, local lad called Paul Spender, works in the local garage, his father's the village carpenter, well, odd-job man. According to the boy they had a row two days before she disappeared, she called it off.' Day stopped for breath.

'Another man?' asked Leo.

'It's not likely,' said Day. 'Nobody knew of it if there was and in a small community like this it's hard to keep secrets. She wasn't too bright perhaps but she seems to have been a normal, healthy, well-adjusted and very pretty girl.'

He took a photograph from his inside pocket and dropped it in front of them. It was a stiffly posed head and shoulders shot of a young girl with dark hair, brown eyes and generous mouth. Joy Prentiss was indeed pretty and not far short of beautiful.

'That was taken a year ago. Anyway, she did shift work. Normally, if she was late finishing, young Paul Spender used to pick her up on his motorbike but since they had the row she took the bus or walked.'

'Hell of a long walk, wasn't it?' asked Bob. 'Bit dodgy too, late at night.'

'It would have taken her about half an hour or so, not long by country standards and she had nothing to fear, nothing ever happens around Bacton Ford.' The irony in Day's observation was not lost on the other two but required no comment.

'A week last Friday she left work at about eleven in the evening and was never seen again . . . at least not alive.'

'Did she get the bus?' asked Staunton.

'We don't know.'

'Okay mate, sorry, you were saying?'

'The following morning her father reported her missing and at that stage we simply treated her as a missing person.' Day became a little apologetic, 'After all she wouldn't have been the first girl to take off for the bright lights.'

'Nor the last,' said Leo, understanding Day's dilemma. Staunton nodded.

'Fair enough,' he said, and indicated for Day to continue.

'We made local inquiries and found nothing either way. After three days we circulated the photograph in our police area and two days later it was published all over the country in the Police Gazette. We had a few possible sightings but nothing came of them of course. We had the boy friend in but he couldn't help.'

'I see from his statement he reckoned she was involved with some other bloke,' said Staunton, tapping the bundle of papers on the table.

'Yes, he seemed genuinely worried. Anyhow, things stood like that until last night. Young lad named Brian Cavell was out after pigeons on land belonging to a farmer called Cracknell, sort of north-east of the village about three miles. He found the body in a ditch.'

'Strangled by ligature,' said Bob, in thought.

'Subject to what Professor Galloway says after the P.M. It seems she was strangled with her own tights, they were wrapped round her throat with a knot by the carotid artery.'

The three men sat in silence for a moment, absorbing the information. Staunton was the first to move. He scraped back his chair and stood.

'Right, let's get our backsides moving. Leo, Bruce and me are going down to the scene. Don't forget the press blokes and I'll want some maps of the area.'

'Right sir.' Leo stood briskly. 'I'll get on then, if there's nothing else.'

Staunton nodded at him and he left the room to start the unenviable task of breathing life and urgency into the empty and echoing hall next door.

A few moments later Staunton and Day were being driven out of the village by Sergeant Cobbold, retracing their path of the previous night, back to the main road. Bob Staunton plied the other two with a continuous stream of questions, checking how much had already been done, how much remained to be done and how much would have to be done again.

They turned right on to the main road and headed towards Felixstowe. The summer sun was gaining strength, dappling the road as it filtered through the tall trees on either side of the road and delicately touching on an enormous bank of rhododendron bushes on one side. It was a tranquil and beautiful scene but Bob Staunton saw none of it.

'There's no other road to this field then, we've got to go this way?'

Day hesitated for a moment, seeking the best words to describe the topography.

'The village is roughly in the centre of an oblong. The two longer sides are this road and the river Orwell. The two short sides are minor roads that run from this road down to other villages actually on the river's edge.'

'What about the road down to Bacton Ford then?'

'That just runs through the village and to a yachting marina at the river.'

'No roads running sideways, I mean like parallel with this one?'

'No, sir. Well, there are farm tracks, rights of way and so forth, you could get through to the murder spot from the village, but there are no roads.'

Two articulated lorries closed up behind their car, jockeying for position to overtake. Cobbold watched them in his mirror and made an angry face. 'Look at they, don't want to live, they don't.'

The huge vehicles pulled out and thundered past them no more than fifteen feet separating the rear of the trailer of the first from the cab of the second. The writing on the side of the containers was Spanish. Bob Staunton stared at them as they disappeared ahead. Day saw his interest.

'There's a multi-million pound dock at Felixstowe, it takes a lot of the container traffic to and from the continent,' he said.

Bob was thoughtful. 'This their regular route?'

'It's the only road to the dock from Ipswich.'

'Right, we'll have a road block on here and run it every night for a week. I'll get Leo to make up a questionnaire.'

'Just the lorries?'

'No mate, stop everything. Run it say . . . 6 p.m. to . . . 2 a.m. That should be long enough. You never know, somebody might have seen something.'

'That's going to take a lot of men, sir.'

'We'll use the Crime Squad. I'll fix it up when we get back to the office.'

Cobbold turned the car off the main road and soon they were back deep into the countryside. A few minutes later they approached a group of cars pulled half off the road nose to tail. A group of eager pressmen were being held at bay by a sturdy uniformed constable who guarded the entrance to a field. Bob Staunton grunted. 'Wondered where those bastards had got to,' he said.

As the car pulled up and Bob got out, the pressmen gathered round. He recognized some of the faces. The questions rained in on him, Bob looked carefully at his watch. 'I'll tell you this,' they fell silent, intent on his words, 'if you lot don't get back to the village you'll miss the press conference.'

They crowded him again, each asking just one more question, the result a cacophony of sound. It was too much for Bob. 'Look here you lot, get off my bleeding back, I've got work to do.' He immediately regretted his outburst, he might need them later. 'Look, do yourselves a favour, leave me in peace for today then we'll have a chat later, split a beer, right?'

One of the older men took charge. 'Right, lads, you heard what the boss said.' They followed the lead and disappeared back to their cars.

Bob led Bruce Day into the field and walked towards the roped off spot a few yards away. It was getting hot, he ran his fingers round his collar, felt the sweat building up under his armpits. As he approached the spot he saw that the area had been heavily trampled by many boots. Under his breath he cursed all thoughtless policemen and their regulation footwear. 'Bleeding idiots,' he said, aloud.

'I beg your pardon, sir?' said Day.

'Eh? Oh nothing.'

The murderer pulled hard on the oars and the six-foot dinghy moved quickly into the main flow of the river. The sun beat on his bare neck and arms and his mouth felt dry. He looked over his shoulder, lining the dinghy up from a mark on the shore, then pulled hard on the oars again.

Between his feet was an old, worn grinding stone and a little further aft a brown paper parcel, tightly wrapped and attached to the stone by a short length of half-inch rope. He was in a hurry, conscious that he could not be away too long, anxious not to be missed. A fishing rod, made up ready to use, stuck up over the transom, a mute alibi for his presence on the river.

There were men in the village now who spelt danger for him. He was angry. These men would try to hunt him down and it wasn't his fault. They would put him in prison, lock doors against him and he had done nothing. Another had used his hands, his body and done this bad thing. It was always the same, always he that was wrong, always he that had to lie and cover up. His eyes blurred with self pity.

He rested the oars inboard and looked around him. In the distance a dredger clanked its slow progress back up river waiting for the tide to fall, empty barges towed behind it like baby ducklings in file.

He grasped the grinding stone and the bundle and heaved them over the side. As they sank they took his anger and fear with them. He let the boat drift for a moment then took up the oars and pointed the prow of the dinghy back to the marina. It was all right now.

Leo was in the centre of a scene of frantic activity. Officers were assembling trestle tables round the walls of the village hall and in a double line down the centre of the room. Others were bustling about placing chairs, typewriters, filing cabinets and other administrative paraphernalia. Four post office workers were running cables along the walls, installing extra telephones. A desk, tables, chairs and cupboards were being set up in the back room Bob Staunton had chosen for his office.

In the sister room on the other side of the stage, now in use as a rest room for the staff, a plump and homely looking lady was setting up a portable gas stove and laying in enough stores to make a thousand cups of tea, as much the daytime fuel of the policeman as beer is the evening panacea.

It was a scene of chaos, seemingly no order would ever emerge. Periodically groups of officers arrived from Ipswich H.Q. and milled around until Leo found time to allocate them their tasks.

In the midst of it all he had found time to unpack the murder bag. That suitcase alone contained all the essentials to conduct the first couple of days of a murder inquiry, even if other assistance and materials were not available.

Its contents ranged from test tubes to statement paper and from index cards to thermometers. Most of these items Leo had already put aside. Since the body was already in the mortuary they would only be using the things needed for the administration of the inquiry.

He spent nearly an hour, in between interruptions, explaining the working of the administrative system to a grey-haired officer who had spent most of his service in the clerks' office of the Ipswich Traffic section. Sergeant Worthington did not get bored by paperwork and had no ambition to chase around the countryside tackling suspects. He was dour, humourless, meticulous, ideal for the job.

He soon grasped the basis of the method, a comprehensive card index system for absorbing and collating information from statements, messages, informants and local knowledge and holding it available for instant recall. It was a neat, tidy and highly functional system and it pleased Worthington's passion for order.

He was soon bustling about on his own account setting up his empire on the double line of trestle tables down the centre of the room, thus taking some of the pressure off Leo, who now set about a pile of books which he had brought with him.

They were already ruled up and headed, 'Action', 'Suspect List', 'Press Cuttings', 'Record of Searches', 'Log of Events', 'Record of Publications', 'Inquiry Allocation', 'Correspondence', 'Exhibits', 'House to House Inquiries' and a small one with the more prosaic title, 'Telephone Numbers'.

There would be others, made up as the inquiry proceeded. Leo worked rapidly, dealing with a continuous stream of questions, issuing orders, instructing, cajoling and infecting the others with his enthusiasm.

Despite the pace he remained calm and unruffled. When it came to work he had total confidence in himself and his ability and it was evident in every word, every action.

The press conference was a triumph of brevity. He read a short statement, parried questions for ten minutes then brought it to a close with a promise that Bob Staunton would talk to them that evening. By the time he had smiled the last one out of the building the hall had already taken on an air of purpose and determination.

Leo hesitated by the door, eyes roving the busy scene, mind flickering ahead to the million things that remained to be done. He heard the car pull up outside and a moment later three girls pushed past him into the room, chattering brightly and loaded down with typing and carbon paper. They were followed in by a young uniformed sergeant who grinned at Leo. 'Like you said, sir, I got the prettiest ones I could find.'

Bob Staunton found the Scenes of Crime Officer bent double in the ditch, his ample rear threatening to burst his trousers as he strained forward to take a sample of earth from beneath the spot on which the body had lain.

'Get your bum out of that ditch and let the dog see the rabbit,' said Bob, dispensing with formality. The red-faced officer scrambled back into the field and introduced himself.

'You here last night?' asked Bob.

'Yes, sir.'

'How was the body lying?'

'Flat on its back, half naked.'

'In a tight position, was it?'

'No, sir, splayed out. She died here and stayed here I'd say.'

Bob grinned at this exhibition of professional mind-reading. 'Hypostasis?'

'Yes, sir, the blood had drained down to the back, buttocks and back of the thighs, well fixed.'

'No rigor mortis I suppose?'

'No, limp as a rag doll, I'd say she's been here since the night she disappeared.'

'Reckon. Okay, mate, you get on.' Bob turned away to be faced by a gaunt angular figure whose uniform hung in a dispirited fashion from his shoulders.

'P.C. Trew, sir, plan drawer. Inspector Wyndsor said you'd want me here.'

'Oh, did he?' said Bob, surprised at the speed of the service.

'Yes, sir. That's what he said.' Trew sounded as though he doubted the wisdom of his presence.

'Well, he's dead right. I want a map of the area. Hundred yards all round where the body was in the ditch, right?'

'Very well, sir.' Trew made it sound as if he were being asked to map the catacombs.

'And I want another one of the whole area.'

'Exactly what area, sir?'

'The village. Bacton Ford. It's a sort of oblong, the river, main road and two side roads leading down to the two next villages, right?'

Trew screwed his skeletal face up in an effort of concentration.

'It could be described that way, sir.'

'That's it, then. That's what I want. Everything inside the oblong. Roads, paths, tracks, homes, pubs, farms and public toilets, the lot, right?'

Trew considered for a moment. 'Quite a lengthy task, sir,' he said eventually.

'Well, you'd better get your finger out then, mate. I want them tomorrow.'

Trew made a pained face. 'Very well, sir.' He turned away and walked back towards the gap in the hedge, his gait reminiscent of an undertaker's slow march. Bob stared after him as Bruce Day came up.

'Bit of a nut your plan drawer,' said Bob.

'He is a little strange but he'll do a good job.'

'Yeah,' said Bob doubtfully.

'Anything I can do, sir?'

'Yes, mate, drop the sir.'

Day hesitated, 'If you say so.'

'I do. Now . . .' Bob looked at his watch. 'Give me a few minutes on my own, then we'll go to the P.M.'

'Very well.' Day walked away towards P.C. Trew who was standing by the gap in the hedge, staring morosely along the ditch as if contemplating the enormity of the task he had been set.

Bob walked out into the field, stumbling occasionally as he trod across the dry earth that had been rough ploughed and left fallow. He stopped about twenty yards in, squatted down on his haunches and stared back at the ditch where the girl's body had been found.

It was hot now and he was sweating profusely. He undid the top button of his shirt and pulled his tie down a couple of inches, feeling the coldness of the sweat under his armpits as he moved.

Then he was motionless for a while, absorbing the details of the place, picturing it in darkness, the girl, her screams muffled by the murderer's hand, being dragged along the inside of the hedge, struggling madly in the last moments of her life.

He picked up a clod of dry earth, broke it in his hand and let the soil trickle through his fingers. He spoke out loud, aiming his words at his unknown quarry. 'I'm going to get you, you bastard,' he said.

FIVE

Ted Prentiss stared down at his daughter's body. It lay on the centre of the three raised marble tables that occupied most of the mortuary examination room. He had mentally prepared himself for the moment but it had been of little avail, he was close to breaking point.

There were two other men in the room, Bob Staunton and Professor Galloway, the pathologist. They waited in respectful silence. Her body was covered up to the chin by a white sheet, hiding the worst aspects of her ordeal from her father's gaze. Her face was still flecked with hedgerow debris and her dark hair matted and in disarray but her features were relaxed as if in sleep and bore no signs of the violence that had been inflicted upon her.

Her father's old muddied boots scuffed the marble floor and his ragged shirt cuffs rode up his wrist as he leant forward to touch her hair in a last painful gesture of farewell. His brown lined face was stiff with attempted control, only a flickering of his cheek muscles betraying the effort required.

His hand dropped limply to his side. He seemed to age before the watchers' eyes. He tore his gaze from his daughter's face and looked up at Staunton. He saw sadness, sympathy and determination mirrored in the policeman's eyes.

'It's my daughter,' he said simply.

Bob Staunton took his unresisting arm and led him out of the door.

Professor Galloway cleared his throat loudly to dispel the atmosphere of timeless sorrow, then bustled around preparing the instruments of his trade.

Staunton led a procession back into the room consisting of Bruce Day, Sergeant Cobbold, who had been given the unenviable task of dealing with the samples taken from the body, the police photographer and the mortuary assistant, a thin, stooped man of indeterminate age and unpleasantly eager eyes.

'Right, gentlemen, let's get to work, shall we?' As he spoke Professor Galloway stripped the white sheet off the body. It was still as it had been found, the clothing in disarray, muddied and damp, the only addition a white tag tied to the right big toe stating coldly the name the body had borne in life.

The photographer stepped forward on cue and took the first of a series of pictorial records of the post-mortem. Galloway removed the items of clothing from the body one at a time and handed them to Sergeant Cobbold who placed them in separate plastic bags and tagged them for identification. The body, naked now except for the tights knotted round the neck, stimulated none of them except possibly the mortuary assistant.

Professor Galloway stepped back to give room for the photographer and looked across at Staunton.

'No underpants,' he said.

Staunton looked at Superintendent Day. 'Were they at the scene?'

'No, not to my knowledge.'

Staunton bit down his anger, the man should have known one way or another. He turned to Sergeant Cobbold who was busy stuffing a brassière into a plastic bag.

'Sergeant Cobbold.'

Cobbold looked up inquiringly, 'Sir?'

'Seen her knickers?'

'No, sir,' said Cobbold, looking rightfully puzzled.

'Not in her handbag then?'

Cobbold saw the direction of Staunton's thought.

'No, sir,' I emptied it last night.'

During this exchange Professor Galloway had been bent low over the body, examining every inch minutely, pinching, prodding, pushing arms and legs about with immodest unconcern. He took a vaginal swab and handed it to Cobbold.

'There's bruising round the inside of the thighs and a couple of scratches. I think you'll find there was completed sexual intercourse, probably seminal stains on her clothing and his.'

He splayed the legs open, took a sample of pubic hair, then moved up to the head, leaving the photographer to record the tell-tale marks he had indicated. After this had been done, Cobbold stepped forward to take the dead girl's fingerprints.

Superintendent Day leaned forward towards Staunton and whispered. 'Why should they have been in her handbag?'

Staunton grinned at him. 'Didn't you ever have a bit of nookey in the back of a car?'

'Er, well . . .' Day stopped in confusion.

Staunton saw that he really did not know. 'If they take their own knickers off they always put them in their handbag, don't they?'

'I thought that was a joke,' whispered Day.

'I promise you it isn't,' Bob replied, his attention on the pathologist who had opened the mouth and was fishing about inside with a pair of forceps.

Day leaned close and whispered again. 'How did he pick out those scratches and bruises? The whole body's covered in scratches, bruises and lumps.'

Staunton looked at him hard but Day was obviously genuinely puzzled. For the first time Bob realized the extent of his colleague's inexperience. He sighed inwardly but his reply gave no hint of his annoyance.

'The body's been in an open ditch for a week. Flies lay eggs under the skin, they've hatched out into maggots, that's what most of the lumps are. The other marks are mostly where the animals have been at it.'

Day shuddered visibly. 'Animals?'

'Mice, voles, beetles, birds even . . . it's all meat to them, ain't it? That's why our professor here runs around in a Rolls-Royce . . . he can pick out the natural marks from the unnatural ones, see?'

Obvious though these things were in retrospect there was really no reason why Day should even have considered them before and considering them now in no way helped the feeling of nausea that was gradually overtaking him.

Professor Galloway grunted in satisfaction and straightened up as he pulled a piece of coloured material from the mouth with the forceps. He held it up for them to see.

'I think we've found the knickers,' he said, sounding as satisfied as if he had just filled in the last clue in *The Times* crossword.

Three-quarters of an hour later Professor Galloway stood at the sink washing the blood from his rubber gloves. In the course of his examination he had found two separate bruises to the front of the head above the hairline. He had cut the skin across the forehead, peeled back the skin and hair and revealed the brain by sawing through the skull bone.

There was no sign of damage to the brain and the bruising was only skin deep. The stomach was incised and opened from rib cage to crotch, revealing further bruising and slight internal damage in the area of the lower stomach.

During the post-mortem the conversation had been limited to brief commands and short professional comments. Now the mortuary assistant was sewing up the ravaged body as best he could with quick methodical movements. His hands, lacking the sophisticated barrier of gloves, were reddening as he worked. He did not seem to mind.

Sergeant Cobbold labelled the last of the samples from the body, fingernails ripped from the hands by heavy pincers. These sad relics now nestled, blood flecked, each in its own separate glass phial.

The heavy, sickly smell of partly digested and decomposed food had pervaded the room from the moment the cut had been made in the stomach and it had been the last straw for Superintendent Day. He had left at that moment.

Bob Staunton waited patiently for Galloway to speak. The pathologist stripped off the rubber gloves and started to wash his hands. The mortuary assistant tied off the last knot and set about cleaning off the body, dousing it in water and scrubbing at it with an old cloth.

'I could do with a beer after that,' said Galloway, vigorously drying his hands on a thin cotton towel.

'No doubt, sir,' said Bob patiently.

'My report will say that she was suffocated.' Galloway, having enjoyed keeping Bob in suspense for a few moments, now pushed on with his explanation.

'The ligature round the neck certainly constricted the breathing and would have reduced her capacity to fight back but there are no bones broken and as you could see for yourself, it left only a fairly light bruise ring. Given the amount of pressure applied, it could not and did not cause death. There are some faint marks on the left cheek which may have been caused by him holding her head down with his left hand, and preventing her breathing through the nose. When he jammed her knickers down her throat that was the end.' Galloway flipped the towel aside, removed his white coat and donned his jacket as Bob chewed this over.

'The body was found about two miles off her route home. She was probably picked up in a car, if she didn't go willingly I'd have expected her to put up more of a fight. Somehow he got her off the road, into a ditch, tights off and round her neck.' Bob looked at Galloway hopefully.

'I said the ligature would have incapacitated her but it may not have been the first thing that did.' Galloway stopped, clearly unwilling to speculate further. Bob took his arm and led him slightly away from the others.

'Look, mate, this is just between you and me, one guess from you is worth ten facts from someone else right now. Just give me an idea of how you reckon it happened.'

Galloway winced a little at the familiarity of Bob's approach but was mollified by the implied compliment.

'Well now, it could have happened this way. He stops his car and invites her in, she refuses. He strikes her a hard blow in the stomach, you saw the bruise, a blow that hard would have stopped a horse. It would have been enough to prevent her putting up any real resistance until he had driven to the spot. He probably half carried, half dragged her into the field, hit her twice more on the head . . . and the rest you know.'

Bob mentally cursed for the second time the heavy-footed policemen who had trampled the field before he arrived.

'Are we looking for a weapon?' he asked.

'I doubt it. I'd guess he used his fists.'

'A big man, you reckon?'

'Very difficult to say. It was a tremendous blow to the stomach and from what you say he must have carted her twenty yards or so as almost dead weight. She weighs about eight stone . . . I'd say he's probably of more than average strength but that doesn't help you much, does it?'

Bob scratched his chin. 'Not much,' he said, deep in thought. 'Well, what about the sixty-four-thousand-dollar question?'

'Time of death?'

'Yes.'

'Well. Let's say for the moment . . . about a week.'

'The night she disappeared then?'

Galloway made a face. 'You're trying to tie me down.'

'Right,' said Bob, grinning.

'Probably.'

'Between say, eleven o'clock and . . .?'

Galloway shook his head. 'I can't tell you.'

'If I said she died between 11 p.m. and 3 a.m. on the night she disappeared would you argue?'

'No.'

'That's good enough. One other thing . . . was she a virgin before the attack?'

'No. The hymen had been ruptured some time before but it was well healed. She had had sexual intercourse I'd say but not frequently and probably not recently.'

'Uh huh!'

'Well, if that's all . . .'

'Can you tell me, was this a murderer who threw rape in as an afterthought or a rapist who committed murder?' Bob saw that Galloway was preparing to decline to give an answer. 'Look, I know you're not a headshrinker . . . off the record, just going on your experience and looking at the body . . . eh?'

Galloway looked across the room but the mortuary assistant and Sergeant Cobbold were lifting the body on to a trolley and paying no attention. 'Between you and me . . . I'd say he is a sexual deviant. The ligature wasn't intended to kill, he may be one of those who can only achieve a climax when the female is partly asphyxiated, it's not common but I've come across cases before. If I'm right there would be no question of an intent to kill, he would be incapable of making such a decision one way or another whilst he was in the act.'

'Makes sense. It's obvious we're looking for a nutter.'

'By any definition he will be insane but don't expect to find him drooling at the mouth.'

'Suppose I got six suspects, from the medical angle how do I pick him out?'

Galloway shook his head. 'Sorry, it's not that easy. He's likely to be at least partly impotent, probably schizophrenic, a quiet type perhaps, introverted . . . but these things wouldn't be obvious to even a trained observer if he wanted to keep them hidden and you can't arrest all the introverts in Suffolk.'

Bob grinned and punched him lightly on the shoulder. 'Thanks, you've been a great help.'

'For a moment there I thought you were going to call me "Doc",' said Galloway, moving away.

'I wouldn't do that,' said Bob to his retreating back. 'It wouldn't be polite . . hey, when'll I get your report?'

'Two days,' said Galloway, on his way out of the door.

Bob discovered himself to be alone except for Cobbold, who was packing the last of the sample phials carefully into the large holdall he had brought for the purpose. The room was once more spick and span after the attentions of the mortuary attendant who had wheeled his charge off to the refrigerator whilst Bob was engaged with the pathologist.

'Done this job before, son?' asked Staunton of Cobbold's back.

The sergeant turned to face him and hitched up his trousers which had slipped down below his paunch. He spoke slowly, rounding his vowels in the local accent.

'No, sir, this is the first time and I won't be sorry if it's the last.'

'Don't worry, mate, you've done a good job,' said Bob, suspecting a little encouragement was in order. Cobbold nodded slowly and indicated the holdall.

'Thank you, sir. With your permission I'll take this lot straight to the laboratory. Perhaps Mr Day could drive you back.'

'Yes, mate, you get off, see you back at the office later.' Staunton followed Cobbold out into the hallway where Superintendent Day was waiting for him. He sensed his embarrassment and, remembering back many years to the first time he himself had attended a full-scale postmortem, knew how he must be feeling.

The car had stood for an hour in the hot sun and it was like stepping into an oven. Bob Staunton felt the sweat building up and squirmed in discomfort from his haemorrhoids as they drove in silence back towards the village. Eventually Day spoke.

'I'm sorry . . . I should have stayed.'

Bob wasn't in the mood to play confessor.

'Forget it.'

'It's just . . . I'd have been sick . . . when he cut open her stomach . . . the smell . . .'

Bob stared straight forward through the windscreen, totally unaware of the sunbathed country landscape through which they were driving. His mind was elsewhere and when he spoke his comment was automatic.

'Yeah . . . nasty business murder, isn't it?' he said.

They arrived back at the village hall at noon to be greeted by a scene of chaotic but intense activity. The three typists had been allocated a trestle table apiece along one wall and their machines chattered in rapid staccato voices. On the centre table stood two file cabinets and four uniformed policewomen in shirtsleeves sat in front of them checking the newly typed statements, extracting information from them, entering it on to index cards and filing the cards in the multi-drawer cabinets.

The plump tea-lady was bustling impatiently amongst the action, collecting up empty mugs. On the stage the grey-haired Admin. Sergeant, revelling in his new role, was talking rapidly on one telephone whilst writing furiously on a message pad and beside him another officer was trying to talk into two telephones at the same time, juggling the handsets between ear and chest.

Bob Staunton strode through the hall, eyes everywhere, noting the progress that had been made in his absence. He led Bruce Day straight into the office beside the stage where the change was even more dramatic. In place of the trestle table was a heavy wooden desk with a comfortable chair and two telephones, one an extension from the hall outside, the other a new direct outside line.

There were pencils, ball point pens, correspondence trays and scrap paper to hand on the desk top. The room was furnished with a table, filing cabinets and upright chairs. The inside wall was partially covered by a large sheet of soft-board pinned to which was a large-scale map of Suffolk.

There were curtains at the windows and carpet on the floor. It was the final sign that the empty echoing Bacton Ford village hall had ceased to exist and in its place was the hub of a full-scale murder inquiry.

As they entered the room Leo was sitting at the desk reading through a pile of typed statements. He stood at their entrance and Bob Staunton's grunt of approval as he looked round the room did not escape him.

'How's it going then?' asked Bob.

'Not too bad, sir. We're processing the statements that have already been taken at the moment. I've just finished looking through them.'

Bob took his seat at the desk and felt it for size, then he grinned up at Leo and inclined a thumb towards the hall. 'See you got plenty of crumpet working for you then.'

Leo detected a faint edge in Bob's voice and decided a flippant reply was not in order. 'It has been my experience that women are better than men on the card index. In general they are neater, quicker and they don't get bored with the work as men tend to . . . as for the typists, well, male typists are thin on the ground, sir. . . .'

Bob grinned up at him. 'All right, son, only a joke, don't get all serious on me . . . just teasing . . . you shouldn't have joined if you can't stand a joke. . . .'

Leo smiled guardedly. 'Sorry, I just couldn't think of a funny answer . . . would you like a cup of tea, sir?'

Bob consulted his watch, then shook his head. 'No thanks, mate, we'll have a quick conference, then pop over to the pub for lunch.'

A man walked straight into the office and came to an abrupt halt when he saw the assembled company. He was short, thick set, with stiff bristling grey hair which was at odds with a bushy jet-black moustache.

Leo stepped forward to introduce him. 'Detective Inspector Stan Grace, sir,' he said to Bob. 'Regional Crime Squad. I asked him to pop in to see you in case you wanted to use his lads.'

Staunton and Grace shook hands and took stock of each other the while, both apparently being satisfied with what they saw.

'Glad to have you with us, mate,' said Bob.

'My boss sends his regards, sir,' said Grace. 'Mr Pilborough.'

'Good grief . . . Pinky Pilborough, how is the old devil?'

'In great form I'm glad to say.'

'How many men have you got?'

'None at the moment, sir. I just came to see what you'd be wanting. You can have as many as you like within reason, just by picking up the phone.'

'That fine . . .'

Bob was interrupted by a knock on the door closely followed by the substantial bulk of Sergeant Cobbold. 'Sorry to interrupt, sir, I've got the fingerprint officer with me . . . I thought you might want to speak to him.'

'Yes, mate, wheel him in,' said Bob.

Cobbold entered, followed by a dapper little man in his mid-thirties. 'P.C. Carter, sir,' said Cobbold.

'What you got to tell us?' asked Bob, poking a pencil indelicately in one ear to dig at a reluctant blob of wax.

'Nothing worth the listening I'm afraid, sir,' said Carter, his concentration wavering a little as Bob removed the pencil and examined the waxed end as if he hated it. 'I printed the body and the rest of her family last night . . .'

Bob wiped the pencil with a piece of scrap paper, which he then discarded into a waste bin. 'Yeah?' he inquired, now giving Carter his full attention.

Carter moved forward and carefully placed on the desk the plastic bag he had been holding behind him as he entered. Inside was a black handbag dusty with white fingerprint powder.

'This is all we had to examine. All the prints go out to the dead girl. There are a couple of smudges but I couldn't pick out more than half a dozen points between them, sorry.'

'Reckon they're hers as well?' asked Bob.

'No, sir, they're too large over all, probably male but I couldn't be sure of that even.'

'Okay, mate, we can't win 'em all.'

'If you come up with anything you'd like me to look at, sir, I'd be only too willing to come out any time.'

'Thank you, Mr Carter,' said Bob. 'Let's hope I get the chance to give you a call.'

Carter nodded and left, closing the door behind him and shutting out the clatter of the typewriters.

'Right, get yourselves seated and we'll get down to it . . . open that window, Mr Cobbold, it's getting bloody hot in here.'

They settled themselves into chairs as Bob started to scribble notes.

'Can I cover a couple of things before we start, sir?' asked Leo.

'Yes, mate,' said Bob without looking up.

'The office is ready to roll as soon as the statements start coming in. The statements that have already been taken will have to be taken again to conform to the format required by the Director of Public Prosecutions.' Leo hesitated and looked at Superintendent Day. 'Sorry about that, sir, but no way round it I'm afraid.'

Bob blessed him mentally for letting Day down lightly. In fact they lacked the detail necessary in a murder investigation and a number of important points had been glossed over or omitted. Day gestured with his hands in mute acceptance.

'There is a press conference at six tonight as you asked, sir, and I have prepared a statement for you.' He handed a single typed page to Bob who scanned it quickly. 'Thereafter I told them we'd have two a day until it cools off, 10 a.m. and 4 p.m. when possible, but I can take those if you like.'

'Where do we see them?'

'In the entrance lobby I'm afraid, sir, a bit cramped but we can't have them in here or the main office.'

'Dead right we can't.' Bob discarded the sheet Leo had provided for him and looked up.

'That it?'

'I've prepared a questionnaire in case you wanted to set up a road block on the main road . . . this is a copy for you to check.' He slid a second typed sheet in front of Bob.

'Where d'you keep your crystal ball?'

'In the murder bag, sir, it's part of the standard equipment.' They grinned at each other and for a moment the other officers in the room felt excluded. 'Last thing, sir, there is a photocopy machine at Ipswich H.Q. and we have the use of it at any time we wish.'

'Right . . . now point one arising from the P.M. The bloke we're looking for is a nutter. The doc reckons he's an introvert, quiet type probably, quite normal most of the time but probably gets his pleasures by strangling the women he has when he's on the job – not killing you understand, just enough to take the wind out of their sails – but this time it went wrong.

'He's likely to be a fairly big bloke and it's my bet he's local but we'll keep an open mind on that. Now, time of death was probably between 11 p.m. and 3 a.m. on the night she disappeared. So we start at the beginning. Mr Day . . . I want a statement from everyone who works at Orwell Engineering, from the boss to the floor cleaner, make sure we cover their movements from 6 p.m. that night to 6 a.m. the morning after the murder. Pick up all the gossip you can as well.'

'Very well, sir. What about manpower?'

'Can you arrange that, Mr Grace?'

'I'll do it if you like, sir,' the Crime Squad man offered.

'No, I've got another job for you, put ten men under Mr Day and leave them with him till it's finished.'

'Right, sir,' said Grace, not sorry to have avoided days of repetitive statement-taking in a factory office.

Superintendent Day on the other hand was looking quite happy at the prospect. Staunton had rightly judged that he preferred the more clearly defined and less earthy parts of the inquiry. Bob ploughed on.

'Now, we have to be sure if she boarded the bus home or not, the chances are she walked it and was picked up in a car but we have to know, so we want a public appeal for all the passengers on the bus . . . eleven-ten, wasn't it?' He hunted amongst the statements.

Sergeant Cobbold pulled a dog-eared timetable out of his top pocket. 'Eleven-nine, sir, if it was on time,' he said.

'Right, I'll put that in my statement to the press tonight then.'

'It's already there, sir,' said Leo, 'last paragraph but one.'

Bob hardly stopped in his flow. 'That's it, then. Bruce, your lads at the factory can cover that as well, give 'em some fresh air. So, next we'll have a road block on the main road. That's your job, Mr Grace ... here's the questionnaire, get it photocopied and sort out how many men you'll need. Run it 6 p.m. to 2 a.m. for one week from today. Deal with any follow-up inquiries yourself and liaise with Leo here on it.'

'What about the daytime, I don't want my lads getting soft doing an eight-hour shift, they might get to like it.'

Staunton grinned. 'That's the next bit, mate. Sergeant Cobbold here is a local lad so he's going to be in charge of taking statements from every person in the village and he'll need some help. The only ones you won't do are the parents and any we designate as suspects, like the boy friend for example.'

'D'you want to see him, sir?' asked Cobbold.

'Not yet, if he's innocent tomorrow will do, if he's guilty it won't harm to let him sweat for a day. Leo, get this lot put into the action book after lunch and booked out to these three gentlemen to deal with. Oh, and put you and me down to see the parents this afternoon.'

'Right, sir,' said Leo, scribbling hard.

'One last thing, they say in this game that if you haven't got your villian two weeks after the murder you're in trouble. I've never believed that and it's not so in this case. I've got a feeling in my water we're going to nick him, so get your heads down and your fingers out and we'll be having a drink to celebrate within a month, stand on me.' He looked ostentatiously at his watch. 'Time for a quick beer and sandwich over the road, I'm buying for once.'

Superintendent Day and Inspector Grace made their excuses and declined the offer, each for his own reasons. Day was no great drinker, feared a heavy lunchtime session, and was in any event anxious to get on with his allotted task in order to show Staunton that what he saw as his poor showing at the post-mortem was not typical of his over-all ability. Grace had to round up twenty men and get them to work that afternoon and with him it was strictly business before pleasure.

Bob Staunton led Leo and Roger Cobbold across the triangle of grass from the village hall and down the road to the Haywain. The lounge bar struck pleasantly cool although it was fairly crowded, one section of the bar being completely taken up by a group of about ten reporters.

They looked up as the policemen entered, but no doubt chastened by their first brush with Staunton earlier that day, made no attempt to join them. Bob waved the others to an unoccupied window seat and joined them within a few minutes with three pints of cold draught beer and a large plate of sandwiches.

There was silence as all three savoured the ecstasy of this first pint. Leo rested his three-quarters empty mug first and looked round the bar.

Apart from the gaggle of pressmen there was a fair smattering of what he took to be locals and behind the bar Tom Stack was being kept busy as was the barmaid, a well-built girl of about twenty with short dark hair and a ready smile. Her eyes picked their way through the throng of customers and found Leo's, they made a promise clear and obvious before she ducked away to serve one of the reporters.

The voice in his head woke to the danger. 'She's probably as thick as two planks and doesn't wash her underarms.' Leo grinned to himself and, seeing the others had finished theirs, downed the rest of his pint.

One of the pressmen detached himself from the group and found his way across to the three officers. He looked briefly at Cobbold. 'Hello, Roger.'

Cobbold nodded up at him, a little apprehensively. 'Hello, Dave,' he said. 'Dave Bull, sir, *Ipswich Herald*.'

Bob squinted up at the reporter, empty glass in hand. 'I won't interrupt you, will you have a drink with us though?' asked Bull, seeing no light of welcome in Bob's eyes.

'Yes, mate, three pints,' said Bob, pushing his mug forward. Bull collected the others and left them with a nod. 'What's he like?' asked Bob of Cobbold.

'I think you'll find he don't cause no trouble,' said Cobbold. 'We look after him and he prints more or less what we want. Local lad he is, father's a builder.' Bob grunted in satisfaction.

'I thought you were a whisky addict, sir,' said Leo, who had been watching. Bob squirmed uncomfortably in his chair.

'Too bloody hot, mate.' Bob pulled his tie down another inch. Dave Bull reappeared with the drinks.

'I'll leave you in peace then,' he said, and did just that.

Bob sipped his drink thoughtfully as if doubtful that it would be as good as the first. 'Well, he buys a good pint any rate,' he said with satisfaction as he dived into the sandwiches.

'Get us one for the road then,' said Bob, when the plate was empty, indicating the direction of the bar with his thumb for Leo's benefit.

She was waiting when Leo reached the bar. 'What'll it be then?' she asked. Leo held his silence just long enough to give a mute reply.

'Three pints of draught,' he said, and stripped her with his eyes as she leaned forward to collect the empty mugs. She grinned at him and let her fingers play suggestively with the upright beer lever for a moment, then pulled hard down on it and let her eyes glitter as the beer gushed out at her expert touch.

'Smell her armpits,' said the voice with disturbing vulgarity.

She leaned towards him as she pushed the overflowing mugs across the bar and he caught the whiff of scented soap. The voice subsided.

'You're staying here then,' she said as he handed her the money.

'That's right and I'm beginning to be glad.' She smiled knowingly at him, rang up the till and let her hand touch his for a fraction longer than was necessary as she returned his change.

'I live in,' she said, 'so I'll be seeing you.'

'You will,' said Leo as he turned away, and there was no element of doubt in his voice.

As they settled down to their drinks, two women entered the room and were instantly the centre of all eyes. They knew it and accepted it with easy grace. The older one was in her late forties and at the height of her mature beauty. The lightweight suit she wore fitted loosely on her slight frame and the blouse, open at the neck, added to the impression of cool elegance.

Her daughter, for there could be no doubt as to the relationship, was in her early twenties, a tall lithe beauty sharing her mother's debt to those early invaders, the Saxons, as evidenced by the long fair hair, wide blue eyes and generous mouth.

Her flowing figure was emphasized by the thin summer dress she wore, displaying the elegant simplicity which only money and innate taste can buy. They shared that inner certainty of superiority which is at the same time the most evident and the most irritating characteristic of the English upper class.

'Who's the crumpet, then?' asked Bob. Sergeant Cobbold was stunned for a moment by Staunton's turn of phrase.

'Mrs Orton, Commander Orton's wife, sir, and their daughter Janie.' He was unable to keep the note of deference from his voice.

'Local squire, is he?' asked Bob, screwing round in his chair and making his inspection of the two women so obvious that Leo and Cobbold squirmed in embarrassment.

'Yes, sir . . . suppose you could say that.'

'What d'they do for a living then?' Staunton turned back to his beer, leaving the question in the air.

'Well, they don't do anything. . . .' Cobbold paused, finding some difficulty in explaining a feudal concept to such as Staunton. 'Commander Orton owns most of the land round here, he lets it off to tenant farmers . . . they do a lot of good work, charities and such like . . .' Cobbold trailed off feeling he had not justified the Ortons' position in the community.

'Do they live locally?' asked Leo, seeing Cobbold's difficulty.

'A couple of miles, sir. Bacton Hall fronts on to the river, at least the grounds do.'

'Drink up, lads,' said Bob, tired of the discussion, 'we've got work to do.'

When they arrived back at the village hall there was no sign of either Superintendent Day or Inspector Grace but the incident room was buzzing with activity under the sharp eye of the grey-haired Clerk-Sergeant who gave them a curt nod as they passed through on their way to Bob's office.

The dead girl's handbag was still sitting on the desk in its plastic covering. Bob took it out and emptied the contents on to the desk top, then his forehead creased in puzzlement. 'How's it get so damn mucky inside?' he asked of no one in particular.

'The contents were dropped out in the field, sir,' said Cobbold, and seeing Staunton's anger added, 'I'm sorry, sir, but a P.C. picked them up and put them back in the bag before I got there.'

Bob controlled himself with an effort. 'Get a statement from that officer. I want to know exactly where each item was and whilst you're about it give him a lecture on how to behave at the scene of a crime, bloody idiot.'

'Yes, sir,' said Cobbold somewhat chastened.

'And you should have told me, you should have known how important it was.' Bob dumped himself angrily into his chair and poked unenthusiastically amongst the contents of the handbag as Cobbold stared blankly at him. 'Anything missing from it?' Bob asked after a moment.

'No, sir,' said Cobbold quickly, 'I checked with her mother, she doesn't think anything is missing. The boy who found the body picked up an eyebrow pencil but I got that back.'

Leo stepped forward to Cobbold's aid. 'If the contents of her handbag were scattered about, it means almost certainly that violence was used on her before she reached the spot where she was found.' Cobbold still looked puzzled.

'But the post-mortem told us that, sir,' he said.

'No. It told us violence was used on her but not when. It could have been at the moment they met or any time thereafter until the time she died, perhaps even afterwards. Now, do you know where exactly these items were found?' Leo looked inquiringly at Cobbold who scratched his head in thought.

'They were more or less in a line between the entrance to the field and the body,' he said slowly.

Leo nodded. 'So she was in distress before she entered the field and some violence had probably already been inflicted on her before then. It helps.'

Suddenly Cobbold banged his forehead with the palm of his hand in an expressive gesture. 'I'm right stupid, aren't I?' he said, as enlightenment dawned, 'she didn't go there willing that's what it means, isn't it?'

'Allelujah,' said Bob somewhat unkindly.

'I'm right sorry, sir,' he said dejectedly.

'Forget it, mate,' said Bob, shovelling the items back into the handbag. 'You'd better get this lot over to the lab.'

Sergeant Cobbold replaced the handbag in its plastic container and left the room without a word. Bob drummed his fingers in irritated fashion on the desk.

'I'll bet you the unidentified finger marks on the handbag were down to that bloody P.C.,' he said to Leo who was now engaged in entering the responsibilities handed to Day and Grace before lunch into the action book. Leo closed the book and looked across at him.

'He's a good lad, Roger Cobbold,' he said, 'I hope that ticking off doesn't take too much steam out of him.' Bob flicked morosely through a number of routine messages that had been left on the desk for him to see.

'I've not got time to teach 'em their job. I'm running a murder inquiry,' said Bob firmly and without looking up.

'I wasn't criticizing, sir,' said Leo hastily.

'I should bloody well think not. Oh, I'll buy him a beer sometime, he'll be all right, they've got to learn to take it.' He pushed the message pad aside and looked up. 'Ready?'

The Prentiss' home was a small three-bedroom farm cottage set back off the road that led from the village of Bacton Ford down to the river. Leo and Bob pushed through the wooden gate and walked up the carefully laid path of concrete slabs which led as straight as a Roman road through the carefully tended garden to the front door.

Mrs Prentiss led them into the small front parlour that was obviously the Sunday's-only room. She excused herself and returned a few minutes later with her husband, a pot of tea and a plate of biscuits. Ted Prentiss shook hands with them both with slow dignity. They waited patiently through the ritual of the serving of tea in the clearly much-prized china tea cups.

For half an hour Bob and Leo questioned gently, probing into every aspect of the dead girl's background, her hobbies, friends, attitudes, likes and dislikes and many other seemingly unimportant areas of her personality and life style which served to give them a rounded picture of the girl they had only known in death.

Then they started again at the beginning. This time Leo wrote their statements as Bob led the couple by judicious suggestions to cover the points he needed recorded on paper for what he hoped would be the subsequent trial.

When June and Ted Prentiss had finally appended their signatures, all four felt worn and drained. Mrs Prentiss in particular was showing evident signs of stress. She was a small wiry woman with short, almost black hair and deep dark eyes revealing her ancestry among the people who had been old in their tenure of East Anglia before the Romans came. Although the cares of a hard and mostly impoverished life had left its mark upon her, it was easy to see that it was from her that her daughter had inherited her dark flashing looks.

The statement told Leo and Bob little of a factual nature that they did not already know. By her parents' account Joy Prentiss was revealed as a quiet girl with her roots firmly planted in the home. When others of her age had turned from the church when they had outgrown the mandatory attendance at Sunday School, she had not and had remained a member of the choir at Bacton Ford Parish Church.

She had apparently shown none of the wilfulness sometimes typical of the only child and had come late to an understanding of her attraction for men. There had been a number of boy friends, all local or semi-local, and the parents had not been aware that she had recently broken off her association with Paul Spender, whose interest in their daughter had by no means met with opposition from them.

The over-all picture was of a happy and attractive girl firmly set in a secure family background and there was nothing here to suggest any reason for her untimely death.

Bob sank back in the comfortable old armchair as Leo stuffed the statements away in his briefcase. 'Lucky to find you in, weren't we?' he asked, looking across at Prentiss, the real question implicit in the words.

'They gave me a few days off, good like that they are,' said Ted, straightening his shoulders as if to shift the burden of sadness. 'Though to tell the truth I'd as soon be at work.' He scratched his chin slowly and looked at Bob. 'Think I'll be a-going back tomorrow.'

Bob nodded and turned his attention to Mrs Prentiss who was collecting together the empty cups. 'Just one last thing, I'm afraid, luv.' She looked up at him and there was cold emptiness in her eyes. 'We got to have a look at her room.'

'Why?' The question was automatic, without real inquiry.

'Just in case she kept a diary, perhaps a name on a piece of paper, in a book, a telephone number, anything that might help, it's worth trying, isn't it?' said Leo gently. She turned and led them out of the room and upstairs.

'She didn't keep a diary,' she said flatly.

The officers searched the bedroom with minute thoroughness but it revealed absolutely nothing that was of assistance to them. Mrs Prentiss saw them to the garden gate and closed it firmly behind them.

'You must come again if you need, don't mind for us,' she said. 'It's not for Joy, we can't help her, but you must lock this man away before he does it again.'

'We don't know that he will, Mrs Prentiss,' said Leo, not wishing to add to her burden.

'He may not be from round here,' said Bob, picking up the cue, 'and it may just have been a fit of madness.'

'He's local right enough,' she said, 'and he'll do it again because he's that sort of man and he's got the taste of it now.'

There was a dread finality in her voice, the certainty of inner knowledge. She walked away from them back to the house. Leo stared after her for a long moment before he joined Bob at the car.

It was five-thirty when they arrived back at the village hall to find it surrounded with parked cars. Obviously the crime squad boys had arrived. Some twenty officers were milling about in the main hall and the rest room and Superintendent Day and Inspector Grace were waiting for them in the office.

Staunton took his seat behind the desk and waved the others to a seat. 'Right lads, how's it going then?' he asked.

Superintendent Day was fairly bustling with enthusiasm and seemed to have totally forgotten his experience at the post-mortem. 'There's about one hundred and sixty persons to see at the factory, sir. I've organized myself an office to work from and we'll start work at six tonight when the evening shift comes on. I've arranged the manpower with Inspector Grace here so we're ready to go. By the way, I've had a preliminary chat with some of the staff in the canteen where she worked and it seems that they are somewhat divided in their opinion of the girl. Some thought she was a quiet, modest, pleasant lass, but others thought she was . . . a bit of a flirt.'

'A prick teaser?' inquired Bob, looking straight at Day.

'Well . . . I suppose so, yes. She certainly raised a bit of interest amongst the male staff.'

'Anyone in particular?' asked Leo.

'Just a general thing at the moment, she had a regular boy friend of course and I gather that rather held the wolves at bay.'

'Pretty toothless wolves, then,' said Bob.

'One other thing, sir, she missed the bus home and was offered a lift.'

'Who by?' asked Bob, leaning forward with greater interest.

'I'm seeing him tonight, chap called Brian Ferris, married man does permanent evening shifts, anyway she refused apparently and said she intended to walk home.'

'How do we know about Ferris, sir?' asked Leo.

'When he heard about the murder he talked about it in the canteen, saying if she'd taken his offer of a lift she'd still be alive.'

'He may be right,' said Bob, 'or he may have given her a lift; we've only his word. Take a straight statement at the moment, he's suspect right enough but we'll give him his chance to lie first. If he begins to look likely we'll lean on him.'

Day, who obviously had not taken his information to its logical conclusion, was relieved that Bob had assumed that in fact he had.

'What about you, Mr Grace?' said Bob turning his attention to the impassive crime squad man.

'I'm ready, sir. If you agree we'll block the main road about twenty yards either side of the Bacton Ford turn-off.'

'That'll do fine. I don't want to teach my grandmother to suck eggs but don't forget it's questionnaire's for everyone you stop and statements from those who were on the road the night of the murder.'

Grace looked a little pained. 'I do understand, sir. With your permission I'll get started.'

'I'd better get going with my lads too,' said Day.

'Right, off you go and good luck to you,' said Bob. When they had left he looked across at Leo and grinned. 'Got a big job for you, son.'

'Yes, sir?' said Leo suspiciously.

'Organize some sandwiches from the pub.'

The meeting took place at nine that evening in the room where they usually met for purposes other than discussion. There were seven men and six women. The last to arrive had murmured his apology to the acknowledged leader, who sat on a raised dais at one end of the room, and joined the others sitting cross-legged on the floor.

The Master's voice had the ring of one used to authority. 'I have called this meeting because of an unfortunate occurrence in our community which may affect us all and the practice of our craft. We all knew Joy Prentiss and naturally we regret her passing but for us regret may not be enough. The police are searching for her murderer and it is certain that they will ask where we were on the night of her murder. We know we were met together and that therefore none of us could have any knowledge of the crime but to tell the truth would mean the end of our work and that is unthinkable. It is therefore essential that we unite in brotherhood and sisterhood to preserve our future for the work as yet unaccomplished.'

He paused for breath and there was a stir of apprehension amongst the listeners.

'It seems likely that the police will look for their suspect among the male population so it is necessary we should agree first on suitable alibis for our brothers. As far as possible we must rely upon each other for our alibis but if it is possible to provide corroboration from outside without prejudicing our cause this would be to our advantage.

'A word of caution, do not underestimate the police for they will be men of experience and no fools, do not lie to them on any matter except your whereabouts on the night of the murder, help them if you can so long as it does not harm us. My own alibi is already agreed, consult amongst yourselves and in the name of Him we serve guard your tongues and preserve unity.'

They spoke quietly amongst themselves for a while, then a woman rose to her feet and waited patiently to be acknowledged.

'I see you, sister,' said the leader eventually.

'Master, we are agreed but for minor details.'

'It is of the minor details we must be most careful.'

'There are some who may be able to take advantage of the unknowing assistance of outsiders as you suggested but we cannot be certain of this tonight.'

'So be it. Should any problems arise, be sure to inform me at once and all alibis must be finalized by tomorrow morning.'

'It shall be so, Master.' The woman respectfully inclined her head towards him, the movement awkward and unsure as if the formality of the action embarrassed her.

'You will stand,' said the Master, and the others shuffled to obey. 'There will be no further meetings until the police investigation is complete and the safety of our work ensured. Go now your separate ways and you will be called together in due time and by the usual method.'

The ill-assorted group drifted out of the room engaged in muted conversation. The Master was the last to leave and it was he who replaced the heavy metal bar across the entrance, lifting it with effortless ease.

At ten o'clock Bob and Leo called it a day and taking the still chastened Sergeant Cobbold with them retired to the Haywain. They had spent four hours wrestling with the gradually mounting piles of paperwork, stopping only for the press conference, and were feeling somewhat jaded.

The press had been eager for copy and after Bob had read the prepared statement, had bombarded him with questions, few of which he could answer. Between them Bob and Leo had successfully trod the tightrope between revealing or promising too much and alienating the reporters by denying them enough information to satisfy demanding editors.

The bar was fairly full when they arrived, due mainly to the presence of the reporters who, having filed their copy were chewing over past successes. When Leo and the others reached the bar Tom Stack came over to serve them bringing with him a plumply pretty middle-aged lady whom he introduced as his wife Rita.

'I'll be getting breakfast for you all mostly,' she said, 'but I've been something queer the last couple of days. It's a bug going around they say, gone now though.' She smiled happily at them clearly none the worse for having played unwilling hostess to the bug in question.

'The press boys have put one in the pipe for you,' said Tom. 'What'll it be?'

They ordered and settled in at the bar, relaxing in the ancient comfort of the room. After a few moments the gentlemen of the press joined them and the conversation became general, with Tom and Rita Stack joining in as work permitted.

Bob Staunton seemed much taken with the bubbly Rita Stack and rather monopolized her, leaving Leo and Roger Cobbold to the mercy of the journalists.

Leo noted the absence of the eager-eyed barmaid but she appeared after a few minutes clutching full bottles of spirits to her chest. She flashed him a look of renewed promise but the presence of the Stacks at the bar kept her serving and away from Leo.

The locals in the bar paid little or no attention to the group of outsiders, apart from Ray Colville, the vicar of Bacton Ford Parish Church, who abandoned his pint of bitter long enough to introduce himself and offer them, if a little diffidently, the facilities of his church during their stay.

At exactly ten-thirty Tom Stack called time and ten minutes later only the three police officers were left. He saw the last of the reluctant journalists off to their hotel in Ipswich and grinned across at them, 'Have a nightcap on me, it's another day over.'

As Bob pushed his glass across the counter for a re-fill he grinned at Leo, 'Well, son, it's the end of our first day – seems like a lifetime don't it?'

Leo looked around him. 'It does. It's mainly because we've been made so welcome and so comfortable,' he said, politically raising his glass to Rita Stack. He caught an impish grin from the barmaid as she turned away to tackle a mountain of dirty beer glasses. Rita looked pleased and joined them at the front of the bar with her drink.

'I could have let the other room to the press chaps but when Roger said you all wanted to stay I knew you wouldn't want them here as well,' she said, settling herself beside Bob.

'I hope you're not keeping the room vacant for our sakes,' said Leo politely.

'No, my pretty,' said Rita. 'I'll let it to a casual but not to the press.'

'You're a darling girl,' said Bob warmly. 'Let's buy you one for the road.'

By eleven-thirty Leo had washed and was arranging his underclothes in a neat pile on a chair in his tiny bedroom to the muted sounds of Bob Staunton's similar preparations in the room next door. He slid naked and thankful into the welcoming sheets, lying back on the pillows with his hands behind his head, staring at the ceiling as his mind ranged ahead to the next day's work.

She came quietly into the room and closed the door behind her. A full-length dressing gown gave a false impression of modesty, for it was patently obvious that she wore nothing else. Leo levered himself up into a sitting position and patted the bed beside him. As she sat, the dressing gown fell aside revealing sturdy, shapely legs. 'I came to see if there's anything you want,' she said, straight-faced. She caressed his muscular bare chest with her eyes. 'Mr and Mrs Stack said you was to be looked after like, so I thought you might like a hot drink?'

The voice in his head burst into action. 'Don't crap on your own doorstep, Leo, she'll want it every night if you give it to her now. How many times do you have to be told, lay off when you're working.'

Leo said nothing but stared at her as if transfixed. When he moved it was to reach forward and slide a hand inside the dressing gown and down on to her left breast until he held it cupped. She did not move.

'Don't do it, Leo, let her down lightly if you like, be polite but tell her it's not on. Leo . . .'

The voice was smothered as the wave of sensuality covered him with its familiar exciting warmth. He released her breast just long enough to use both hands to pull her dressing gown open. He held it apart, his eyes devouring her body, savouring the delights to come. She shivered under his openly lustful gaze but did not move.

He slid the dressing gown off her shoulders and it fell in disarray around her hips. In slow motion he took her face gently in his hands and pulled her towards him to kiss her chastely on the lips. He felt her rigid nipples on his chest, the quivering of her body as desire mounted in her in tune to his own. His hands slipped expertly down her body, rising over her firm breasts, dropping down to the stomach taut with anticipation, hesitating there to heighten her desire before just one reached down to the warmth between her legs. She stiffened, then relaxed and mewed her pleasure as his expert fingers flickered and teased.

He pulled away from her and pushed her on to her feet. For a moment she was nonplussed but only until he ripped the bedclothes back and held up his arms to her. She hesitated for a moment then her mouth formed a delighted round as she looked down at the hardness of him.

There was a moment of confusion as he raised himself awkwardly to allow her to slip in beneath him in the narrow confines of the single bed. He pulled the bedclothes over them and settled between her legs as they opened to receive him. They lay quietly for a moment savouring the anticipation, then he slid his hand between their bodies, directing himself into her with practised ease. His movements were slow but strong, warning of things to come. She writhed in delight under him.

'God that's beautiful, Leo . . . that's bloody lovely, darling . . .' Her hands caressed his back, fingernails tracing light patterns across the moving muscles, her breath came more quickly as she moved with him.

Suddenly he stopped, propped himself on his elbows and stared down at her face. 'What's your name?' he asked.

'Anne . . . Anne Partridge,' she gasped, frustration mounting fast at the interruption, 'Now come on . . . come on.'

He dropped his mouth to hers, his tongue forcing a way between her lips. She pushed herself up on to him. He stopped again.

'Are you on the pill?' he asked.

She dug her fingernails into his buttocks and bit his lip. It seemed as good an answer as any.

SIX

She was gone when Leo woke the following morning. He hurried through his toilet but even so was only just in time to meet Bob Staunton on his way down the stairs.

'Have a good night?' asked Bob, by way of greeting.

Perhaps it was only guilt but Leo seemed to sense an imp of mischief in the older man's eyes.

'Yes, thank you, sir.'

'Comfortable in that bed?'

'Er ... yes, sir.'

'Any good?'

'Well . . .' Leo hesitated, uncertain if fervent denial or outright admission was indicated. Bob only dug him heavily in the ribs.

'Saw her going in your room, mate, nice bit of stuff . . .'

Leo smiled uncertainly. 'She came in to see if there was anything I wanted,' he said and even to his ears it sounded lame. Bob laughed.

'Tell him the truth, you lying bastard,' said the voice.

'She did stay, actually,' said Leo.

'That's all right, son,' said Bob. 'It's not good for a healthy young lad to be without, just don't let it interfere with work and don't put her in the club, that's all.' Leo heaved a sigh of relief.

'I thought you might take exception to the idea.'

'I'm not that old fashioned, mate, besides if you've got her you won't be after every other bit of skirt in sight, will you?'

'Not bloody much he won't,' said the voice, viciously.

'No, sir,' said Leo.

'Let's get some grub then.' Bob led the way into the bar.

Breakfast had been laid for them on the same table in the bay window and the morning sun bathed the room in a mellow glow. They had no sooner taken their places than Rita Stack appeared as if by magic.

'Morning, gentlemen, and lovely too, you'll see.' She bustled around them pouring milk over cornflakes.

'All the better for seeing you,' said Bob, with heavy gallantry. Rita dimpled back a smile at him.

'You city gents shouldn't tease us poor country maidens,' she said, with artificial coyness and waggled her bottom rather obviously as she left the room.

Leo, who had followed the exchange with some amusement, indicated the door with his spoon. 'I think you have found favour there, sir.'

Bob ceased his attack on the cornflakes and looked hard at Leo. 'Don't get it wrong, son, when I chat up a female it's strictly business.'

Leo spread his hands in a gesture of acceptance but was unable to keep a suggestion of amused disbelief from his voice.

'Of course, sir.' The faint inference was not lost on Bob.

'I mean it, mate. Use your head. Who picks up most gossip? I'll tell you, women and publicans . . . and she's both.'

Leo grinned, 'I had noticed, sir.'

'Even if they want to help, people only tell you what they think is important. They may know some little thing that's vital but if it don't seem important to them they don't tell you and since you don't know what it is you can't ask them and that's why I chat up Mrs Stack . . . right?'

'Okay, sir, okay,' Leo made a face, 'I suppose I asked for that.' Bob grunted and returned to his cornflakes, firing one parting shot.

'We're not all as randy as you, mate.'

The voice giggled in Leo's head. 'You hit a nerve there, Leo, take a good look at him, that's a real live faithful husband, they're a dying breed. He's got you dead centre too. He doesn't need to lay females left, right and centre just to prove he's a man – he knows he is.'

It was an unfair attack. Leo resented these outdated and prim feelings of guilt which none of his contemporaries seemed to suffer. He looked across at Bob who was squirming uncomfortably on his chair and felt the need to assure him that the reputation that he imputed to Leo was not well founded.

'I know there have been some pretty lurid things said about my private life, sir, but the truth is very ordinary you know.'

Bob replied through a mouthful of cereal. 'Don't give me that educated bullshit,' he said, spraying the tablecloth, 'if there was nothing else available I wouldn't trust you with a knothole in the fence . . . you're a good lad but you know what you're like and so do I, so don't try to snow me . . . and another thing, when we're alone don't call me sir, it gets on my tits.'

Despite himself Leo laughed aloud and for the first time spoke without prior calculation. 'There's an outside chance I might enjoy working with you . . .'

'Cheeky sod,' said Bob, but he was not displeased.

Rita Stack brought in full plates and took away the cereal bowls, tutting in annoyance to herself as she did so.

'What's up, luv?' asked Bob.

'Oh, the place is that dirty.'

'Didn't notice it, looks all right to me.'

'That poor girl's mother does our cleaning, you know, so I couldn't ask her to come in to work like that, could I?'

'Mrs Prentiss always cleaned here?' Bob asked.

'Why yes, ever since we came, as good as gold she is, keeps the place like a new pin . . . I hope you get that rotten bastard. I'd put him out of business if I could get my hands on him, I'll tell you.'

There was clearly a hidden metal in the normal bubbly and light-hearted Rita Stack.

'We'll do our best,' said Bob. 'We saw Mrs Prentiss yesterday, I think you'll find she'll be back at work soon.'

'She might be better doing something at that . . . have your breakfast before it gets cold then.' She bustled out of the room with noticeably less of a waggle.

Bob moved uncomfortably on his chair as he set about his food. Leo noticed and felt that their relationship had developed to the stage where he could afford to mention it.

'Will you give me a straight answer to a straight question?' Bob looked up at him in surprise.

'Of course.'

'Are you suffering from haemorrhoids?'

Bob applied himself to his meal in silence, as if he had not heard. 'Yes,' he said finally.

'They can be cured.'

'I'm not ill, I don't want doctors playing about with me, thanks. It don't stop me working.'

'The cure is a little painful but it is fairly quick and you'd feel a lot more comfortable afterwards.'

'Look, Leo, thanks, I know you mean well but I can't afford the time. Anyway like I said, I'm not ill and if a man can't put up with a bit of discomfort he's not much of a man.'

Leo shrugged, 'On your head be it then,' he said, resignedly.

Bob grinned, 'No thanks, mate, I've got enough trouble with them on my backside.'

They arrived at the village hall just before eight o'clock but even so Sergeant Worthington and most of the office staff were already present and hard at work. Bob and Leo stopped for a chat with them, a few moments well spent in ensuring those officers did not feel that they were the unconsidered poor relations of the inquiry.

In Staunton's tiny office a pile of typed statements awaited them, some from Sergeant Cobbold's efforts in the village, some from Superintendent Day's late evening work at Orwell Engineering and a couple from Detective Inspector Grace as a result of the road block.

Bob and Leo read them through quickly but thoroughly. That dealt with, they tackled the separate file of messages received during their absence and by a quarter to nine they were up to date.

Leo took the statements and messages and put them to one side, ready to be returned and filed in the office for easy reference. With masterly timing a pale-faced constable entered at that moment with two cups of tea, the quantity of liquid in the saucers evidence that he would never make a head waiter.

'Thanks, mate,' said Bob, tipping the contents of his saucer back into the cup. 'Ask Sergeant Worthington to pop in and see me, will you?'

When Worthington entered the room Leo was in the act of placing his tea-filled saucer on the window ledge and avoiding the drips from the bottom of his cup. Worthington frowned in annoyance.

'I shall have to speak to that young man, sir,' he said sternly.

'Who?' asked Leo, in between sips.

'P.C. Callum, he's tired out, white as a sheet and can't carry a cup of tea without slopping it.'

'He's a policeman not a flunky,' said Bob, missing the point.

'He has a girl friend, sir,' said Worthington, 'not a nice girl if you see what I mean. He doesn't get his sleep.'

'He's only young,' said Leo, 'he'll get over it in time.'

'You supercilious two-faced bastard.' Leo ignored the interruption in his head and applied himself to his tea.

Staunton grinned knowingly at Leo. 'I've never known anyone to die from it,' he said.

'I'll have to speak to him,' said Worthington, passing final judgement.

'Well, he's your lad,' said Bob. 'Now, there's a few things I'd like you to do for me.'

'Yes, sir.'

'I want to see the files on all the unsolved murders in the last five years involving sexual attacks.'

'There won't be many of those, sir,' said Worthington with conviction.

'Right then, extend it to include all unsolved cases of rape, attempted rape, indecent assault . . . any marriage of violence and sex, right?'

'Very well, sir.'

'I've already applied for the criminal records of sexual offenders in the county for the last five years, sir,' said Leo.

Worthington nodded. 'They should be here today, sir.'

Staunton finished his tea noisily and put down the cup. 'Let's see them as soon as they arrive.'

'Yes, sir.'

'Next, check all the mental institutions, I want to know who's absent without leave and details of any who might have been out on temporary release at the time of the murder.'

'Shall I put these straight in the action book and allocate them to Sergeant Worthington, sir?' asked Leo.

'Eh? Oh yes, might as well.' Bob sat back in his chair and scratched his jaw in thought as Leo wrote quickly in the hard-backed book marked 'Action'.

'One other thing, get me a list of all males over the age of . . . say fourteen, who're on the missing persons list, we'd look right fools if our bloke's done a bunk and we didn't know he'd gone.'

'That the lot, sir?' asked Worthington.

'Yes, mate . . . that should keep you busy for half an hour.'

'A little longer, sir, I should think,' said Worthington with no trace of humour.

As Worthington opened the office door to leave, Chief Constable Edward Boulton walked in. The sergeant rightly judged from Staunton's expression that he had no idea who his visitor was.

'Good morning, sir,' said Worthington.

'Good morning, Worthington,' said Boulton, already reaching for his pipe.

'May I introduce Chief Superintendent Staunton...' he stood aside as the two men warily shook hands.

'...and Detective Inspector Wyndsor.'

'Pleasure to meet you, sir,' said Leo.

'Creep,' said the voice.

'I won't stop long,' said Boulton, looking round for a chair. Worthington bustled around and seated him in front of the desk.

'Stop as long as you like, sir, you're always welcome, it's your inquiry after all,' said Bob, lying in his teeth.

Boulton stuffed tobacco energetically into the bowl of his pipe. 'Just thought I'd see how you were getting along... if there's anything you need.'

'I don't think so, sir,' said Bob, and then to Leo, 'Anything you want on the office side, Leo?'

'Not for the office, sir, but there is one thing which would be of considerable assistance, although not absolutely essential...'

Boulton flapped at the cloud of smoke he had created in lighting his rough cut and beamed at Leo, recognizing in him a fellow upper-class mate.

'Anything at all, dear boy,' he said, 'if it's in my power, anything at all.'

Bob Staunton saw that there was a club here to which he would never belong and to which his rank alone did not qualify him for membership. He dropped back into his chair and stared hard at Leo.

'We have transport here, sir,' said Leo, ignoring Bob's stare, 'but it would be most convenient if we could have a vehicle for Mr Staunton's exclusive use.'

'Why certainly,' said Boulton, relieved his magnanimous offer of unlimited assistance had involved him in nothing more difficult or expensive, 'I'll send my own reserve car over this afternoon... driver as well if you'd like?'

'Thank you, sir,' said Leo, 'just the car would be fine, we can always raise a driver from amongst our staff.'

'So be it,' said Boulton amicably. 'How are we progressing then?' He looked across at Bob, the question hanging in the air.

'Well...' said Bob stiffly, 'it's a bit early yet...'

'Of course, of course.' Boulton's acceptance was too quick, too automatic and it betrayed his lack of real interest in the mechanics of the inquiry.

'You'll be the first to know if we come up with anything that's promising,' said Bob.

'That's fine,' Boulton puffed hard.

He had come only because he felt he should show interest, he did not wish to get too deeply involved in the inquiry. He was aware the other two were waiting for him to speak but he had difficulty in thinking of anything that would not sound inane to these two men who were experts in a field in which his knowledge was limited.

'Well, Mr Staunton,' he said finally, 'I see myself as a kind of father figure to this inquiry. A benign and understanding father, I hope, one who is not afraid to let his children develop in freedom but who is ready with timely . . . and one would hope helpful, advice when and if it is needed.'

He stopped in mid sermon and looked at his pipe with raised eyebrows as if surprised at its presence in his hand. Leo stole a look at Bob and was not surprised at the blank and stony gaze with which he was regarding the Chief Constable. Even Leo winced. Colonel Boulton accepted the pipe as a friend and returned it to his mouth, then immediately took it out again as he continued.

'So, basically, you'll not see much of me but I'll be there whenever needed. My door is always open.'

He beamed at them. He was vaguely conscious that his words had not had the effect he intended. He felt uncomfortable. Finally Bob found words.

'That's very comforting to know, sir,' he said, trying not to allow sarcasm to show.

Boulton got to his feet and the others followed suit.

'I'll be off and leave you chaps to it then,' he said with false bonhomie.

'Good-bye, sir,' they chorused in dead voices.

'Good hunting,' said the Chief Constable on his way out of the door.

Bob and Leo seated themselves and there was silence for a long moment. Bob picked up a pencil, played with it idly, then broke it viciously in half and threw it in the wastepaper bin.

'I don't criticize senior officers,' he said, tight-lipped.

'No,' said Leo, aware this was not a moment to make observations.

'Not in front of junior officers anyway.'

'No.'

'But it would be bloody obvious to anyone that that bloke is a weak, pompous, Eton and Harrow berk of the first water.'

'Yes.'

Bob looked at him hard. 'Oh, you agree do you?'

'Yes, sir.'

'I thought you and him were talking the same language.'

'We're not all like that, sir.'

'So it *is* we, is it?'

'Eton, sir.'

'Yes?'

'Yes.'

'I should have known.'

'I'm sorry.'

'Don't worry, son, it's not your fault, you can't help the way you were brought up.' It was obvious Bob did not intend this as a joke and Leo did not feel inclined to let it rest.

'I'm not sorry to have been to public school, only that you bracketed me with him, because he would be the same whatever his background.'

Bob moved irritably on his chair. 'You're right, mate, he just got up my nose that's all.'

'At least he will not interfere and we can get anything we want from him.'

'That's a bit bloody cynical. He's probably a good Chief Constable, he's just not a detective that's all. All right so he's weak and pompous but that don't matter to us, you don't have to be Genghis Khan to push papers round a desk . . . bloody hell, you've got me defending him.'

Leo grinned. 'No, you just put things in perspective for both of us. By the way if it helps, I was only at Eton for two years. Father made some bad investments, we finished up pretty well broke.'

'No, mate,' said Bob, wagging a warning finger, 'don't do that. Don't deny yourself. You're what you are so learn to live with it. I did.'

Leo stared at the wall, deep in thought. Bob's words had struck home. Perhaps to be adaptable, to try hard to fit in wherever you were, whoever you were with, to deny your upbringing to facilitate your work, make others feel relaxed or slip unnoticed into any social milieu was in fact weakness.

Perhaps Staunton's uncompromising approach to life was the answer after all. He was filled with a sudden deep uncertainty. Was he then weak, vacillating, over-concerned with what others thought of him and was he after all right to have these frequent feelings of guilt about his actions and motivations?

His troubling thoughts were interrupted by a sharp knock at the door.

'Come in,' barked Staunton, who had been deep in thoughts of his own.

P.C. Trew entered the room slowly and carefully, as if he feared it were booby-trapped. His long angular face was whiter and the black rings under his eyes even darker than when Staunton had last met him at the scene of the murder.

He was carrying a large envelope with great care, hugging it to him with bony arm and skeletal fingers. He held out the envelope grudgingly to Staunton.

'I was up all night, sir,' he said, giving no clue as to whether this was a complaint or an excuse for his appearance.

'You've met our plan drawer,' said Bob to Leo as he ripped open the envelope. 'How'd it go, mate?'

P.C. Trew acknowledged Leo's greeting and winced at Bob's rough handling of his work. 'I've not had time to make any copies, sir,' was his only answer to Bob's inquiry. He leaned forward on the balls of his feet and peered anxiously at Staunton looking much like a uniformed crow in doubt about its next meal.

When Bob came to the plan of the Bacton Ford area he whistled in surprise. Like the others it was drawn with meticulous care but here Trew had surpassed himself. Although the lines were in black and white he had used colour on the tiny frothing beer mugs that marked the public houses, he had drawn and painted the tiny trees, shrubs, animals and the larger individual dwelling houses. He had picked out every right of way and farm track. The main road was populated with a variety of vehicles exquisitely drawn and the river and marina were alive with boating traffic. It was not just a stark graphic statement, it was a work of art. Staunton looked anew at the unlikely frame that housed this talent.

'Is it all right, sir?' asked Trew anxiously.

'When this job's over,' said Bob, 'I'm going to take this home, have it framed and hang it in my sitting room . . . it's bloody beautiful.'

A suggestion of a pleased smile flickered across Trew's face.

'Thank you, sir.'

'You're wasting your time in this job, mate, you should be doing this full time, you've got bloody talent,' said Bob, with the total conviction of the man who knows what he likes.

Trew looked uncomfortable. 'Well . . . if there's nothing else, sir . . .'

'No, mate, go and get some kip . . . you look as if you need it.'

Trew nodded uncertainly at them both, permitted himself a grimace that might have been intended as a smile and sidled out of the room.

'Bloody talent that is,' said Bob, pointing at the door.

Leo took a good look at Trew's masterpiece. 'It's a pity. He must be as frustrated as hell drawing accident scenes day after day,' he said.

'Like I said, he should jack it in and take a chance painting. Right, what's the time?'

'Five to ten, press conference at ten.'

'Oh hell.'

'I'll take it if you like.'

'Yeah, do that. I want to go over the statements again.'

'I'd like to pop out for an hour afterwards. . . .' Leo hesitated.

'What for?'

'To go to church.'

Bob stared at him in blank astonishment.

'Do what?'

Leo shrugged. 'Not for the good of my soul, I'm not a believer. It's like you said about publicans picking up local gossip, that goes for the vicar too I should think. We met him briefly in the Haywain, remember? Ray Colville.'

'Just about, yes, that's right, nice bloke. Might be worth a try. Don't be too long.'

'I'll be back by eleven, it's not far.'

'He could have you for a week if I thought he'd convert you.'

'No chance of that,' Leo grinned, 'but I might convert him.'

Bob grunted. 'Bloody heathen,' he said to Leo's departing back.

Leo dealt quickly and efficiently with the gentlemen of the press. There was little to tell and he noticed that there were fewer faces present and some of their earlier eagerness had gone. To the journalist no news is bad news. He gave them time to disperse, then wandered out of the village hall, across the sunbathed village green and down the main street. There were few people about and those that were ignored him.

The church was a patchwork of periods. The original building was sixteenth century but it had been repaired, partially rebuilt and considerably added to over the years. It sat with solid determination in the midst of half an acre of ancient graveyard, sunning itself among the dead.

Leo walked up the path to the heavy wooden door and stood there for a moment undecided. There was a strange lethargy upon him. Perhaps it was the heat. He turned the heavy metal ring that lifted the latch and entered the church.

It was sparsely elegant and pleasantly cool. He walked slowly up the aisle and stood looking at the altar. Involuntarily he bowed his head and closed his eyes. He took a seat on the front pew and looked around. A feeling of peace and contentment settled over him like a warm blanket. The quiet acted on him like a drug, dulling his senses and for a few moments he sat inert, breathing in precious silence.

When he emerged into the sunlight again the mood was still upon him and he sat on one of the old stone lintels that flanked the entrance porch.

A thrush was prospecting for worms among the drunken decaying gravestones. As he watched, the bird dived a stabbing beak into the turf and began a short and violent tug of war with its victim. Death among the dead. It cut the worm into neat pieces, swallowed them and flew up on to a gravestone where it fluffed out its chest and whistled and warbled in delight of living. Was it worth a death to hear that song? Leo shuffled his feet and the thrush flew off, its alarm call ringing in his ears.

He was just able to make out the wording on the nearest stone: 'Here lies Leah Martin beloved daughter. Born 1st July 1798 died 4th September 1802. We are all God's children.'

She had died at the age of four. Why? Who was she? Was she really beloved? Would she have been beautiful, talented? Might not Leah Martin have changed the world? God in heaven, death is a waste.

Leo heard the crunch of footsteps on the gravel path but did not look up until Ray Colville stood in front of him.

'Inspector Wyndsor.' It was a statement of fact rather than a question of identity.

Leo squinted against the sun. 'I came to see you,' he said.

The priest took a seat beside him. 'For spiritual guidance or temporal information?' There was no hint of prejudgement.

'Information,' said Leo. 'Joy Prentiss attended this church.'

'She did.'

'You must have known her well, what sort of girl was she?'

'Quiet, helpful, loving and kind. That was the Joy Prentiss I knew.'

'Was there another?'

'I don't think so.'

'Then I don't understand.' Leo hunched himself round to look at the priest who was picking absent-mindedly at a loose button on his jacket.

'You meet me and you form one impression, someone else will form another opinion perhaps quite different. We all have many facets to our personalities and at different times, under different circumstances with different people we show different charactersitics. That was all I meant. I did not intend to imply Joy was anything but good.'

The explanation comforted Leo more than the speaker could have known. He relaxed against the warm stone wall behind him and found some difficulty in formulating his next question. There was a moment of companionable silence, then Colville waved a hand.

'Beautiful, isn't it?'

'Yes,' said Leo. 'Strange how we can find peace and beauty in a place of death.'

'Not so strange when you know of the joy of the hereafter.'

'But you don't know, you can't and yet you preach certainty where there is none.'

'You want proof?'

'No, just some logic, something other than blind faith.'

'Ah, Thomas again.'

Leo looked at the priest in puzzlement. 'Thomas? Oh, Doubting Thomas you mean.'

Colville nodded, 'Yes. He also wanted something more than blind faith. Like Thomas you desperately want to believe but logic assails you. God is not to be found through logic but through love.'

'I'm sorry but those are just words and too much of church language has no real meaning. Even you yourselves have fought bitter battles over matters of dogma. Is there one God or three? Does the holy spirit qualify as a God or is it the essence of God used only as a vehicle to deify in life the body of a low-born carpenter? The list of arguments is endless and it seems only to confuse any truth there might be.'

The priest pursed his lips. 'So, at least you are sufficiently interested to probe the wounds of the Church to see if they still bleed.'

'It is a matter of history and it is not the Church that is wounded it is the countless millions of ordinary people it has deceived and deluded. History is an indictment of the established Church, it claims to be the oracle of God yet it despoiled the poor while its priests were clothed in luxury. It has waged war, and so-called men of God have murdered, tortured and exploited. Even today the Church finds excuses to meddle in politics and if it doesn't actually kill it condones killing, after all God was on our side in every war, or so we are told.

'No, Mr Colville, organized religion doesn't represent God, it's a power block and I wouldn't want to be in your shoes and have to answer for two thousand years of deceit.'

Colville scratched his chin and looked up to the sky as if for guidance. 'Well now . . .' he said, transferring his gaze to his feet, 'you have just dealt with two thousand years and hundreds of different religions in one breath. There is no way of presenting reasoned arguments against that kind of generalization. At least we have established you believe in God, I have seldom heard his case presented more vehemently.'

'No, I do not believe in God but I do believe in a Creator.'

'We don't make that distinction.'

'I do. Logic tells me that there must have been a Creator. I am here. I stand on a lump of matter circling a sun that is the merest dot in the universe. There are too many miracles, it cannot be blind chance, there is no logic in that. So there must be a Creator but I cannot accept that he sees every sparrow fall.'

'Do you say then that the Creator has no interest in that which he created? Where is the logic in that?'

'If he has any interest at all in this insignificant speck of dirt we inhabit it could only conceivably be an interest in the survival of the human race as a whole, not in individuals. The artist is not interested in the molecules that make up the materials he uses, only in the effect of the finished product.'

'The human artist maybe, not an artist of infinite power and wisdom.'

'Try convincing those who are born maimed or mentally retarded, or innocent victims of war. It strains belief in an all-powerful individual god when blind luck hits good and bad alike. What about Joy Prentiss? Quiet, helpful, loving and kind you said, where was God when she was being raped and murdered?'

His fingers shook with the depth of his bitterness as he pointed to the nearest gravestone. 'And where was he when Leah Martin aged four died. Don't tell me this life is a trial between good and evil, what choice did she have, aged four?'

Silence fell again between them but now it was strained and uncomfortable. Leo felt his recent passions abating and wondered at his lack of control. He relaxed and leaned back against the wall again. Guilt at this uncharacteristic outburst flooded over him. After a moment he spoke.

'I'm sorry. Never in my life have I spoken to anyone like that. I can only apologize.'

Colville joined him in leaning back against the wall. 'No,' he said sadly, 'it is I who should apologize. I should have ready answers to the questions you raise but I cannot reply without using the language of the Church and that you deny has meaning. If it is true that without belief the words we use are meaningless then it is a horrifying failure on our part and I cannot accept it.'

Leo felt drained, unwilling to prolong the discussion any further. 'It is only my opinion and I do not ask you to accept it. I was riding a hobby horse of mine, that's all.'

The priest steepled his fingers and looked straight ahead. 'There is one thing I think you've overlooked,' he said.

'That is more than possible.'

'The power of evil in this world.'

'I have not overlooked it but if there is no individual God then equally there can be no individual Devil. Evil is a human condition and what is or is not evil is determined by the social mores of the day. It is the Church that needs the Devil, it was the early Christian Church that created him, without him how could they explain the failings of an allegedly all-powerful and personal God? I'm sorry, I'm off again.'

The priest ignored the apology and demolished his steeple. 'Then how do you explain the basic human need to worship a power beyond them, be it God or the Devil, or in your case a Creator?'

'I don't know. I'm afraid I have no answers to anything, only questions. As for those who worship the Devil, I have met some and they are either sensation seekers, sexual deviants or mentally ill.' Leo hesitated, '. . . and there are some who genuinely seek pure knowledge and are prepared to despoil themselves to that end.'

Colville looked at him thoughtfully. 'You are seeking knowledge, you have said so . . .'

'Not that way.'

'But you could have been involved at one time?'

'No. I have looked in from the outside. As I said I have met some people who are involved.'

'If you stay long enough in Bacton Ford you may meet some more.'

Warning bells rang in Leo's head. He sat up sharply and looked at Colville. 'There is a coven here?'

The priest shrugged. 'I don't know what they call themselves but there is something.'

'You're sure?'

'You want evidence?'

'Well . . .'

'This time I can provide it, come with me.'

Colville led the way to the rear of the church then picked his way through the ancient stones to a far corner of the graveyard. He stopped and pointed. Two headstones were lying flat on the ground and the graves themselves were loosely covered with fresh soil. Between them was a charred and blackened area in the grass, the remains of a fire.

'Someone opened these graves, scattered the bones about and took some of them away. There must have been a dozen or more people here. The grass was flattened all round this area. They seem to have held some sort of ritual round the open graves.'

'When was this?'

'About a month ago, but it's been happening on and off for the last ten years. We can't guard this place twenty-four hours a day all year.'

'Did you inform the local police?'

'Oh yes. There is little they can do. They haven't even managed to find the chalice . . . er, not that I mean any criticism,' he added hastily.

'Things have been stolen from the church as well?'

'The chalice, a cross, candles, baptismal water, vestments . . . quite a list. We are not alone, other churches hereabouts have suffered.'

'What do your parishoners say about it?'

Colville shrugged. 'The newer arrivals are outraged. The old families . . . well, they cross themselves and turn away. Old beliefs die hard, unlike you they have a healthy respect for the Devil and his disciples.'

'Well,' said Leo thoughtfully, 'it looks as if you're right. Who carried out the investigations?'

'Well, recently it was Sergeant Cobbold from the C.I.D.'

'And he has made no progress?'

'Apparently not.'

Leo looked around, noted with wry amusement the yew tree that helped to prop up the old stone wall. Its lower leaves had been burnt and shrivelled by the fire. He pointed at it.

'Your guardian got its fingers burnt.'

'Guardian?'

'It is an old belief that the yew tree has magical properties. Weren't they planted in churchyards to ward off evil? Some of your predecessors obviously thought God needed some help in his fight against the Devil.'

Colville shook his head sadly. 'Perhaps he does. Perhaps I should plant some more.'

Leo held out his hand. 'Mr Colville, thank you. You've been a great help. Sorry about the lecture.'

The priest gave a wan smile as he took his hand.

'Thank you. I've become too used to ministering to people who want only confirmation of what they already believe. What a pity it is always easier to provide proof of the work of the Devil than the love of God.'

SEVEN

It was a thoughtful Leo that arrived back at the village hall shortly after eleven o'clock. He found Bob Staunton wading through an impressive pile of paperwork that littered his desk and overflowed on to the floor around him. He looked up as Leo entered.

'Hello, mate, how's the vicar?'

Leo hesitated. It did not seem a good moment to start talking about witches, warlocks and the machinations of the Devil. He had a fairly good idea of what Bob's reaction would be and somehow the ideas that were formulating themselves in his mind seemed unlikely and unreasonable away from the persuasive atmosphere of the churchyard.

'Somebody stole his chalice. He's a bit upset,' he said.

'Waste of time then,' grunted Bob.

'No. We made contact. You never know.'

Bob rooted among the papers on his desk and came up with a bulky folder. 'Here. Give your eyes a treat, the P.M. report.'

Leo settled into a chair to read the post-mortem report prepared by Professor Galloway. It was lengthy and detailed but told little that they did not already know.

Also in the folder Leo found the report from the police Forensic Laboratory. It was much shorter but made rather more interesting reading. After dealing with negative findings it disclosed that some of the outer clothing examined had contact traces of heavy-duty engine oil.

In addition there was on her overcoat the blurred outline of a quarter footprint. The suggestion was that it might have been a heavy shoe or light boot, about size nine.

Leo replaced the folder on Staunton's desk. Bob pushed aside the papers he had been reading and pointed an accusing finger.

'Know where I've been this morning?'

'No?'

'The Coroner's inquest.'

Leo stared at him, stunned.

'I knew nothing about it. I had half an hour to get there. So why didn't you tell me, eh?'

'I didn't know. Good God, you'd think someone would have told one of us.'

'It's your job to know, not wait for someone else to tell you. You dropped a bollock, my son, and I don't want it happening again, right?'

Leo made a face expressive of self-disgust. 'Yes, sir. You're right I should have remembered.'

'So while you were wasting time frigging about with the vicar I was tearing about here like a blue-arsed fly.'

'I'll make sure nothing like that happens again.'

'Right. Now the funeral's tomorrow. We'll both be there.'

'Yes, sir.'

Leo mentally kicked himself. It wasn't like him to forget such an obvious event as the inquest.

'Right idiot, aren't you?' said the voice. 'Too busy scoring cheap points off a country vicar to get on with the job. Why do you always have to prove how bloody clever you are? Grow up and leave theology to those who're qualified . . .'

The harangue was interrupted by Bob Staunton.

'Young Cobbold wants us to interview the local squire, Orton. He's got a point, bit awkward for a local to deal with the likes of him. We've got an appointment for two this afternoon.'

'Right, sir.'

'Cheer up, mate, we all make mistakes, even me.'

He grinned at Leo, not unhappy to have caught him out. A brisk knock on the door heralded the entrance of Superintendent Day and Detective Inspector Grace.

'You two are beginning to look like a double act,' said Bob. 'What you got for us?'

'Not a great deal, sir,' said Day, apparently not in any way put out by the fact, 'but you expressed an interest in the man who offered Joy Prentiss a lift home from the factory.'

'So I did. And . . .?'

'No go, I'm afraid. He didn't give Joy a lift but he did pick up an old friend on his way home and took him in for a drink and a chat.'

'Is that confirmed?'

'Yes. It was one of our lads. Sergeant Walsh from the traffic division. They were at school together apparently.'

'That's that, then.'

'I think so, yes.'

'What did he say about the girl?'

'After I promised him that whatever he said would be treated in confidence he was quite forthcoming. He seemed to quite enjoy it all. He admits he tried to get her to go out with him.'

'Did she?'

'Well, apparently she spent one afternoon with him. He has a small boat, potters about on the river, does a bit of fishing. He asked her out on other occasions but she refused. He says she was a nice girl.'

'Too nice for his liking by the sounds of it. Was he upset when she refused?'

'I don't think so. He just kept trying.'

'Did the other workers know what he was at?'

'Some of them. He wasn't the only man that tried his luck but none of them seem to have got anywhere. You'll see from the statements some of them thought she was a flighty piece but it seems like sour grapes for the most part.'

Bob grunted and scratched his chin. 'Okay, mate, keep at it. What about you, Mr Grace?'

'Well, I've got six men with Mr Day, ten with Sergeant Cobbold in the village and five of those ten doing shifts on the road block. We found two regular travellers last night but you have the statements, neither saw anything unusual on the road on the night of the murder.

'We traced the driver and conductor of the bus she should have taken and six passengers, which we think is the lot. We showed them her photograph, some of them knew her but they all say she wasn't on the bus that night. I've left the statements outside to be processed.'

'That was quick work.'

Inspector Grace nodded. 'We were lucky, the conductor knew most of the passengers by name. Not many strangers take a bus round here that late at night.'

'D'you think you'll have time to look at this lot for me?' Bob Staunton tapped a heap of Criminal Record Office files on one corner of his littered desk. 'They're all your friendly local sex fiends, see where they were at the time, eh?'

Grace picked up the files. 'We'll have a look at them, sir.'

Sergeant Worthington poked his head round the door and hastily apologized. 'Sorry, sir, didn't realize you were busy.'

'Come in, old fruit,' said Bob, 'join the club, there ain't no state secrets being discussed. What you got?'

As Worthington edged into the tiny room Superintendent Day and Inspector Grace bid Staunton goodbye and left.

'These searches you asked me to do, sir,' said Worthington, placing his burden of files on the already crowded desk.

'These are the correspondence files on the unsolved murders, rapes and sexual assaults. I had them brought over from Ipswich H.Q. by car.'

'Nothing like a bit of light reading is there?' said Bob. 'What's that you got there?'

Worthington waved the message sheets he was still holding. 'Missing persons, sixteen males over fourteen missing in the county but only one disappeared since the murder, a lad of fifteen. He was seen by an uncle in London and he had a good reason for going, his father caught him stealing from the gas meter at home and gave him a good hiding. From his description he's five foot two and weighs about seven stone.'

'Well, he's not our man,' said Bob, picking absentmindedly at his teeth with a paper clip, 'we'd better have a statement from him when he's picked up though.'

'Very well, sir, I'll tell H.Q. to make a note for us to be informed when he turns up. Now, the mental homes, nothing there at all. At the moment there's only one absent without permission. He went two years ago and is reliably believed to be in Australia.'

'How the hell did a mental escapee manage to get to Australia?'

'They believe he joined a party going overland in a converted London Transport bus, sir,' said Worthington as though this was an everyday occurrence.

Half an hour later Worthington returned bringing them a large plate of sandwiches. Bob and Leo munched their way through them as they continued to read the files on the unsolved sexual cases with which the sergeant had provided them.

By the time the sandwiches had disappeared Leo had returned all but two of the files to the main office. These two they re-read with great care. One concerned the rape of a young married woman a year before on the outskirts of Pin Mill, just across the river Orwell from Bacton Ford. A heavily built man had hit her once on the jaw as she walked home late at night from a visit to her mother's house. He had partially strangled her with the belt from her raincoat whilst he raped her.

The other told how, just three months previously, a seventeen-year-old girl was walking home along a lonely road near the village of Bucklesham when she was struck from behind, dragged into a field and indecently assaulted by a tall dark-haired man. He had tightened her own scarf round her neck and only stopped short of rape because of a premature ejaculation.

'Where's Bucklesham?' asked Bob when they had replaced the files on the desk. Leo consulted the small-scale map of Suffolk pinned to the wall alongside P.C. Trew's masterpiece.

'About five miles, and Pin Mill is just across the river, say two miles as the crow flies.'

'I reckon we lied to Mrs Prentiss,' said Bob thoughtfully, 'this bastard is going to do it again if we don't stop him.'

'Two in a year, same method, similar description, such as it is. I agree he's our man, it's too much of a coincidence.' Leo returned to his seat. 'At least we can be pretty sure he's a local.'

'Or a regular visitor,' said Bob.

'Yes, good point. I suppose he could come from as far as London if he had a car. Perhaps he only uses this area as a hunting ground. He may not be a local after all then.'

'But he is.'

'Yes.'

'I had that feeling from the start, Leo. The bastard's probably not more than a mile away from us at this moment.'

The Chief Constable's reserve car was an opulent saloon; a far cry from the utility models in common use as C.I.D. cars. Leo drove sedately through the village and along the single track tarmac road that led to Bacton Hall, home of the Orton family. Bob squirmed uncomfortably on the plush seat beside the driver, moving his weight from one side to another, unappreciative of that part of England's green and pleasant land through which they were passing.

They entered the grounds of Bacton Hall through a huge crumbling archway of stone guarded by a substantial lodge built in the style of the main house but it was another half mile before Bacton Hall itself was in sight.

The Hall had been built by Montague Orton in 1723 and had the almost mandatory tradition of ghostly visitations. The Orton family had in the past carried the taint of madness and in 1813 the then squire, Joshua Orton, had climbed the front of the house, cut his throat with a kitchen knife and thrown himself to the ground, giving rise to the legend that a bloodied, partly decapitated figure still stalked the house and grounds.

Even in the bright summer sunshine the turreted façade and small leaded windows surrounded by thick grey stone gave the impression of brooding, hooded watchfulness.

Leo parked the car ostentatiously in the centre of the gravel drive, right in front of the massive main doors of the house. They were admitted by an elderly, sour-faced housekeeper and shown into the library, a room of heavy drape curtains, dull wood panelling and old leather furniture.

It had an atmosphere of dust, damp and disuse.

'Bloody hell,' said Bob in a whisper when they were left alone, 'I didn't think anybody lived like this any more. It must cost a fortune to keep this place up.'

'I think they are struggling,' said Leo looking around, 'the grounds are pretty overgrown and this room hasn't seen a duster for weeks.'

'You do the talking when he comes in, you know what we want.'

'Okay, if you like.'

'You might get more out of him being one of the clan.'

Leo looked hard at his senior officer. Bob caught his look and grinned. 'Relax, I wasn't being funny. I just don't believe in keeping a dog and barking myself.'

Commander Orton entered the room at this juncture. He was a man of imposing stature and his dress proclaimed him to be very much the country gentleman. He was in his middle fifties but his ramrod straight back and light step showed he was still physically fit. There was about him the positive aura of mental and physical strength that is often a characteristic of those bred for power and leadership.

Leo extended his hand. 'Detective Inspector Wyndsor, sir,' he said with a formal smile.

'Wyndsor,' said Orton, as though addressing a fellow but junior officer.

'May I introduce Detective Chief Superintendent Staunton who heads the inquiry into the death of Joy Prentiss.'

'Mr Staunton.' The slightly more formal greeting recognized Staunton's rank without granting it any enhanced standing.

'Pleased to meet you, sir,' said Bob, his normally heavy cockney accent noticeably less in evidence.

'Please be seated,' said Orton, waving them somewhat imperiously to chairs, 'and tell me how I can help you.'

Leo relaxed into an enveloping leather armchair. 'Firstly, sir, it is necessary for us to interview every resident in the immediate neighbourhood of Bacton Ford, so please understand that our visit here is a matter of general necessity rather than particular purpose.'

Orton settled himself into a chair facing them, the position of which somehow seemed to place him in the role of inquisitor.

'Can all the villagers expect a personal visit from the senior officers on the case then?' Orton's face revealed nothing but his tone indicated delicate disbelief.

'Our presence here only reflects your substantial standing in the community, sir,' said Leo, to whom words were an old and trusted weapon.

Only Orton's eyes revealed that he recognized in Leo a worthy antagonist. He moved slightly in his chair but said nothing.

'It is necessary for us to see everyone to establish their whereabouts at the time of the murder,' Leo continued. 'We work on the premise that only by eliminating the innocent can we isolate the guilty.'

'Then initially we are all suspect?'

'In a very general sense, yes.'

'A somewhat uncomfortable feeling,' said Orton, looking not in the least uncomfortable.

'Indeed. However, we try hard to prove a man's innocence.'

'Surely you should try to prove his guilt?'

'No. Ours is a fairer and more certain way. Only if we are totally unable to prove a man's innocence are we justified in seeking further evidence which might convince a court beyond reasonable doubt that he is guilty.'

'Forgive me . . .' Orton managed to sound faintly bored, 'but that smacks of the lecture room.'

'Then please accept my apologies. It seemed to me that you invited an explanation.'

On the loss of this debating point Commander Orton seemed for the first time to lose a little of his certainty. Bob Staunton scratched his cheek and behind the cover of his hand smiled to himself with the simple pleasure of a trainer whose favourite dog had just successfully performed a particularly difficult task.

'Perhaps I did,' said Orton. 'So you wish to know where I was at the time of the murder?'

'If you would be so kind. From 6 p.m. that evening until 3 a.m. the following morning . . . and the names of those persons who can verify your statement.'

'Then you will need to see my wife and daughter.' Orton started to rise but Leo put up a hand to stop him.

'There is no immediate hurry, sir. If we could just go through it with you first, then we shall only need to bother them for a few moments. We do not wish to cause undue upset, no doubt it was a shock.'

'Why, of course. We've known the family all our lives. Good people, a terrible thing, terrible.'

Whilst there was no warmth in Orton's words, they had the ring of honesty.

'Then if you could tell us . . .?' asked Leo gently.

'Yes, I was working in my study until seven, accounts you know . . . then I bathed and changed, we dined at eight and were together until about nine-thirty in the drawing room.'

'With your wife and daughter, sir?' asked Bob.

Orton looked at him in some surprise, as if he had forgotten his presence. 'Why, yes.'

'And then, sir . . .?' prompted Bob.

'Then I went out.'

'Alone?' asked Leo.

'Yes, we've had a lot of trouble with poachers on the estate lately. I take the dogs out now and again just to let them know I'm about.'

'What time did you return, sir?' asked Bob.

'About 1 a.m. My daughter had gone to bed but my wife was waiting up for me. We had some cocoa and went to bed about two.'

'Did you meet anyone, sir?' asked Bob.

Commander Orton looked blank. 'Pardon?'

'Poachers, sir.'

'Oh, no. Not that night.'

Bob Staunton dropped back in his chair, by this act removing himself from the conversation.

'Do you have any personal views as to who might be responsible, sir?' asked Leo, looking innocently at Orton.

Commander Orton stared into the middle distance, apparently deep in thought. When he spoke, it was slowly and carefully, choosing the words one by one.

'The short answer is no. However, knowing the local people as I do, I cannot imagine any one of them being responsible. It would seem to me most likely that whoever killed the Prentiss girl was a stranger, perhaps an occasional visitor, a travelling salesman or someone of that order. Also, from what I have read in the newspapers, it would seem that the murderer was mentally ill, no sane person could have attacked that girl in the manner he did. Regrettably I can think of no one who fits the bill.'

Leo nodded in mute acceptance of the Commander's reasoning.

'Perhaps we could take a written statement from you now, sir, just dealing with the points we have already covered.'

'Certainly. You may use my desk,' said Orton as though bestowing a monumental favour.

Half an hour later Commander Orton signed the statement form and left them to find his wife and daughter. As soon as he had gone Leo looked across at Bob. 'What do you think?'

'I think you're doing a good job,' said Bob enigmatically. 'We'll talk later.'

Orton returned with the women and the two officers stood as they entered. The introductions were brief and formal. Mrs Orton sat near her husband, legs crossed elegantly at the ankles, hands resting loosely together in her lap, an example of naturally correct deportment.

Janie Orton sat opposite Leo. She was wearing a crisply ironed cream blouse and a lightweight pleated skirt. She sat on the edge of the chair, her legs apart, elbows on her knees, face in her hands and stared with frank and uninhibited interest at Leo. She was seemingly unconscious of the fact that from where he sat he had an uninterrupted view between her legs. She had an aura of sullied innocence, of spotless white depravity, of virginal abandon and the effect on a man of Leo's susceptibility was devastating.

'Concentrate,' said the voice, 'you can't think while you're looking up her knickers.'

Leo turned away from her, but it was an effort.

'I understand from my husband that you wish us to confirm his presence here on the night the poor girl was killed.' There was in Mrs Orton's voice a clear indication of the absurdity of the request.

'A matter of formality only, madam,' said Leo, 'it will not take long.'

In fact twenty minutes later they had completed the two further statements which exactly dovetailed with the explanations given by Commander Orton.

As the officers drove away the Orton family stood on the step outside the massive front door, watching their departure. Leo watched them in return in his rear view mirror. Orton stood tall between the two women, his left arm round his wife, his right arm round his daughter. It should have been a still picture of a united, loving family yet it seemed to Leo that it was as much a façade as the gloomy backdrop of the house. He had a feeling of wrongness about the scene that he was unable to define.

'There's something wrong there,' said Bob, echoing his thoughts.

'Yes, there is.'

'I've been thinking. Reckon I know what it is.'

'Well I certainly don't.'

'There's no love there, mate. There's a house and a family and they all make the right noises but it's all on top. There's no love in the place, that's what it is.'

'Perhaps you're right. Certainly there is something strange about them, they made me feel uneasy.'

'I tell you they're cold fish. That's besides the fact that they weren't telling the truth.'

'Yes, and that's what's really bothering me.'

'We may never know the truth, mate, because he didn't kill her.'

'No, I don't think he did. I don't know why I'm so sure though, because he has no alibi that stands up.'

'If he was guilty he *would* have an alibi that stood up. That's partly why I don't think it's him.'

'I didn't have to refresh his memory at all. He knew the date and the day of the week she disappeared. He assumed that was the day she was murdered and his wife and daughter corroborated every word he said, every single word.'

Leo slowly negotiated a narrow bend in the road, then relaxed as he continued at crawling pace towards the village.

'One witness who remembered exactly what he was doing ten days before would be a miracle but three of them I do not believe. It doesn't help us though.' Bob bit thoughtfully at his thumbnail. 'See, they've worked it out together. They're word perfect. He was up to something they want kept secret but it could be something simple, something we wouldn't consider important at all, maybe he was at a meeting, maybe he's a mason?'

'No, he's not,' Leo spoke without thinking.

'No?' Bob grinned to himself. 'Well, I'm sure you're right.'

Leo threw him a quick, uncomfortable look, then shrugged. 'He's not a mason,' he said, turning his eyes back to the road, 'but he probably has got a tractor.'

'You're thinking about the oil on her clothes?'

'Yes.'

'Yeah, I've been thinking about that. It could point to anyone. Think about it, it was on the murderer's shoe, even office workers can tread in a patch of oil. That don't help us either. It's no good trying to make it fit him, we don't work that way, remember?'

Leo grinned. 'Ouch,' he said.

'No, our Commander Orton is worried about something but not about getting nicked for murder, that's for sure.' Bob looked at his thumb, then went back to biting it. 'If we're going to think about that oil at all it makes sense to start thinking about the place you'll find most of it, the local garage.'

'The boy friend.'

'Right. He's got a motorcycle and he works at the garage. He's still first suspect.'

'Maybe.'

'You're in a funny mood.'

'It's just that I don't see how he carried her two or three miles on the back of a motorcycle when she was at least partly unconscious.'

'I've got enough problems,' said Bob, giving up on his thumb, 'don't make any more. We'll have him in I think.'

'Yes,' Leo pulled up in front of the village hall. 'What about the other lad?'

'Who?'

'Cavill, the boy who found the body.'

'Yeah. Right, well we'll do the boy friend today and him tomorrow.'

'That's if the boy friend doesn't admit it.'

'Oh, you've cheered up then have you?' said Bob.

'I'm not usually despondent, Bacton Hall gave me the creeps that's all.' Leo combed his lengthy fair hair with his fingers. 'It's only half past three. If we pick him up now we'll have at least two hours at him before he's expected home.'

'Right, mate, off we go.'

'D'you want to go into the office first?'

'No. We'll only get stuck there if we go in. Drive straight down to the garage and we'll bring him back here with us.'

As they drove on to the forecourt of Bacton Ford garage the vicar, Ray Colville, was driving out in a small elderly saloon. He waved cheerily at them.

'That's your mate the vicar, isn't it?' asked Bob, peering at the departing car.

'Yes.'

'The hottest informant in the village,' said Bob, with a sly grin.

'That's all right, sir,' said Leo, with mock humility, 'knock poor old Leo, that's what he's paid for.'

They parked on the forecourt away from the petrol pumps and walked across to the office-cum-accessory shop that stood beside the single service bay. In the bay two overalled figures were guiding an engine, suspended on a hoist by chains, into position over the front of a car that looked to be the twin of Ray Colville's.

In the office a woman of about thirty was sitting at a desk poking delicately at an adding machine, careful not to damage her nails which were long and expertly painted. She stood up as they entered and looked inquiringly at them.

She was out of place here. Obviously a city girl. She was of medium height and slim, almost too slim. Her hair was dyed blonde and pulled back tightly behind her head. She had thin features which on close inspection gave her a slightly mean and strained look. She had a nervous habit of tightening her lips then relaxing them. Her clothes fitted her small but impressive figure perfectly and they were without mark or crease, as though she had ironed them after she had put them on. When she spoke her voice was high, tinged with the nervous edge of the shy person forced into public speech.

'Can I help you?' she asked.

Bob introduced them.

'You've made a mistake,' she said with certainty.

'Why's that, luv?' asked Bob.

'My husband and I have already been seen . . . by Sergeant Cobbold, he took statements from us both.'

'Ah, it's not that we've come about,' said Bob, 'you're Mrs . . .?'

'Salmon,' she said. 'Mrs Salmon.'

'And you and your husband run the garage?'

'Yes, well he does, I just do some paperwork now and again.'

She spoke quickly, in short bursts of words as though in a hurry to get the conversation done with.

'Could we see your husband, please, Mrs Salmon?' asked Leo.

'Yes, I'll call him.'

She went to the door and shouted 'Roy' in a voice that was harsh and strangely unfeminine.

Roy Salmon appeared a few minutes later. He was in his middle thirties, with a bronzed country face smeared with engine oil. He smiled amiably at them.

'Some more policemen,' said his wife, 'they want to see you.' She retired to a corner of the office where she sat side-legged on a table, setting a neat ankle to advantage. Leo caught her looking at him. There was the familiar flicker of interest in her eyes as she appraised him.

'I won't shake hands,' said Salmon, in his slow Suffolk accent, 'changing an engine, see.' He wiped some of the oil off his hands with an already filthy rag hanging from his overall pocket. 'What can I do for you-all?'

'Young Paul Spender works for you,' said Bob as a statement.

'So he does.'

'It's him we came to see. We've got to take another statement from him,' said Bob.

'She were his girl,' said Salmon, as though rationalizing this request to himself.

'Yes. Is he here?'

'Helping me change the engine. He be long with you, will he?'

'A while,' said Leo, 'he probably won't be in time to come back today.'

'You'll not keep him will you? He'll be back tomorrow? That engine, it's a two-man job that.'

'Oh, I shouldn't think so,' said Bob.

'Could do it myself perhaps,' said Salmon reflectively. He looked big enough. 'He won't get paid if'n he's not here,' he said as an afterthought.

'That him in the bay?' asked Bob.

'That's him. In the bay, that's Paul.'

'Thanks,' said Bob, 'we needn't bother you any more.'

'Good lad that Paul,' said Salmon, as they went out.

They found Paul Spender bent double with his head in the empty stomach of the car he and Salmon had been working on.

'Paul,' said Leo.

The boy straightened up and looked at them. He was tall, slightly built and had a shock of unruly brown hair. There was a certain listlessness in his manner and a blankness in his eyes. He did not know who they were but they looked as if they were people of authority and there was deference in his tone when he answered.

'Yes, sir,' he said.

'We are police officers, Paul,' said Leo. 'We're in charge of the investigation into Joy's death.'

Paul rubbed his oil-streaked hands uncertainly down his overalls. 'Yes, sir?' he said, his eyes flickering from Bob to Leo and back again.

'You made a statement to Detective Superintendent Day didn't you, my son?' said Bob.

'Yes, sir, I did that.'

'We'd like you to make another statement now, cover a few things we found out about since.'

'You mean right now, sir?'

'Yes, son, right now.'

'But I'm working now. I finish at six like.'

'We've seen Mr Salmon,' said Leo. 'He says he can spare you.'

'Well, if he says so,' Paul hesitated. 'I'll just take these off then,' he said, getting out of his heavily oil-stained overalls and throwing them across a work bench. He took a packet of cigarettes and a box of matches from a shelf and stuffed them into a pocket, then turned back to the officers.

'Should I tell my parents where I'll be like?' he asked.

'You'll be home for tea,' said Bob calmly, 'no need to bother them, eh?'

He led the way back to the car. As they drove away Leo saw Mr and Mrs Salmon standing side by side in the office watching them go. They looked an ill-assorted couple.

As Bob and Leo led Paul Spender through the village hall everyone working in the incident room watched them in curiosity and anticipation. When the door of Bob's office closed, they turned to muted speculation.

Leo placed a chair in front of the desk and motioned to Paul to sit. The boy sat bolt upright with his knees together and fidgeted nervously with his hands. Bob took off his jacket and hung it over the back of his chair before sitting down. Leo selected three statements from the pile on the larger of the two tables that flanked the wall opposite the desk and laid them in front of Bob.

'Mr Spender's first statement and those of his father and mother,' said Leo, as he took a chair for himself and placed it behind the desk beside the rather more comfortable one Bob occupied.

'You comfortable, son,' asked Bob of the boy.

'Yes thank you, sir,' he replied.

'Well I'm bloody not,' said Bob, 'open another window for me, Leo, it's like a bleeding oven in here.' Bob pulled his tie down an inch as Leo did his bidding.

'Right, let's get started shall we?' said Bob, smiling in friendly fashion at the boy who was still sitting rigid in his chair facing his interrogators. 'Relax, mate, we won't eat you, it's just a friendly chat.'

Paul seemed not in the least reassured.

'Now, according to this,' Bob tapped the statement, 'you've known Joy Prentiss all your life.'

'Yes, sir, I did.' He hesitated, grinding his hands together in his lap. 'Can I smoke, sir?'

'Fill your boots,' said Staunton, pushing an ashtray towards him and watching the boy like a hawk as he fumbled with the cigarette packet. Paul lit up with an unsteady hand.

'Why are you so nervous, my son?' Bob smiled, but only with his mouth.

'You think I killed her,' said Paul through a cloud of smoke. It was a statement of fact.

'We are trying to prove you did not kill her,' said Leo, toying with a pencil and not looking at the boy. 'After that we can set about finding out who did.'

'I didn't,' said Paul, shaking his head to add emphasis to his denial, 'but you won't believe me.'

'Why not?' asked Bob.

'Because . . .' the boy shrugged half-heartedly, 'because she was my girl, we had a row like and I was on my own when she was . . .' He faded into silence and stared down at the tip of his cigarette.

'What was the row about, Paul?' asked Leo.

'I saw her talking to another bloke one night when I went to pick her up from work.'

'And . . .?' prompted Bob.

'She said there weren't nothing in it and I didn't own her.'

'No more you do, mate,' said Bob.

'You don't understand . . . everybody knew. She had no right . . .'

'To talk to another man?' Bob relaxed back in his chair, Paul leaned forward to stub out the cigarette.

'She told me she went out with him and he took her out in his boat. She shouldn't have done that, sir. He were a married man and all.'

'We spoke to the man and it was all quite innocent,' Leo said, 'also she told you the truth; don't you think you were being a little unfair to her?'

Paul picked at a spot on the back of his hand and looked sullen. 'She didn't have no right.'

'You were angry?' asked Bob innocently.

'I were that but I got over it like. T'were too late then. She were missing . . . she were dead then.'

'On the evening she was killed you went out on your motorcycle. Just riding around you said . . . why was that?'

'I were angry inside. I took the bike up to Foxhall Heath and tore it around for a bit. I felt better after that. Then I rode up to Orford. I come home about half past ten. I was going to see her next day, apologize like, even though it weren't my fault.'

'Why apologize if it wasn't your fault?' asked Leo gently.

Paul fidgeted on his seat and was clearly finding an answer difficult. Eventually he said, 'I missed her like . . . I missed her that much it upset my stomach.'

'Did you see anyone who knew you at Foxhall Heath or on the way to or from Orford?' asked Leo.

'No, sir.'

'You sure?' Bob butted in.

'Sure, sir,' said Paul.

'So we have to rely on your word don't we, son?'

Paul slumped silently in the chair.

'Were you angry enough to kill her?' asked Bob, suddenly loud and harsh.

The boy jumped at the sudden change in tone and had answered before the full implication of the question hit him.

'No . . .'

'She wouldn't let you have your oats . . .'

'What . . .?'

'You wanted to go to bed with her . . .'

'Well . . . yes, but . . .'

'She wouldn't have it.'

'No.'

'Then you found out she was seeing another bloke and you thought he was getting it, so you killed her.'

Paul came slowly, white-faced to his feet. He stood before them mouthing words that would not come.

'Want to tell me about it?' asked Bob, gentle again now.

'Joy...' Paul fought to get the words out, 'I could not kill Joy. Not her.'

'Why not? She was seeing another man.'

'Not my Joy, not her.' Paul sat down suddenly on the hard chair, limp and defeated.

'But why not?' Bob persisted.

'Because she was the most beautiful thing in the whole world,' said Paul simply.

Bob and Leo exchanged glances and arrived at a mutually understood decision.

'Relax, Paul,' said Leo, 'we have to ask these things. We can't let the murderer go free, can we?'

For the first time Paul showed some animation. 'I could kill him that did it,' he said, and raised strong hands with thumbs arched outwards and fingers straining towards each other.

'I could choke that bastard to death, I could.'

He dropped his hands and screwed up his eyes. His body shook. Tears coursed down his face.

They gave him time to recover, took a lengthy statement from him and at six-thirty they sent him home.

'Fancy him?' asked Bob, when they were alone.

'Not my type,' said Leo, with a grin.

'You've a dirty mind,' said Bob. 'Well?'

'He's either innocent or a consummate actor,' Leo shook his head, 'and I don't rate him as a thespian somehow.'

'He's a big lad,' said Bob, thoughtfully.

'It seems there are not many dwarfs round these parts,' said Leo, 'even Tom Stack at the Haywain throws barrels of beer around as if they were powder puffs.'

'You're not seriously putting his name forward are you?'

'No. He was at a licensed victuallers' meeting in Ipswich that night. I read his statement yesterday. No doubt that's where he was, his name appears in the minutes of the meeting.'

'So you did reckon him then?'

'Not really. I just didn't ignore him that's all.'

'Well,' said Bob, rising from his chair, 'let's go and see if he's poisoned the beer.'

The reporters clustered round them as they entered the Haywain.

'Heard you had someone in for questioning, sir,' said a large man from a Sunday horrible.

'Just for a statement,' said Bob.

'Care for a drink, sir?' asked another.

'Thought you'd never ask,' said Bob, 'large Scotch.'

'Can we expect an early arrest?' asked another.

'You've been reading too many papers,' said Bob, 'I'm afraid not.'

'It was the boy friend wasn't it?'

'Look lads,' said Bob, 'we spoke to young Paul Spender. We already had a statement from him but it only covered two pages. Now we got another and it's six pages but if you say any more than that he'll sue you and I'll help him.'

The large man from the Sunday pushed forward as Staunton sipped his drink.

'Look, sir. You cancelled the press conference tonight, then we hear you'd had the boy friend in, you can't blame us for thinking can you?'

'No,' said Bob.

'The story's pretty dead,' said the big man, 'can't you give us something to keep it going?'

'Wish I could,' said Bob, 'fact is, it's all hard slog at the moment and that's the truth. Some of you know me, if there was anything, I'd give it to you but there isn't. The boy is no more suspect than anyone else.'

The long faces among the reporters showed their disappointment. Bob ordered some sandwiches for himself and Leo and the conversation became general. An hour later they returned to the office and buried themselves in the latest batch of statements Sergeant Cobbold had taken in the village.

Just after ten o'clock they called it a day and after a nightcap with the Stacks they both retired to bed.

Leo was fast asleep when Anne crawled into the bed beside him at eleven-thirty. He mumbled blearily as he moved across to make room for her.

'Tired,' he said indistinctly.

Her hand slid between his legs, warm and encouraging.

'Very tired,' he said.

'That's all right, lover,' she said as she moved into position and sank herself down on to him, 'you just lay still a minute.' She moved gently up and down, finding pleasure in his quiescence.

Detective Inspector Stan Grace sat in a crime squad car parked on the verge of the Ipswich to Felixstowe road. Beside him the driver was crunching loudly and happily as he made rapid inroads into a large bag of crisps.

They were some thirty yards beyond the road block which consisted of a traffic patrol car and crew, commandeered for the job, and six of his own men in two nondescript cars.

Grace looked at his watch. It was nearly midnight. He settled more comfortably into his seat and stared out of the window thinking of nothing in particular.

'Want a crisp, sir?' Grace shook his head in refusal. The driver shrugged.

'They're good,' he said, tipping up his face and emptying the bag into it.

Grace stared moodily out into the night. The tall trees on either side of the road drew faint outlines of themselves on the road in the moonlight. There was the harsh rattle of a diesel engine as a huge container lorry pulled away from the road block and accelerated away past them.

'Noisy bastards,' said Grace.

Peace settled on the road again as the noise of the lorry receded towards Felixstowe and its destination at the docks. The officers on the road block milled around leaning against their cars and talking amongst themselves, waiting for their next customer.

A pair of headlights showed in the distance headed towards the road block. Grace looked across at his driver in disgust as that officer noisily picked his teeth and swallowed the treasures he found, intent on getting value for money.

The headlights slowed down as the oncoming car approached the road block. Grace watched it idly then alarm bells rang in his brain as he saw the car was maintaining speed.

'Start the engine,' he said sharply.

The driver obeyed by reflex. The oncoming car was gaining speed now and the traffic patrol officers at the road block were waving frantically at it as the crime squad men raced for their vehicles.

The uniformed officers dived out of its path as the car smashed through the road block, its engine screaming under full acceleration.

'Get after the bastard,' said Grace, as the powerful saloon flashed past them. His driver swung them out in pursuit, moving quickly through the gears, the car steady as a rock under his hands as the speedo reached up towards its limit.

Angelo Quantez was not a brave man. When the police stopped him at the road block his heart stopped as well. He had been sure they would search his cab and find the plastic wallets the man in London had paid him so much to deliver. But they had only asked him questions, they had not searched his cab and he had been allowed to go. Now, as he drove away, the reaction set in. He felt an overwhelming desire to pass water.

The road was deserted and he pulled his large container lorry to the side and stopped. It was not a good place to park, being one of the few stretches of two-way road on this route, but he could not wait. He jumped down from the cab and hurried into the bushes.

As he did up his flies and lit a calming cigarette he heard the scream of approaching engines. He walked back towards his lorry and saw two sets of headlights approaching at high speed. Suddenly he realized that in his haste he had switched off the lights of his vehicle. It stood seventeen feet high, ten feet wide, completely blocking one side of the road and would be invisible to the oncoming cars. He started to run.

The leading car was only thirty yards from the parked lorry when its headlights picked up the huge wall that was the rear of the container lorry. It was too late. The driver spun the wheel desperately to the right and the car careered onwards at an angle for a second, then turned over just before it struck. It spun into the air and the driver was thrown out, his body cartwheeling in a loose flurry of arms and legs, finally coming to rest in the bushes beside the road. The car flew through the air, struck a telegraph pole five feet from the ground and burst into flames.

Angelo Quantez began to shiver uncontrollably. He was not a brave man.

EIGHT

Bob and Leo left the Haywain just after eight o'clock the following morning and walked in companionable silence up the main street of the village.

When they reached the small parade of shops near the village hall, Leo hesitated.

'Anything you want? I need another razor.'

'No, mate, you carry on. I'll see you in the office.'

Bob wandered on and Leo turned towards the tiny general store. The exterior paintwork of the shop was faded and cracking and the name above the door, 'A. GATWOOD', was difficult to pick out. The windows were a jumble of grocery and toilet items, no attempt apparently having been made at a tempting display.

Inside, the shop was cool and clean, a delight of old-fashioned trading. The stock overflowed from the shelves and counters on to the floor leaving only a small space in the centre for the customers to stand. It smelt of fresh vegetables, confectionery, cheese and uncut bacon.

The couple behind the counter spoilt the effect. Gatwood was a fat man with greasy black hair plastered across a balding pate and small piggy eyes. His wife was slightly taller, greying hair pulled back in a tight bun. Her face had a mean look emphasized by close-set eyes. There was an unsightly mole on her left cheek from which two hairs grew.

There were two customers in the shop as Leo entered, both women of middle age and alike enough to be sisters. He did not recognize them but it was clear that all four knew who he was. The intense conversation that had been taking place stopped instantly and there was a moment of silence that screamed 'stranger'.

Gatwood put on his false, trading smile.

'Good morning, sir. Can I help you?'

Leo gestured politely to the two women.

'That's all right, sir. These ladies are just deciding.'

Leo made his purchase, conscious all the while that the women's hostile eyes were upon him. He was glad to be back on the street again and was aware without looking or hearing that the interrupted conversation continued on his departure.

The morning sunlight was warm but he shivered. For the first time he felt how these people saw him, an outsider, an alien.

When Leo arrived in the village hall he found Bob Staunton deep in a pile of statements and in an uncommunicative mood. He left him to it and spent half an hour with Sergeant Worthington and the office staff.

He noticed the tubby figure of Sergeant Cobbold ensconced at a table in one corner sorting out some of the statements he and the crime squad men had taken in the village. Cobbold looked up as Leo took a seat beside him.

'Morning, sir,' said Cobbold inquiringly.

'Something I wanted to ask you.'

'Yes, sir.' Cobbold pushed the statements away and settled back in his chair, glad of a break from the boring routine of checking and cross-checking.

'I saw Ray Colville, the vicar yesterday. He told me you'd investigated the theft of some items from the church a few weeks back.'

'That's right, sir.'

'Get any leads?'

Cobbold shook his head and looked a little uncomfortable. 'I'm afraid not, sir.'

'Roger, this is not the first time this sort of thing has happened at the church and other churches have suffered as well.'

'It's very difficult, this sort of thing . . .' said Cobbold slowly, 'unless you catch them at it that is. Nobody talks you see, not on a thing like this.'

'Why not?'

'Well,' Cobbold stopped to think, 'you see, the people round here, the old families that is, they're a community on their own. They don't let on to strangers nor yet to authorities and they're the only ones who'd know.'

'But you're one of them,' said Leo, 'won't they talk to you even?'

'Not about a thing like this.'

'They could be responsible for the thefts, or some of them.'

'More than likely,' agreed Cobbold.

'So they win,' said Leo, 'they get away with it.'

Cobbold scratched his ear. 'Well not exactly. Don't misunderstand me here, I'd catch them if I could but the fact is they do pay for what they take mostly.'

'How?'

'Well if something goes missing, more often than not there's a big collection in the plate at the church the following Sunday. More than enough to cover what's gone.'

'Ah.' The chair groaned in protest as Leo sat back.

'That don't make it right, mind,' said Cobbold quickly, 'but that's the way it is like.'

'How did they pay for the graves they dug up and the headstones they smashed?' asked Leo, leaning forward to look hard at Cobbold.

'Ah, well that's another thing,' said the Sergeant evasively.

'No it's not,' said Leo, 'it's the same thing, the same people. You know that as well as I do. There's a coven operating here and it's almost certainly made up of people from the village. Witchcraft, Roger, nothing else fills the bill.'

Cobbold wiped a dry hand across his mouth. 'Yes, sir, I reckon that's about it.'

'Why were you so reluctant to talk about it?'

'Seems a bit daft, doesn't it, sir? Policemen talking about witches and suchlike in this day and age.'

'So long as a single coven exists and a single person believes in the Devil then policemen are entitled to take it into account. Suppose it had some bearing on this inquiry?'

Cobbold looked puzzled. 'Don't see how it could, sir.'

'She dies within an hour of her twenty-first birthday which also happened to be the feast of Lammas. Does that mean anything to you?'

It obviously did. Cobbold stiffened and looked away. Leo waited.

'I see what you mean, sir.'

'So, can you think of anything at all that might help us? Anyone we could start with?'

Cobbold looked him straight in the eye. 'I can't, sir. Could be anyone in the village and that's the truth. I'll mind what you've said though.'

'Sergeant Cobbold.' Bob Staunton stood in the door of his office, beckoning. Leo followed the sergeant into the office.

'I want you to bring young Brian Cavell in to see me,' said Bob to Cobbold.

'Very well, sir, right now?'

'No, make it . . .'

'Funeral at ten-fifteen, sir,' Leo reminded.

'Yeah, make it eleven-thirty then.'

'Yes, sir.'

'Right, off you go, son.'

As Cobbold left the room Bob suddenly clutched at his throat. 'Bloody hell, I haven't got a black tie.'

Leo pulled two from his pocket and handed one over.

'There you are, I brought a spare just in case.'

'Oh, right then. Thanks.' Bob returned to his pile of papers without another word.

Only three reporters turned up for the press conference that morning. Leo had little to offer them and they agreed that there was little point in continuing with regular meetings. Only Dave Bull, the local man, asked if he could pop in from time to time. The others indicated that they were heading for pastures new.

Bob and Leo left immediately afterwards for the church. They stood together beside the churchyard gate as the cortège wound its way up the main street of the village towards them. Leo's gaze strayed inadvertently towards the far corner of the graveyard where he knew there was a blackened patch of ground. Was there some deep irony in the fact that the girl was to be buried here?'

They followed the mourners to the graveside where Ray Colville performed the burial service. It was another very hot day and Leo could see the sweat running in rivulets down Bob Staunton's face and disappearing beneath his collar.

As the vicar's voice droned on Leo's eyes wandered around the faces of the mourners, resting at last on the distraught parents. In a tree above them a blackbird was in full song, oblivious of the drama being enacted below. Was there really the body of a dead girl in that wooden box? It hardly seemed possible.

The coffin was lowered into the gaping hole. Colville picked up a handful of earth.

'Ashes to ashes, dust to dust . . .'

Would someone look at this grave in a hundred years' time and wonder why Joy Prentiss had died before the full bloom of womanhood, wonder at the futility of it, the horror of an unfulfilled life? Was Leah Martin, aged four, murdered also? The gravestones would not say, they would only record the fact of death not the manner or the reason. They pose questions for the thinking man but offer no answers. Nobody has any answers.

They were filling in the grave. Ray Colville was standing with the parents, his head bent towards them as he mouthed words of comfort. The mourners broke up into small groups and began to move away. Leo saw Bob Staunton go to the father and take his hand.

'We'll do our best,' he heard Bob say. There was a look of painful gratitude in the man's eyes but his wife was marble-faced and dry-eyed in her grief.

The gravedigger was shovelling hard at the diminishing pile of earth beside the grave. A blackbird hopped around his feet, its beak already half full of grubs. Leo felt the flush of anger. Nature could be obscene. He wanted to run across and kick out at the bird. Instead, he turned away and joined Bob Staunton for the walk back to the village hall.

Detective Inspector Stan Grace was waiting for them when they arrived back at the office.

'Hullo, mate,' said Bob without his usual ebullience.

'They told me you were at the funeral, sir. Thought I'd hang on till you got back.'

'I could do with some good news. Got any?'

Grace shook his head. 'Not for the inquiry but we did have a bit of excitement last night.'

'Yeah?'

'Chap jumped the road block. We took off after him and he hit a parked lorry and wrote the car off on a telegraph pole.'

'Dead?' asked Leo.

'No. He had more luck than he was entitled to. He was thrown clear before the car caught fire.'

'What's his game then?' asked Bob.

'He'd nicked the car and done a shopbreaking in Nottingham. On his way to see his girl friend in Felixstowe. He'll be in hospital for a couple of months they say.'

'Sure he can't be our man?' Leo inquired.

'Definitely. He was doing the job in Nottingham that night. Incidentally we had another tickle. Remember I said he hit a lorry?

Well, the lorry driver had been through the road block and stopped for a slash. Parked the bloody thing right across the road with no lights, that's why our friend hit it. The driver was pretty shaken up, Spanish chap he was, had six packets of heroin under his seat. So we had him as well and could be more to come in London.'

Grace looked well pleased with his night's work.

'Well it's an ill wind, they say,' said Bob.

'Bit hard on him though, gets through the road block then gets arrested by accident as it were. His guardian angel must have had a night off.' Grace did not sound at all sorry.

'Well that's his worry,' said Bob sourly. 'Nothing for us, then?'

'We found seven more who were on the road on the night of the murder but they saw nothing.'

'You mean that,' said Bob, 'they really saw nothing at all going on on that road?'

'My boys are pretty thorough,' said Grace, 'they've done this before. You can take it for certain that these people saw nothing.'

'Yeah.' Bob rounded his desk and plopped into his chair, pulling off his black tie as he did so. 'I'm sure you're right. Just seems odd. She was walking home and she met the murderer on that road. You'd have thought someone would've seen them, wouldn't you? Her or him or his car, something.'

'We may pick up something yet.' Grace did not sound very hopeful.

'We'll give it another couple of days, then we'll see,' said Bob, struggling to get his own tie back on.

A knock interrupted them and Sergeant Cobbold's rotund face appeared round the door. 'I've got young Cavell here, sir.'

'I'll pop in tomorrow, sir,' said Inspector Grace.

'Okay, mate,' said Bob, and then to Cobbold, 'Wheel him in, my son.'

Cobbold held the door open for the departing Inspector then closed it firmly behind him. 'D'you want a lever with young Cavell, sir?' he asked.

'A what?' said Bob.

'Well, sir, the time he found the body he were trespassing on old Cracknell's land and he had a twelve-bore after pigeons but he don't have no licence,' Cobbold explained. 'He reckons he's in trouble like, so if you want to lean on him you've got a lever.'

'Sergeant, you've got an evil mind,' said Bob, but grinned his approval. 'Let's have him in.'

Leo laid the boy's statement in front of Bob as Cobbold brought him in and stood him by the chair in front of the desk.

Bob left him standing there for several minutes after Cobbold had left without acknowledging his presence. The boy began to fidget, holding his hands together in front of him and picking at the dirt under his fingernails.

'Know who I am?' asked Bob apparently still reading the statement.

'Yes, sir.' Brian Cavell tried his hands at his sides but they didn't seem right there. He crossed his arms in front of his chest but that seemed worse so he took them down again.

'Sit down,' said Bob, still not looking up.

Cavell sat down gratefully. It was something to do.

Bob looked at him for the first time. His nose twitched as he caught the aroma of the farmyard. 'Let's see your gun licence,' said Bob, holding out his hand.

'Ain't got one, sir,' said Cavell.

'You were trespassing on Mr Cracknell's land and you had a shotgun with you,' said Leo coldly.

'Yes, sir . . . well I've been meaning to like.'

'Meaning to what?' asked Bob.

'Get a licence. It sort of kept slipping my memory.'

'Stop picking your nails,' ordered Bob.

'Yes, sir.'

'You found the body.'

'Yes, sir.'

'D'you know the girl?'

'Yes, sir, we . . .'

'Don't tell me,' Bob interrupted, 'you went to school together.'

'We were cousins,' said Cavell.

'Kissing cousins?' Leo put in.

'What?'

'How close were you?'

'I didn't fancy her if that's what you mean . . .'

'Why not, she was pretty enough wasn't she?' asked Bob.

'Too skinny for my liking,' said the boy defiantly.

'Can you drive?' asked Leo.

'Yes, well tractors like.'

'Got a car, motorcycle?' from Bob.

'No sir, can't afford that.'

'According to this,' Bob tapped the statement in front of him, 'you were at home the night she was killed.'

'Yes, sir.'

'You sure about that?' from Leo.

'Yes, sir. My father kept me in.'

'Eh?' Bob looked blankly at the hulking eighteen-year-old six footer, 'your dad kept you in?'

'Yes, sir. I broke the chain on my bike so I borrowed his to go to the pub. He didn't like that so he kept me in. Said I should've asked like.' He sounded suitably contrite. Bob raised his eyebrows and tried another tack.

'Any ideas who might've killed Joy?'

Cavell sucked in air through his teeth and shook his head. 'Can't say I have,' he said, and then remembering his lack of a gun licence added 'sir'.

'What about her boy friend?'

'Paul?'

'Yeah, Paul.'

Cavell shook his head. 'Soft as lights, him. Suffin' daft over that girl, he were. Couldn't understand it, I couldn't. That weren't him done it.'

'Why not?'

'Like I said, soft as lights he is. He come over ours one day when I was drowning some kittens. Sick as ought he was, right over my boots.'

They spent half an hour taking a detailed statement from him then told him he could go.

'What about the other thing then?' he asked nervously.

'What?' said Bob blankly.

'That about the gun licence.'

Bob sighed. 'Listen, mate,' he said, 'when we catch this bloke you turn up in court and give your evidence like in the statement, nice and clear and we'll forget all about it. How about that?'

Brian Cavell grinned in relief, showing off his lack of interest in dental hygiene.

'We're fast running out of suspects,' said Leo when Cavell and his aroma had left the room.

'Now tell me news,' said Bob glumly.

'Time for lunch,' said Leo.

Anne Partridge was serving in the saloon bar of the Haywain when they arrived. She gave them a smiling welcome that didn't betray the close relationship between her and Leo. Bob was appreciative.

'Good girl that,' he said in a huge whisper, 'doesn't show owt does she?' Leo winced but miraculously no one else in the bar seemed to have heard.

Anne put down drinks in front of them and waved in the direction of the window. Dave Bull, the local reporter, nodded at them and Bob raised his glass in thanks.

'Not a bad lad that,' said Bob, 'I'll go over and have a word. We haven't given them much on this job.'

He left Leo alone at the bar.

'Be back in a minute, lover,' said Anne and disappeared in the direction of the cellar.

'I tell you I want another one.' The voice was high-pitched and querulous. It struck a chord of memory and Leo looked across to the corner of the bar.

It seemed the local garage was left in the care of young Paul Spender. Mr and Mrs Salmon were engaged in a bout of in-fighting. She was clearly the worse for a few, her thin face flushed and animated, her lips a narrow line of determination. Her husband held up a hand to hush her.

'I want a drink,' she said, enunciating too carefully and trying unsuccessfully to lower her voice.

Salmon took her firmly by the elbow and stood her up. She did not try to resist but anger blazed in her eyes. As he led her along the bar towards the door their faces were fixed in lying half smiles for the benefit of the other customers. Leo noticed that Salmon's fingers were digging into his wife's arm. She'd carry a bruise for that.

'She's a bitch.' Anne had reappeared behind the bar.

'Because she has one too many?' Leo pushed his glass over for a refill.

'Not specially. She just is.'

'I feel sorry for her.' As he said it Leo realized that he did.

Anne put the full glass in front of him and took his money. 'So long as that's all you feel,' she said.

'Not my type.' Leo took a sip, 'I like a woman you can get hold of.'

He did not hear her come in but he smelt the scent and sensed the rustle of silk. Even had he not, the look on Anne's face would have signalled her presence.

Janie Orton took a seat at the bar beside him. 'Vodka and lime, please, Anne.' The words were innocent, her tone polite but the imperious demand was edged with malice. Anne turned away.

Leo put money on the bar. 'May I?'

She nodded acceptance. Anne dumped the drink on the bar with unnecessary violence and took the money.

'A nice little dress, Anne.' With a smile that had all the warmth of a striking cobra.

Anne smiled back in like manner. 'Yes,' she said, 'I bought it at the last church jumble sale. The vicar said you gave it . . . I had it taken in a little.'

'Ah yes,' Janie hesitated beautifully, 'I remember now, it belonged to cook. It did rather hang on her after she went on a diet.'

Anne picked up a glass and rubbed furiously at it. Janie sipped her drink and eyed Leo. She inclined her head towards Anne.

'She does that beautifully doesn't she? Perfect action with the fingers. Practice, I imagine.'

Leo remained silent. He had an acute sense of self-preservation and clearly Anne was near flashpoint. There was no way he could win if he opened his mouth, so he settled for an enigmatic smile.

'Two pints, luv,' Bob's strident voice interrupted Anne as she was about to reply. She slammed her mouth shut and moved away to fulfil the order.

'Lower sixth stuff that,' said Leo mildly.

'Yes,' said Janie, 'rather juvenile, I'm afraid.'

'So why?'

'We both enjoy it. It livens things up. I can't be too clever or it goes over her head.' She eyed him inquiringly.

'You've had her of course or she wouldn't have been quite so jumpy.'

'Of course.'

'Are you a good lay?' She asked much in the way she might have inquired about a stallion's stud performance.

'I'm told so.' Leo was a little sharp in his reply. Suddenly he was off obvious women, even one this beautiful.

She explored her lips with her tongue as she looked at him. 'You're rather pretty,' she said.

Leo was beginning to feel like a zoo exhibit. 'Thank you, gracious lady,' he said, in a half mocking tone.

'I think I might have you,' she said, 'if a suitable occasion arises, and I think it will.' She finished her drink, slid off the bar stool and was gone before Leo could recover his composure.

He was taking a much-needed swig when Anne reappeared behind the bar.

'She's a bitch,' she said venomously.

'You're not having a good day, Anne.' Leo drained his pint. 'Every woman that comes into the pub is a bitch according to you.'

Anne leaned across the bar towards him and stabbed his chest with her right forefinger. 'If you bed her, Leo,' she said quietly, 'so help me, I'll cut your equipment off.'

When they reached the village hall Bob went straight to his office and busied himself in a pile of statements and messages. Leo spent half an hour with Sergeant Worthington in the main incident room but in fact there was little for him to do. Worthington had the office ticking over in perfect rhythm and in fact had already reduced the staff by one typist and two constables as the initial flow of incoming work had decreased.

Leo wandered into Bob Staunton's office. He was sitting at his desk surrounded by paper, his tie at half mast. Despite the open window it was oppressively hot in the tiny room.

'Anything I can do for you, sir?'

'No, mate, I'm going to work my way through all the statements again. There's got to be something we've missed.'

'Will you want the car?'

'All I want is a couple of hours' peace and quiet.'

Leo told Worthington that Bob was not to be disturbed then drove off through the village in the direction of the river. He had no set plan in mind. He felt lethargic and not a little depressed. The inquiry seemed to be settling into a stalemate situation and he had the feeling they were going to need a huge slice of luck if they were to get a result.

Almost in sight of the river the road forked right and left. He turned right following the singpost directing him to the marina.

He parked beside the clubhouse and walked down to the wooden pilings that protected the river bank. There was no one in sight. The sun seemed to have drawn the energy from the river which moved sluggishly on the ebb tide. The boats drawn up on the hard and bobbing gently at anchor ranged from tiny fishing skiffs to ocean-going yachts and motor cruisers. There was a lot of money around here somewhere. Clearly not much of it was in the village so the marina must draw its custom from a large surrounding area. More suspects?

He returned to the car and retraced his route to the crossroads. The left fork simply said 'To the river'. After a moment's heistation he turned in that direction. A small estate car pulled out from the entrance to a field where it had been hidden from his sight and followed him.

The road soon became single track then turned sharply left and right and degenerated into a pot-holed, rutted path that meandered through overhanging trees and a wall of thick shrubs.

The path ended suddenly at the river's edge. Leo turned the car and parked on the grass verge. He threw his jacket and tie into the driving seat, locked up and set off along a narrow path.

The river was to his right and to his left a field of wheat, beyond which could just be seen the grim ramparts of Bacton Hall. In the foreground, beyond the wheatfield, he caught sight of a low stone building part hidden by trees and shrubs. It looked like an unusually substantial summer house.

Leo began to sweat as the path led him upwards to a cliff top some fifty feet above the level of the river bank. When he reached the top he was amongst trees and low grasses. The view up and down the river was one of startling beauty. Both banks were a medley of greens and the river bent slowly away, dappled white on blue as the sun reflected each eddy and ripple.

A wave of desperate tiredness flooded over him. Late nights, intense concentration and considerable sexual athletics had taken their toll, the stiff walk up to the cliff and the hot sun had drained the last of his energy.

He left the path and sat down between the trees in a secluded oval patch of sunlight and drank in the view. Despite his inaction it was still uncomfortably hot. He looked quickly around him. Only birds singing and scuffling sounds in the undergrowth.

He stripped quickly, placing his clothes on the ground to form a barrier between his naked body and the stiff bladed grass, then sank back, stretching his muscled body one limb at a time like a settling feline. The sun bathed him in warm assurance. A heavily loaded bumble bee droned around him, seducing the wild flowers in seemingly untiring abandon, each conquest denoted by a brief cessation of the monotonous deep hum of its wings. A cotton-wool cloud of gnats collected above his head, soundless, mindless communal movement. His eyes closed and almost instantly he slept.

Leo had no idea for how long he slept. His first impression was that he was chained to the ground between two tight brown marble columns in a world of dim, diffused sunlight. As he struggled to consciousness he heard the soft feminine laughter.

Janie Orton stood above him, one leg on either side of his head, her loose dress almost obscuring his face from her sight. She saw his eyes distend in horror as he realized who she was and that he was lying naked beneath her.

Leo lay stock still, staring up at her. His brain refused to act, no words came. A slight breeze billowed out the skirt of her dress and his eyes followed the inside curve of her legs to their meeting point. It was a further shock to see the smudge of fair hair and above that the naked swell of her breasts. She was wearing nothing but the dress, which from his privileged position hid none of her secrets. She laughed again, low and conspiratorial. His cheeks flamed with embarrassment and he struggled for words.

'You've got no clothes on,' he said, and could immediately have bitten out his tongue. She laughed again.

'One more item than you,' she said.

'Let me get up.' God this was ridiculous.

She moved back, placing her feet beside his chest, pinning his arms to his side. Her tongue flickered round her lips.

'I let you sleep,' she cocked her head on one side, 'I thought you'd like to be woken like this.'

Leo looked desperately around him. He could hardly wrestle the girl off him could he? Pretty undignified that.

'It's all right,' she said, 'there's nobody about.'

'Let me get up, Janie.' He sounded to his own ears like a cringing third former bested in a playground tussle.

'Let me get up, Janie,' mimicked the voice.

'Not yet.' She moved her feet further back, level with his thighs, then knelt forward on to her knees, sitting on his stomach.

He felt the silky warmth of the inside of her legs against his side, the moistness between her legs.

'Look . . .' he got no further.

'No, you look,' she said. She crossed her hands across her chest, clutched the dress and pulled it off in one swift movement. Her breasts bobbled enticingly in the sunlight.

'She's going to rape you,' said the voice, 'what a joke.'

Unreasoning panic set in. 'For Christ's sake, Janie, not here.'

'It's for my sake and I say here and now.' She reached back and ran her hand down his naked stomach and between his legs.

He felt his panic subsiding in inverse proportion to the rise of his desire. His stomach muscles flickered in anticipation as she caressed him.

'There's a big boy,' she said, as much to herself as to him.

'Do something, Leo,' begged the voice. Leo did nothing.

Janie moved her body and guided him into her. At first her movements were slow and careful. She sat on him, watching him, an arrogant, confident half smile on her face. Then she moved faster, pushing hard down on him, willing him to action.

'I won't be long,' she said, the insult as much in her look as in her words. Suddenly Leo woke from his torpor, anger adding spice to pleasure. He reached up and grabbed her hair, pulling her down on to him, his tongue locking their mouths together. His hands reached for her breasts, his back arched and he thundered into her.

He was rewarded by a slight moan and later the squirming tortured movements of delight as she achieved climax. He allowed himself to relax and exploded into her.

After a few moments she sat up. He felt himself shrinking inside her.

'I imagine that's that,' she said, but her voice was a little shaky and the attempt at arrogance fell a little flat. They lay side by side soaking up the sun, bathing in the afterglow of passion.

Leo rolled on to his side and picked a piece of dry grass from her breast.

'How did you know I was here?'

'I followed you.'

'Why?'

She laughed up at him and he could not help but join in.

'Have you lived here all your life?'

'Apart from university.'

'I want to ask you something.' He bent down and nuzzled her breasts with his nose.

'The answer's yes.'

Leo sat up. 'Not that.'

'Too soon for you?' The smile and the arrogance were back.

'Do you know how I might make contact with the witchcraft coven here in Bacton Ford?'

She stiffened and her eyes went stony. 'What makes you think there is one?'

'There is.'

'Are you one of those people?' She was picking her words with care.

'No.'

'Why are you interested then?' She sat up on her elbows and looked hard at him.

It was an awkward question. He wasn't even sure why he had broached the subject with her. He had given it no prior thought and now he wished he had.

'Acquiring unusual knowledge is a sort of hobby of mine.'

It sounded as weak as it was.

'What makes you think I would know?'

'Find an answer to that one without showing your hand,' said the voice. 'Better make it good.'

'I'm not sure. Perhaps the way you make love . . .'

'Good grief!' said the voice.

'I've met people who were involved, they have an attitude of superiority . . . arrogance almost.'

'Keep trying,' said the voice in false encouragement.

She stood up with an easy supple movement, slipped her dress over her head and pushed her feet into open sandals. 'You're a poor liar,' she said coldly, 'and we didn't make love, we had sex. I should have thought you would know the difference.'

Leo sensing the advantage she had taken by dressing, scrambled for his clothes.

'I'm sorry, Janie . . .'

'You bore me,' she said and walked quickly away, leaving him in an undignified pose, hopping on one foot with his underpants halfway up his legs.

He dressed quickly and took the path back to the car. Janie Orton had long disappeared.

'She used you like a six-inch Woolworth's candle,' said the voice. 'About all you're good for.'

She had too. He wasn't egotistical, she had not just been after his body. What then? She had arranged the whole scene to give herself the maximum advantage throughout. Why? Did she find out what she wanted to know?

'She found out you're anybody's,' the voice tittered.

Suppose she was a member of the coven. They'd all know he was interested now, they'd go to ground. If she wasn't what the hell would she think? That was the lesser of the two evils. Either way he hadn't been very clever, in fact he'd made a complete mess of it.

'Not surprising if you carry your brain between your legs,' said the voice acidly.

By the time Leo arrived back at the village hall he had been gone for over three hours but Bob was still immersed in paper and did not seem to have missed him.

Leo busied himself in the main office until six-thirty then sent a constable across to the Haywain for sandwiches for himself and Bob.

In the next hour Sergeant Cobbold, Superintendent Day and Inspector Grace all returned with further batches of statements from their various activities and Bob and Leo spent the rest of the evening going through them.

They stopped work at ten o'clock and repaired to the pub. Both bars were full. It seemed most of Bacton Ford was represented there that night.

Anne was serving but they didn't get the usual smiling welcome. She seemed cool and distant.

Rita and Tom Stack were busy behind the bar but near closing time Leo found himself alone in conversation with the publican and the local reporter, Dave Bull. He steered the conversation on to the subject that was occupying his mind more and more.

'I had a chat with Ray Colville the other day.'

'Good lad that,' said Stack approvingly.

'He was telling me about the trouble he's had there.'

'What trouble?' asked Bull.

'Stuff stolen from the church, desecrated graves . . .'

'Ah, that . . .' Stack shook his head. 'Bad business.'

'Seems beyond belief in this day and age . . . people dancing naked round fires in the woods and all that rubbish.'

'It's not rubbish, believe you me,' said Stack. 'There're folk in these parts that take it seriously.'

'Really?'

'Goes back into history round here . . . strange thing would be if there wasn't someone still at it.' Stack looked round then edged closer. 'Wouldn't be surprised if some of them aren't in this pub right now.'

'You know who they are?'

'Good Lord no.' Stack took a swig of his beer. 'I'm an outsider, only lived here fifteen years. They're not likely to advertise, are they?'

Leo turned to Dave Bull who had remained silent and thoughtful.

'Isn't there a story in this somewhere?'

'If I'd thought so I'd have done a piece on it by now,' said Bull shortly.

'The Sundays like that sort of thing,' prompted Leo.

'But the people round here don't,' said Bull, 'and I've got to live and work here remember.'

Leo left it at that but he was faintly disturbed by Bull's terseness and apparent lack of interest.

The murderer walked home from the Haywain. He had drunk nine pints of beer. He did not usually drink that much. Just five pints mostly, he had to be careful. The beer distended his stomach, he felt heavy and slow.

People bid him good-night, smiled at him, waved hands. He acknowledged them with a fixed smile on his face. As he walked a little unsteadily away the homeward-bound customers thinned out and he was alone.

Anne Partridge. Skirt riding high up her legs as she bent over behind the bar. Swelling breasts pushing at the front of a flimsy low-cut blouse. Plump white throat pulsating as she laughed.

He felt the familiar uncontrollable urge. His fingers flexed in anticipation. No ... not yet. It was too soon. The urge was becoming stronger year by year, the periods between shorter. Not yet, it was dangerous. Too dangerous.

He had seen them in the bar. He had felt sick deep in his stomach. They were after him. He was the prey, they were the hunters. Questions in their eyes, confidence in their voices, the casual certainty of the carnivore. No, not yet. It was too dangerous.

He was near the outskirts of the village now. The moon had gone into hiding behind a bank of cloud and it was dark. He felt the urgent need to relieve himself, looked round and stepped off the path behind a tree. The flow reduced to a trickle, a drop. A flick. Another. Gentle massage with the hand. Almost erection. Almost.

Anne Partridge. Squirming under him. Muffled cries of distress. Exciting cries. Rising panic, rising excitement. Don't breathe, Anne, don't breathe. Now into her. Yes. Tight on her neck, tight. She's given in. Now ... take her. Yes. Take her ... take her ... serves you right, serves you right. I'm not to be laughed at ... ah ... God Almighty.

He leaned back against the tree as he did up his flies. Eyes squeezed tight shut. It would be all right now. It would be all right now. After a while he pushed himself off the tree and resumed his walk home.

He was almost sober. Just very tired. It would be all right now. Until the next time.

When Anne came into Leo's room shortly after eleven-thirty she was still fully dressed. She sat on the edge of the bed and looked hard at him, doubt and simmering anger in her eyes.

'What is it, Anne?' Leo put out a hand, stroked her knee. She ignored his approach.

'After you left here lunchtime I went up to the shops ...' she hesitated.

'Yes?'

'I saw Miss smelly knickers in her car parked by the green. Was she waiting for you?'

'Who?'

'Janie Orton, who else, lover?' It was not an endearment.

Leo looked away, uncertain what to say.

'Was she?'

Anne wasn't going to leave this thing alone. Leo felt suddenly very tired and unwilling to surround himself with lies.

'I think so.'

'You must know.'

'She said she was.'

'You must know. Did you meet her after lunch today?' Her voice was dangerously quiet.

'Yes.' Some justification seemed in order. 'But not by arrangement. She followed me.'

'Where to?'

Leo was suddenly angry. 'What the hell, Anne. I can do without all this.'

'Coward,' said the voice.

She leaned forward. 'Leo, tell me the truth. Did you make love to her?'

'No. I did not make love to her.'

'Liar.' The voice gloated.

'She seduced me if you must know. I was . . . well, practically raped.'

Anne sat stock still for a moment. Eyes dilated, lips a thin line, face white with anger.

She hit him just once with the flat of her hand. A hard stinging blow to the side of his face that set bells ringing in his head. The shock stunned him and before he had recovered she had gone.

'Hell hath no fury . . .' the voice quoted in obvious glee.

Leo dropped back on to his pillow and closed his eyes. Taken on the whole, it had not been a very good day.

The next three days were no better.

NINE

On the Sunday morning Leo woke feeling thick-headed and tired. Long hours of intense concentration and a shortage of sleep had drained him of energy.

The drought was broken, the sky dull and overcast, moderate rain drumming in repetitive rhythm against the window. He heard the church bells, muted by distance, an endless succession of low, mournful sounds in keeping with the grey morning. With a slight shock he realized that they had been in Bacton Ford just one week.

He felt only marginally better by the time he joined Bob Staunton for breakfast. He ate little, drawing anxious inquiries from Rita Stack.

Bob was in an unusually quiet mood. He moved constantly on his chair, clearly suffering badly from his perennial complaint. As they left, Rita came hurrying up with the loan of an umbrella. Mrs Prentiss was at work in the saloon bar, on her knees cleaning the heavy brass fire irons in the capacious old hearth. They bid her good morning but she only nodded curtly in reply.

They walked close together, huddled under the umbrella. It was raining harder now and the church bells seemed louder, a more urgent appeal to the faithful, as if the ringer were in doubt as to the efficacy of the call.

Bacton Ford on a wet Sunday. Grey, dismal, deserted. The atmosphere of depression seemed to have infiltrated the village hall. The typewriters were silent, there was none of the bustle and briskness that had become a backcloth to their work. Even the ill-painted backdrop behind the stage seemed a joke in bad taste now.

Superintendent Day was waiting for them in Bob's office, the last of the statements he had taken from the dead girl's workplace in his hand. He laid them on the desk as they entered.

'Morning, sir. That's the lot.'

If he was waiting for a word of praise he was out of luck.

'Anything?' asked Bob.

Day shook his head. 'Not that I can see.'

'No.' Bob sat at his desk. 'We're in the sticky bit you get sometimes when nothing seems to happen.'

'We need a stroke of luck,' said Day.

'Indeed we do. Look, Leo and I are going to the special memorial service for Joy Prentiss at the parish church at eleven. It'd look right if you showed up as well I reckon.'

'Of course I will.'

Leo raised an eyebrow. It was the first he'd heard of it. Bob addressed him.

'Leo, send most of the lads home. They could do with a break. Just keep a skeleton staff.'

'Right, sir.' Leo left to do his bidding.

'What about the Crime Squad men I've had at the factory, sir?' asked Day. 'I've finished with them now.'

'Send them back. It doesn't look as if we're going to need them any more.'

The church was almost full. The rain pattered on the roof and windows, keeping monotonous time with Ray Colville's voice. He spoke of Joy Prentiss, her goodness and faith.

Her parents sat in the front row. After a while the father's head sank to his chest but Mrs Prentiss sat rigid, her eyes never leaving Colville's face.

Bob sang loudly in a surprisingly melodious baritone voice. Day joined him an octave higher. Leo mouthed the words. He felt depressed, inadequate, out of place and ill at ease. They sang of hope, of love and, with painful lack of tact, of the joy hereafter.

Day joined them for lunch at the Haywain on Bob's invitation, then went home. After his departure they went to Bob's room and spent nearly two hours completing their official diaries. A separate entry for each day, every person seen, every visit made, every penny spent, every waking minute was accounted for. It had to be done with care. An innocent mistake and in a year's time they might have to account for it. It might not seem so innocent then.

Leo took a chance and lied. He felt that officialdom would take unkindly to the two hours he had spent with Janie Orton the previous afternoon. Local inquiries in the vicinity of marina. It sounded a hell of a lot better than the truth.

Bob threw his completed diary on to the chest of drawers and flopped on to his bed.

'We'll have to have a conference Monday, bring things up to date.'

'I'll arrange it. Afternoon, say . . . two-thirty?'

'Yeah, that'll do.'

'I saw Sergeant Cobbold briefly this morning. He said he'd be finished this afternoon.'

'Thought so.'

'We'll call off the road block in the morning?'

'Yes, and the rest of the Crime Squad as well. They can't help us now, we're on our own.'

'Anything else?'

'No. Get lost. I want to think.'

Leo went to his own room. There had been no malice in Bob's voice. It was just that sort of day.

He flipped off his shoes and lay back on the bed, staring at the ceiling. It wasn't going well. Both of them were facing their first major failure. If you don't get a lead in the first two weeks you're in trouble. That's the rule they say. It seemed to be holding good.

When he woke the room was in darkness. Leaden-limbed, he pulled off his clothes and crept into bed.

The sun was steaming moisture off the fields when Leo woke next morning. The starlings had resumed their meeting on his window sill but he left them in peace. He felt rested and relaxed, ready to face the world again.

For once he beat Bob Staunton down to breakfast. Bob had also benefited from the rest. He was bright eyed and bushy tailed. By mute consent they avoided mention of the grey despair that had affected them the day before.

The reassuring clack of typewriters greeted them when they entered the village hall. They spread words and smiles of encouragement round the room on their way to Bob's office.

The overnight messages were few and uniformly uninteresting. Leo looked at his watch. Eight forty-five.

'We'd better get going.'

'Where?' Bob looked blank.

'Ipswich General Hospital. You've an appointment with Doctor Ryan at nine-thirty.'

'Don't talk wet.'

'It's in your diary if you look.'

Bob did. The entry was there all right. He scratched his ear. 'Damn funny. Looked in there yesterday, didn't see it. What's it all about?'

'He put me straight on to his secretary. I had no real conversation with him. I just made the appointment since it seemed necessary.'

'Well, we'd better get going then. Next time find out what it's all about, mate, I like to know who I'm seeing and why.'

'Yes, sir.'

Leo drove as fast as the traffic permitted, leaving Bob little time to speculate. He parked near the out-patients' department and ushered Bob inside.

'Mr Staunton. An appointment with Doctor Ryan,' he said, to the receptionist.

'Straight ahead of you. The waiting room is on the right.'

Leo led the way.

'I hate these places,' said Bob, *sotto voce*.

The waiting room was empty. They sat on moulded plastic chairs. Bob sniffed the antiseptic air.

'Smells like the poorhouse kharsie on open day,' said Bob, wrinkling his nose.

A staff nurse entered, scowling at a clip-board. She would have graced any shot-putt ring.

'Staunton?' She looked at them accusingly. Bob stood up.

'I'm . . .' he began.

'This way.'

She led him into one of three curtained cubicles lining one of the walls. As if by magic a thin sandy-haired doctor appeared and followed them in. Leo listened to the ensuing three-cornered conversation with growing apprehension.

'Take your trousers off.'

'Just a minute, nurse . . .'

'Staff nurse.'

'Right then, staff nurse. Now, there's been a mistake . . .'

'There's been no mistake. We're going to treat those haemorrhoids for you. Be a good boy and take your trousers off.'

'Not likely, missus.'

'Do as you're told, Mr Staunton. I'm busy.'

'No!'

'You need treatment. Grow up and behave like a man.'

'Trousers off.'

'I'll kill him.'

'Later. Trousers off or shall I do it?'

'Leo,' a shout, 'LEO, YOU HEAR ME, I'LL KILL YOU.'

'Right off, please.'

'Turn round then.'

'What've you got I haven't seen before?'

'I'll kill him!'

'Underpants off, please.'

'Don't stand there like a goldfish. Here . . .'

'Lot of fuss about such a little thing, wasn't it?'

'Up on the table.'

'What the hell's that?'

'Just a syringe.'

'What for, a bloody horse?'

'Adopt a foetal position.'

'Move! Curl up like the baby you are.'

'You could do with losing some weight.'

'AH!'

'Just a local anaesthetic.'

'Lubricant, please, staff nurse.'

'I'm going to insert this metal lining. It might hurt a little.'

'JESUS CHRIST!'

'Now let's have a look . . . uh huh . . . quite a collection. Syringe.'

'There's a brave boy. Bite on this.'

Whatever it was she gave him to bite on apparently did the trick. There followed only Bob's muffled groans. He emerged from the cubicle quarter of an hour later with a look of bitter hatred on his face.

'That's it. All finished,' said Leo tentatively.

'Oh is it, mate,' said Bob ominously. 'That's what you think.' He attempted to stride off down the corridor but was soon reduced to a bandy stiff-legged waddle.

He said nothing on the way back in the car, refused Leo's assistance on arrival and banged the door of his office behind him. Leo wondered if he had gone too far. Sometimes the rewards of virtue seem to be less than those of sin.

There was just about enough room for the five of them in Bob's office. He and Leo sat behind the desk, Superintendent Day, Sergeant Cobbold and Inspector Grace in front of it. Bob opened the proceedings. He seemed much recovered and in good spirits.

'Gentlemen, we have reached that stage in the inquiry when we have to assess the position and set ourselves on fresh lines. Before I start let me just check. You've finished, Mr Day?'

'Yes, sir. Everyone on all shifts in the factory has been seen.'

'And you, Sergeant Cobbold?'

'Finished yesterday afternoon, sir. Not just the village, we did every house on that plan there.'

He pointed to P.C. Trew's masterpiece adorning the wall behind Bob and Leo.

'Right.' Bob changed direction. 'The road block is off as of now, Mr Grace. So thank you for your help, give my regards to all your lads – they've been a great help.'

'Sorry we didn't come up with anything. Ah, just remembered. I left the C.R.O. files outside, you asked me to check them out.'

'Yes, the boys with convictions for sexual assaults.'

Grace shook his head. 'All alibied up to their armpits.'

'Not surprised.' Bob seemed unperturbed. 'This job isn't going to be easy.'

'Well I'll push off, sir, if there's nothing else I can do?'

'Hang about. Stay for the conference, you've been in it this long, might as well keep in touch. You never know what you might come across in your travels.'

The door opened. A pipe entered, closely followed by the Chief Constable.

'Ah, picked the wrong moment I see.'

Leo was first to his feet. 'Would you like to take my chair, sir?'

'They'd never keep you in prison,' the voice leered, 'you'd crawl out under the door.'

'No, no. Just passing. Any news?'

He looked hopefully at Bob, now standing with the other officers.

'Mid-term conference, sir,' said Bob, 'correlating what's been done. Sorting out the strands.'

Colonel Boulton nodded knowingly as if he understood what Bob was talking about.

'Excellent. Don't forget, anything I can do . . .'

'Have you time to sit in on the conference, sir?' asked Bob, hoping fervently for a negative reply.

' 'Fraid not, old chap. You'll ring my office if . . .?'

'Of course, sir.'

'Right. Good luck, then.' The Chief Constable nodded briskly round the room and left. They shuffled around regaining their seats, then looked expectantly at Bob.

'Now,' he said, sorting the papers on his desk into order, 'the position as I see it is this. We've now completed the first part of the inquiry. The taking of statements from the village area, the factory, the road block. Also sundry items like the post-mortem and forensic and fingerprint examination are dealt with and tucked away.

'Some of you may think that because we haven't put him on the sheet at the end of all this it means we aren't going to. Cobblers. We've only just started. This bloke isn't going to put his hands up, we've got to find him. Every statement we've got is a bullet in our gun, the real work is just starting.

'I don't want to deal in guesswork but I am making one assumption that don't have a real basis in fact. I think our man is a local. If he is it means that we've already taken a statement from him. Somewhere in the thousand-odd statements outside is one made by the murderer. Now I've been through every single one and on their own they all stand up and all the alibis are good.

'We've got a real chance though because one of those statements is a pack of lies. It has to be. So all we have to do is find which one and we're home and dry.

'All right, so it's not just that easy. For a start he probably isn't the only one who lied. Someone may be covering up for him, wife, lover, parents or friend. Other people may have lied to cover some skeleton of their own. What we have to do is dig and dig until we separate the truths from the lies.

'We're going to tackle this two ways. In here and out on the streets. Mr Day, you and Sergeant Worthington are going to sit down and go through the index and the statements until you find the one that doesn't stand up. I'll make just one suggestion, separate those males who don't have an alibi from those that do, then reduce all the information on to some form of comparative grid, right?

'The rest of us are going to make ourselves a bloody nuisance round here. We're going to poke and pry, talk and question until the people in this village are sick of us. I don't care who you talk to or what about, the weather, the harvest, gossip, who sleeps with who, anything goes. Then we talk amongst ourselves, pass on all the tiny unimportant titbits we've picked up. Sooner or later we'll find something that doesn't jell. Then we're in business.

'One last thing. Time isn't on our side. There's been two similar sexual assaults in this area in the last year. Each one could have been a murder. I'm certain myself it's the same bloke. This bastard is going to do it again and we've got to get him first. That's it. Any questions?'

The murderer stood on an area of concrete just off the main road through the village. The sun beat down with stunning ferocity. He wiped the sweat from his brow with the rolled-up sleeve of his shirt.

Anne Partridge appeared round the bend in the road, her skirt just out of time with the swing of her hips. She acknowledged him as she passed, addressing him by first name but she did not smile. She seemed anxious and preoccupied.

His eyes followed her, watching her buttocks moving in light sensuous rhythm. She was heading out of the village. The bus stop on the main road. She used to make the trip to Ipswich frequently. She had family there. She had not been out of the village for the past week. Perhaps she would resume her usual pattern now. Perhaps he would see her one day, away from the village. Somewhere quiet.

His mouth felt dry. He searched in his pockets for a packet of mints. He found a slip of cardboard, pulled it out and looked at it. Panic struck him. He thought he had destroyed it. A mistake like that and they would . . . He walked quickly away behind the buildings, entered the male toilets. His fingers shook as he watched the cardboard burn. He dropped the fragments into the pedestal and flushed them away. He felt sick.

'I was wondering if there was any way we could use the press a little more.' Superintendent Day looked inquiringly round at the others.

'There's nothing we can give,' said Bob. 'We can't use the press unless they can use us. What can we tell them?'

The conference had already lasted an hour and despite the wide-open windows they were all feeling the effects of the heat. A moment's silence followed Bob's last question.

'I went into the general store the other day,' Leo said into the vacuum, 'the conversation stopped instantly. It happens in the Haywain too. If we appear the subject changes. I'm not paranoiac about it but it smacks of a cover-up. It's a sort of us and them atmosphere and we're them.'

'That's just the way they are,' said Sergeant Cobbold, flapping his shirt front over his ample stomach, 'it's not just you, it's any strangers. Leastways with the old folk anyhow.'

'I've noticed this before,' said Day, 'they're polite but they exclude you somehow. They put up an umbrella and only the locals can get under it.'

'Well somehow we've got to get under it as well,' said Bob determinedly, 'otherwise half the village is a closed book to us and that's no good. Push a few beers into some of them you never know your luck.' He hesitated for a moment in thought. 'Tell me something, Mr Day, why isn't Commander Orton a local J.P.? I looked him up and he isn't.'

Day looked puzzled, 'I really don't know.'

'I mean he's a logical bloke for the job, isn't he? Local Squire and all that. Family goes back hundreds of years. Pots of money, plenty of time I should think. So why not?'

Sergeant Cobbold cleared his throat. 'It goes back about seven years, sir, before Mr Day came.'

'What does?'

'Commander Orton was a J.P. but there was a little difficulty arose like.'

'Well don't be bloody coy about it, Roger. What happened?'

'He caught that Cavell poaching see . . .'

'The boy that found the body?'

'His father.'

'So?'

'Well, he shot him with a twelve-bore. Put him in hospital like.'

'Was he charged?'

'Well yes, but he weren't convicted. Cavell refused to give evidence against him. Commander Orton resigned though.'

'Good old-fashioned English cover-up,' said Bob in disgust.

Cobbold shrugged. 'The Cavells lived pretty well for a time after that. Nobody really suffered like.'

'Anything else from anybody?' Bob looked round but no offers were forthcoming.

'We'll call it closed then. Just remember this when you're poking your noses around. We're looking for a nutter who seems normal. Keep it in the back of your mind what sort of man he is. Everyone's a suspect,' he grinned across at Leo, 'even the local vicar.'

The conference broke up just after four o'clock and Bob and Leo were left alone in the office.

Leo telephoned the Divisional office at C.I. Department, New Scotland Yard and asked for the Deputy Commander's clerk. He spent quarter of an hour trying to get some more money sent down to them. It was as though that officer was paying out of his own pocket. In the end they settled for half of what Leo was asking. It was not important since he had taken the precaution of doubling his requirement beforehand.

Bob listened to the exchanges with wry amusement as he tidied up his post-conference clutter. Leo replaced the phone, eyed Bob for a moment, then decided to take a chance.

'How's your rear end now?' he asked.

'Fine,' said Bob, 'much better, thanks.'

It seemed he had forgotten his earlier threats. Leo dropped into a chair and inspected his hands thoughtfully.

'There's something I want to talk to you about.'

'Fire away, son.' Bob occupied his chair and sat back waiting.

'I didn't bring it up at the conference because it's a little . . . speculative.'

'Do get on with it, mate.'

Leo put his hands away and looked straight at Bob. 'It is my belief that there are a number of people in this village who practise black magic.'

'Good grief,' said Bob, with the start of a smile.

'There is in my opinion ample proof of an active coven at work here.'

'Do me a favour, Leo . . .'

'I'm serious and I think it could have a bearing on this inquiry.'

'What now? Ritual murder, human sacrifice, come on . . .'

'No, not that. The forensic evidence rules it out. Clearly this was a one-man sexual murder. If you'll just hear me out.'

'I'm listening.'

'The local church has had a number of items stolen over the last few years. Priest's clothing, crosses, chalices, sanctified water, the sort of thing a coven would want for its rituals. Other churches round here have suffered as well. The last episode in the village was just a month ago. The vicar showed me a spot at the back of the churchyard where two graves had been opened and the bones scattered about. The headstones were thrown down and smashed. Someone had lit a fire, you can still see the ashes and Ray Colville says when he found it, the grass was still trampled down. He thinks at least a dozen people were there.'

'Thirteen to a coven, right?' said Bob, thoughtful now.

'Exactly. Roger Cobbold investigated this last incident. He got nowhere and clearly he didn't expect to. He seems to accept the fact of witchcraft round here as if it were part of the normal scene. Even Tom Stack at the Haywain knows about it. Nobody talks about it though, it's one of the things that is kept under the umbrella. I said earlier I thought there was an atmosphere of cover-up in the village. I think this is the reason. Even people among the old inhabitants who are not members of the coven seem to give it their tacit support.'

'When their churches are being thieved from?'

'It seems that after each theft extra money appears in the collection box. The coven doesn't seem to do anybody any actual harm, if you discount desecrating the graves that is.'

Bob scratched his ear thoughtfully. 'These people exist all right. Every now and then there's a story in a Sunday paper, fat ladies dancing around campfires at dead of night and all that. No reason why there shouldn't be a local branch here I suppose.'

Leo leaned forward intently. 'What happened in the churchyard is fact. That means the coven is a fact. We're not dealing in wild theories. I'm not asking you to believe in black magic, I'm only asking you to accept that there are other people who do and that they practise it here.'

Bob considered for a moment. 'All right,' he said, 'I'll go along with that. So now tell me what it has to do with this inquiry.'

'There are several possibilities. First, what kind of person would be a member of a group like this?'

'Bloody nutcases.' Bob was emphatic.

'My point exactly. Magic attracts all kinds of people, including inevitably some who are mentally unbalanced. Perhaps even a psychopathic killer.'

Bob was interested now. 'But he'd still need an alibi for the night of the murder.'

'We have to start guessing now. If the murderer is a member, perhaps the rest of the coven is made up of people mad enough to lie for him. Perhaps they had a meeting that night and he slipped out without them knowing. It's anybody's guess.'

'If he wasn't a member of this lot the whole idea falls flat. Why should they cover up for him then if they're not involved?'

'I don't know but that raises another point. Suppose there was a meeting of the coven the night of the murder. It doesn't matter if he was a member or not. They could not tell us what they were up to. It means we may have as many as thirteen statements or more out there which are a pack of lies, apart from the murderer's, anyone who is covering up for him, or anyone else just keeping a skeleton buried.'

'Oh, that's great.' Bob relapsed into thought. 'Just a minute, suppose there wasn't a meeting that night. What then? Coven or no they could have told the truth about what they were doing.'

'I'm not a betting man but I'd wager a year's salary that there was. Joy Prentiss died on the night of the thirty-first of July and first of August. Lammas. One of the biggest days in their calendar. They wouldn't have missed that.'

Bob chewed absentmindedly at the stub of a pencil. 'If you're right we've got a bloody big problem. How do we get in amongst them?'

'I've given that some thought,' said Leo tentatively. 'No one is going to talk and we can't put an ad in the local paper. We may be able to do it though.'

'How?'

'We need an intermediary. Someone outside us, outside the coven, outside the village. Someone they will talk to.'

'They'll only talk to one of their own.'

'Or someone who knows enough about it to convince them they are talking to a friend.'

'Even so, how could he make contact? Where could he start?' Bob had made an assumption.

'She,' said Leo.

'She?'

'And she starts with Janie Orton.'

'Why Janie Orton?'

'We have to start somewhere. I met her casually the other day. It was something she said, in retrospect I think she's the most likely starting place. Anyway she's all we've got.'

'Who've you got in mind as this intermediary then?'

'A woman named Carrie Fuller. I've known her for five years or so.

She's a freelance journalist and she's spent most of her adult life studying the occult.'

'A journalist,' said Bob thoughtfully.

'Yes, a good one.'

'Don't like it,' said Bob.

'We're in trouble. What can we lose?'

'What's in it for her — this Carrie Fuller?'

'If we fail, nothing. If we get him — the story of a lifetime. She'd take the gamble.'

'I'm not agreeing, mind . . . but what d'you want to do then?'

'Go up to London and see her. Bring her back here and put her to work to provide us with the names of the coven members. We can then check the statements they made and lean on them. We only need one to break and we can uncover the lot.'

'They won't talk if they know she has anything to do with us. She'll need a cover.'

'She comes as herself. That's the beauty of it. A freelance lady journalist takes up residence at the Haywain with the object of writing a piece for sale to the Sundays. She also happens to be an initiate.'

'Is she?'

'I'm not sure. Maybe at one time she was one of them. I think she's grown out of it now.'

'If she's one of them she could turn the coin. Inform on us not them.'

'To tell them what? That we're after them? Fine, that would put the cat among the pigeons and we might get a whisper. As I said, how can we lose?'

'Don't like it, Leo. It's hardly orthodox is it?'

'Put it this way. She's just another informant. We take chances on informants every day of the week.'

He watched anxiously as Bob chewed it over. Finally he discarded the mangled pencil stub and sat up briskly.

'Take the car if you like,' he said.

By dint of ignoring the speed limits Leo was in Bayswater at seven-fifteen that evening. He crossed his fingers as he pressed the doorbell. He hadn't telephoned. Carrie Fuller was not a lady to spend too much time at home and it had been three years after all.

Her eyes widened in surprise when she saw him.

'Well now, the three-legged wanderer,' she said.

'Hello, Carrie . . .'

'Well, don't stand there like yesterday's milk, come in.'

The flat was more opulent than he remembered. The décor and furnishings more extreme, purple black and light brown, hidden lighting, subtle decadence.

She was wearing faded jeans and a man's shirt open low at the front. Her long dark hair tumbled about her shoulders and framed the long face with the huge brown eyes, Carrie Fuller was a looker. He had almost forgotten.

'Come and tell mummy all about it,' she said, leading him to a low chair.

'You're looking fabulous,' said Leo, in frank admiration.

She smiled her thanks and showed a flash of very white teeth. 'Scotch?'

'Fine.'

She handed him the drink and took hers to a rocking chair opposite. She cocked her head to one side and looked at him.

'You're not much to look at . . . but I'm pleased to see you again.'

'I was a fool,' Leo said.

She waved a dismissive hand. 'No thanks. No scenes of painful regret. We both had some growing up to do.'

Leo sipped his drink and looked at her over the rim of his glass. He stripped her in his memory, wrestled again with that creamy white body.

'Put those lustful eyes away and tell me what you want,' she said. 'You didn't come here to bed me, not after all this time.'

'Don't be so sure.'

'Not even you would be that bloody cheeky. You'd be out of luck anyway.'

'A deal then. Strictly business.'

'Doing deals with the press? Tut, tut,' she grinned deliciously.

'How would you like to have the exclusive story of the arrest of a man for a sexual murder?'

She sat up suddenly. 'Pictures?'

'No. At least . . . well maybe. Interested?'

'Of course not, I throw away an exclusive story every day of the week.' Her beautiful eyes clouded. 'What do you want then, Leo? What's your angle?'

'All you have to do is come down to Bacton Ford in Suffolk and stay in this delightful olde worlde inn . . .'

'Leo, what's the catch?'

'Book in under your own name. Tell everyone you're doing a piece for a Sunday or a woman's mag or something. The food's marvellous...'

'Leo...'

'All you have to do is find out the names of the members of a black magic coven that is operating in the village.'

She choked on her drink. He watched the conflicting emotions play across her face, wondered if he had called it right.

'Is that all...?'

'That's all.'

'What makes you think I could do that?'

'Come on, Carrie. You could do it all right. It's just a matter of whether you will or not. A conflict of professional and personal interests.'

'It's that all right.' She took a swallow of her drink and shuddered as it went down.

'Carrie, we'll smash that coven anyway. If you play ball we get our answers sooner, and it's less messy for them. Not to mention your exclusive.'

She ran her tongue along the tips of her teeth as she looked at him. 'Better tell me the story, oh pretty one,' she said.

He told her. Five minutes and a dozen questions later he had a deal.

TEN

Leo pushed the Chief Constable's saloon hard on the way back to Suffolk. He stopped just once on the Colchester by-pass for a brief altercation with an unsympathetic traffic patrol policeman who took exception to his swift passage. He explained exactly where that officer could insert his motorcycle and promptly lost a friend.

On arrival, Leo parked the car outside the village hall and walked down to the Haywain. Despite his hustle he was too late. It had already gone closing time. Customers were passing him on their way home, some less steadily than others. His stomach churned with hunger and he recalled he had eaten nothing since breakfast. Even the prospect of a stale cheese sandwich seemed the height of gastronomic delight.

He found Bob drinking with Tom Stack in the bar. Rita Stack and Anne were clearing up some of the debris from what had obviously been a busy evening.

'All right, mate?' asked Bob.

'Yes, fine.' Leo attracted Rita's attention. 'Rita, I've eaten nothing since breakfast. Any chance of a sandwich or something?'

She clucked in motherly fashion. 'Ruin your stomach you will.' She called across to Anne, 'There's some ham in the fridge, make Leo some sandwiches, dear.'

Anne looked blandly at Leo. 'What would you like with it?' she asked.

He had the impression that ground glass and rat poison were what she had in mind.

'Nothing, thank you, Anne,' he said.

He felt better after the sandwiches and a pint of bitter.

Tom Stack was overtly curious about his absence during the evening. Eventually Bob satisfied his curiosity.

'Leo's had a few hours off.'

'Oh yes?'

'Been to see the doctor.'

Leo looked at him in puzzlement. Bob had an evil look about the eyes.

'Nothing too bad I hope?' asked Tom, solicitous.

'Oh no. Poor lad suffers from piles.'

Bob and Leo spent the following morning in the office. At eleven o'clock Rita Stack telephoned. Was it all right if she let the spare room to a lady writer who was interested in the murder?

They confirmed it was Carrie Fuller, then gave their clear but not too evidently enthusiastic consent.

'Well, we've put your cat among the pigeons,' said Bob, as he replaced the receiver. 'Let's hope she can stir them up a bit.'

At that moment they were interrupted by voices raised in heated argument in the outside office. Prominent amongst them was that of Sergeant Cobbold.

'What the hell . . .' said Bob.

'I'll have a look,' said Leo, but before he could make a move Cobbold, looking heated and dishevelled, entered the room.

'What's going on, Roger?' asked Bob, his displeasure evident.

'It's Mrs Prentiss, sir.'

'What about her?'

'She just attacked Commander Orton outside the Haywain.'

'Did you see it?'

'No, I was just too late.'

'Okay. Just slow down and tell us exactly what happened.'

'Well . . .' Cobbold paused to regain his breath. 'Seems Mrs Prentiss had just finished work at the Haywain. When she came out of the pub Commander Orton was getting out of his car. She just went berserk, scratching and clawing at him. He's got four great scratch marks down the side of his face. I heard her screeching and got there in time to pull her off him.'

'Has she any explanation?' Bob asked.

'No, sir. I can't get any sense out of her.'

'You said she was screeching at him,' said Leo. 'What was she saying?'

Cobbold shrugged. 'I don't know. I couldn't make it out. It didn't sound like English.'

'Orton's not badly hurt?' asked Bob.

'No, sir. A bit shook up and the scratches, that's all.'

'Where are they now?' asked Bob.

'Outside, sir. There's two P.C.s with her and Superintendent Day is with Commander Orton.'

'Bring her in,' said Bob grimly.

Mrs Prentiss was white-faced and tight-lipped but she seemed to have herself under control.

'Pull a chair up and sit her down,' said Bob, and Cobbold hastened to comply.

'Now, Mrs Prentiss, what's all this about?' Bob sounded relaxed and only mildly interested.

'I'm sorry, sir,' Mrs Prentiss stared at her hands in her lap, 'I lost my temper, sir. I'm very sorry.'

'Why did you lose your temper?' asked Bob quietly.

'Very silly, sir, I'm sorry.'

'That's not enough, Mrs Prentiss. I want to know why you assaulted Commander Orton.'

Mrs Prentiss said nothing.

'Is this anything to do with your daughter's death?'

Her dark eyes flashed at Bob for a moment then she dropped her head again.

'Well?' Bob insisted.

'There's things you know,' she said slowly, 'and there's things I know. You sort out your things, I sort out mine.'

'You don't take the law into your own hands,' said Bob, 'and you haven't answered my question.'

'Look, mister,' she peered up at him, cunning and determination in her eyes and the set of her face, 'I did what I did. I said my sorries. That's it and all about it.'

'What chance have I got of catching Joy's murderer if her own mother won't answer my questions?' asked Bob, the exasperation begininng to show.

She sat motionless.

'For God's sake, woman, don't you care?' Bob exploded.

'I care,' she matched his stare, 'I'm helping.'

She said nothing more. She answered none of their questions, just sat completely still in an attitude of stubborn submission.

'Take her out and bring Commander Orton in,' said Bob.

Cobbold saw her out and returned with Commander Orton whose face bore witness to the ferocity of the woman's attack. Cobbold offered him a chair but he declined with a gesture. He was pale and seemed to have lost his arrogant composure.

'The woman won't talk to us, sir,' Bob said. 'Won't give a reason, won't answer any questions in fact. Strange isn't it?' He looked up inquiringly.

'She was always . . . a little strange, that one.' Orton hastened on, 'One must feel sorry for her, obviously the tragic loss of her daughter has left her deranged.'

'You think that's it. She's mentally ill?'

'What else?' Orton raised a hand to his wounds, 'She must not be charged, of course.'

Bob raised his eyebrows. 'Oh, why not?'

Orton shrugged, 'The poor woman needs rest and quiet, it would be inhuman to subject her to arrest and trial on such a trivial matter.'

'Why did she attack you, sir?' Leo put in.

Orton hesitated. 'I'm an authority figure round here, am I not? There would be a sort of twisted logic in attacking me, I suppose.'

'If we let her free I can't guarantee she won't attack someone else, or go for you again,' Bob pointed out.

Naked fear flickered across Orton's face. He spread his hands in a gesture and it was obvious he was trembling.

'I doubt it,' he said, 'it's a small chance and one I'm prepared to take. After all you could not keep her in prison even if she were charged. She'd be out on bail.'

'You refuse to charge her, then?'

'I do.'

'Very well, Commander Orton, that's all.' Bob's tone was curt.

'I'm sorry you have been troubled.'

He left a dead silence behind him. Bob broke it.

'Sure you didn't see the assault, Roger?'

'No, sir, as I said . . .'

'Yeah, okay. There's nothing we can do then. Better read her the riot act, tell her to be a good girl and take her home.'

'Yes, sir. I don't know . . .' he stopped uncertainly.

'Spit it out, mate,' said Bob sharply.

'Well I don't know if it's anything to do with it but . . .'

He fished in his pocket and brought out a crumpled piece of paper. 'I saw her stuff this into his top pocket just before I grabbed her. First thing he did was to pull it out and look at it. Went as white as a sheet he did, dropped it on the ground. I picked it up as I was bringing her in.'

Bob took the paper from Cobbold and Leo moved behind to peer over his shoulder. It was cheap writing paper torn from a pad. At the top a rough diagram had been drawn, a snake swallowing its own tail. Enclosed in the circle was a design of triangles and interwoven squares. Other unidentifiable symbols filled the intervening spaces. The rest of the page was covered with writing in capital letters but they were badly drawn and the language was not English.

'Okay, Roger, thanks, better take her home now.' Cobbold left and Bob turned to Leo.

'What d'you make of that little lot, then?'

'This?' Leo waved the paper that he had been studying closely.

'For a start.'

'I'd like to show it to Carrie. I can't be sure but I think she gave him the black spot.'

'Do what?'

Leo shrugged. 'Notice of intended prosecution if you like. A warning. I'm going to hex you. That sort of thing.'

'This is getting bloody ridiculous.'

'Orton was scared stiff. Didn't you notice?'

'This makes her one of your coven then.'

Leo smiled, 'Hardly my coven. Maybe it does. I don't know but I've no doubt Carrie will find out.' He tucked the paper away in his pocket.

'This is all I need.' Bob sank his head into his hands. 'Bloody fine reading the report on this job is going to make.'

'It may help to stir up the pigeons though,' said Leo thoughtfully.

'Hey, just a minute,' Bob pointed an accusing finger, 'it still don't tell us why she attacked him.'

'I can't see any way it can relate to the murder,' said Leo, 'maybe it's an internal thing, a power struggle inside the coven or something. It's anybody's guess.'

Bob sighed deeply and ran his finger round the collar of his shirt. It was stifling hot again.

'Leo, take me over the road and buy me a beer.'

The Haywain was almost empty. In one corner of the saloon bar

Mrs Salmon was sitting alone cuddling a glass. The vacant smile on her face suggested she had tried to make up in consumption for the absence of other customers.

Anne was serving. She treated Leo to another slice of cold shoulder. Tom Stack appeared from the public bar and joined them.

'You've heard, of course,' he said.

'Yes, mate.'

'I've had to sack her. Went mad she did, ripped his face open. Never seen anything like it.'

'Upset over the girl I expect,' said Bob.

'Commander Orton of all people.'

'Is this a pub or do we make our own beer?' asked Bob.

Anne served them and managed to spill Leo's pint. Tom Stack seemed affected by verbal diarrhoea.

'Right outside my pub. You'd never believe it.'

Leo tried to change the subject. 'Is that lady reporter about?'

'Who?'

'Rita rang the office this morning, asked us if we'd mind if she let the room to a woman reporter.'

'Oh, no. She put her things upstairs and went straight out. Haven't seen her since . . . cut his face open, you should have seen it.'

'We did,' said Leo, and headed out to the gents.

On his way back he bumped into Mrs Salmon who was making hard work of negotiating the door out of the saloon bar.

'Hullo, policeman,' she said with what was presumably intended as an engaging smile.

'Mrs Salmon, isn't it?' said Leo, 'from the garage.'

'Stinking garage,' she said.

'Well it's a pity, but we can't all enjoy our work,' said Leo politely.

'Can't enjoy nothing,' she said with deliberate slowness.

'Except a drink, eh?' Leo smiled and tried to sidle past her.

She put out a hand and stopped him. 'You,' she said, poking a finger at his chest, 'should come see me this day . . . afternoon.'

'Why, Mrs Salmon?'

She laughed and the effort made her stagger slightly. 'Woman asks you round . . . husband out and you want . . . to know why.' She giggled into her hand.

'Mrs Salmon, you've had a drink or two,' he hesitated, not wishing to provoke her into a scene. 'Let's face it, if your husband found me alone in the house with you he wouldn't like it.'

She put one finger alongside her nose and tapped it. The second time she missed. 'He isn't getting it,' she said, 'he never gets it . . . never gets the point.' Apparently this was enormously funny.

'I really must . . .' said Leo.

'You come,' she said demandingly, 'I got something you want.' She tapped her nose. 'I know,' she said, 'I know what you want.'

She weaved her way to the door and out into the street. Leo watched her departure then dismissed her from his mind and returned to the bar.

Bob and Tom were deep in conversation. Anne was sitting on a stool behind the bar. Leo leaned across to her in an attempt at reconciliation.

'Still hate me?'

'Why no,' she said coldly, 'of course not.'

'Are you working tonight?'

'No. My night off.' She did not sound encouraging.

'Things are a little quieter now,' he inched nearer, 'I might be able to get away for an hour.'

'Very gracious of you, I'm sure,' she said, with a false smile, 'but I'm going to see my parents.'

Roger Cobbold burst into the bar and stood irresolute. Bob and Leo went across to him.

'What's up, mate?' asked Bob.

Sergeant Cobbold was out of breath, his chest heaved and his face was red and sweating.

'Trouble?' asked Leo.

Cobbold took a deep breath. 'A man's just walked into Ipswich Police Station and given himself up for the murder.'

Kenneth Barker sat on a hard wooden chair in a drab office at Ipswich Police Headquarters and looked amiably at the two officers who faced him across the desk.

They saw a short squat man of about forty. His clothes were clean but shabby. His domed head was bald but for a monk's fringe of greying hair. A round face, large brown eyes and faint eyebrows gave him a slightly owlish look. He blinked rapidly and waited their pleasure.

'You are Kenneth John Barker?' asked Bob.

'Yes, sir.' His voice was quiet, educated, a surprise.

'Unemployed and of no fixed abode?'

'Yes, sir.'

Bob looked up from the sheet of paper which had recorded these bare facts.

'Tell me about it, Kenneth.'

'I killed her, sir.'

'Who?'

'That girl, sir. Joy Prentiss.'

'Why?'

'I don't know, sir, it just came over me.'

'It just came over you,' said Bob blandly.

'Yes, sir. I get these fits see, I don't know what I'm doing. I'm dangerous, sir, I should be put away.' He looked anxiously at them. 'I'm dangerous see,' he said.

'Did you know the girl?' asked Leo.

'No, sir.'

'You're not from here?'

'No, sir. Bournemouth I'm from. Bournemouth by the sea.'

'How did you know her name then?' asked Bob.

'What?'

'You aren't from around here, you didn't know the girl, so how did you know her name?'

'Ah. I read it in the paper. I kept the cuttings. Look here . . .' He pulled a wad of press cuttings relating to the murder from an inside pocket and laid them carefully on the table. 'My cuttings, see,' he said, 'all about me they are.'

'Tell me exactly how you killed her,' said Bob quietly.

Kenneth Barker licked his lips. 'I saw her at the bus stop see, this girl . . .'

'Waiting for the bus?' asked Leo.

'Yes, sir. She was on her own. I told her the last bus had gone and I offered to walk her home . . .'

'She agreed?'

'Yes, sir. Women do you know, women like me.'

'And then?'

'We walked a long way. Right past her turning. She fancied me see.'

'Where did you go?' from Bob.

'She took me to this field see . . .' his eyes were glinting and beads of sweat dotted his upper lip, 'then I got this fit come on, and I ripped her clothes off . . . ripped them off,' his hands demonstrated, 'stripped her naked I did, then I had her.'

His eyes flickered from Bob to Leo and back. Cunning and lust.

'Right into her see and she screamed . . . I had to stop her, didn't I?

'... stop her screaming ... so I put my hands round her neck ... then ...' He trailed off and the gleam in his eyes flickered out.

'And then?' asked Bob softly.

'I don't remember.'

He sat staring at the floor between his legs. They let him sit. After a moment he looked up, owlish again. Blinking.

'I'm hungry,' he said.

Bob hunched forward on the desk. 'Who's your nearest living relative?' he asked.

Barker considered. 'Sister, sir ... I've got a sister.'

'Her address?'

'Bournemouth by the sea,' he screwed up his face, struggling to remember, 'Twenty eight, The Avenue,' he said distinctly, as if repeating a lesson hard learned.

Bob caught Leo's eye and nodded. Leo left the room.

'How did you come to be in this area?' asked Bob.

'I'm doing research, sir.'

'What for?'

'My book, sir, for my book ... I'm writing a book you see.'

'What's it about?'

'People, sir, it's a book about people.'

'What sort of people?'

'Oh, just ordinary people like you and me. Just people.'

'What did you do with her knickers?'

'Pardon, sir?'

'What did you do with the dead girl's knickers?'

'Ripped them off, sir.'

'Then what?'

'I had her, sir ... I had her hard. That's why she screamed ... I've got a big cock, see. Women like me.'

'I meant, where did you put them?'

'I ripped them off, sir.'

'After that.'

'What?'

'What did you do with her knickers after you ripped them off?'

'Put them in my pocket, sir.'

'What for?'

'To sniff them, sir.'

'Where are they now?'

'Burnt them, sir.'

'Why?'

'They didn't smell right. She'd put perfume on them, see . . . French I think, "La Chanteuse", that means "The Singer", see. It's French.'

'What about her tights?'

'English, sir.'

'What did you do with them?'

'I put them back on her, sir.'

'After you'd killed her?'

'Yes, sir.'

'Why?'

'She was cold, sir.'

Bob sat back in his chair. Barker crossed his legs and stared at the ceiling. He seemed to have lost interest in the proceedings. After a moment he began to pick his nose. Bob said nothing.

Leo half entered the room and beckoned. Bob joined him outside.

'Nutty as a bleeding fruit cake,' he said, shaking his head.

'Right, sir.' Leo consulted a sheet of paper on which he had made notes. 'Bournemouth Police know him well. He's been a voluntary patient on a number of occasions. Suffers from a sexually orientated guilt complex. Lives with his sister when he's not in a mental home. She must be a saint.'

'What's he doing here?'

'He takes off every now and then, usually walks into a police station somewhere and gives himself up eventually for some imaginary rape. The doctors say he's harmless.'

'I wouldn't like to put money on it.'

'He didn't do our job anyway.'

'I know that, he doesn't know enough about it.'

'He definitely didn't leave Bournemouth until two days after the murder.'

'Sure?'

'Positive. I spoke to his sister on the telephone.'

'Okay. Get one of the helmets up here to hold his hand.'

Bob went back into the room. Barker had taken off one shoe and sock and was picking at his toenails.

'Put your shoe on, Kenneth, you're going home.'

'Number One Court. The Old Bailey.'

'Home.'

'A coat over my head. Avoid the press.'

'If you like.'

A uniformed Police Constable entered. Barker tied up his shoe lace, sniffed his sock, then put it in a pocket.

'He's all yours,' said Bob, "bye, Kenneth.'

'Guilty, sir,' said Kenneth.

'This way,' said the constable.

'I'm a dangerous man you know . . . women like me . . . I've got a big . . .'

'Mouth,' said the constable.

Bob and Leo adjourned to the Haywain just after eight o'clock that evening. The saloon bar was almost full and Rita and Tom Stack were loudly bemoaning the absence of Anne Partridge, whose insistence on having two evenings off a week seened suddenly unreasonable.

In a corner Dave Bull, the local reporter, was in earnest conversation with young Brian Cavell. Still dining out on his discovery of the body no doubt. There was no sign of Carrie Fuller.

Superintendent Day and Sergeant Cobbold joined them about nine and they chewed over the events of the day.

Carrie arrived half an hour later, looking her part in a figure-flattering trouser suit. She introduced herself to the policemen and thereafter did not lack for attention. It was nearly closing time before Leo had the opportunity to speak to her separately.

'I've got something to show you,' he said.

'Boasting again?' she grinned.

'I'm serious.'

'What room are you in?'

'Blue door, second right down the corridor.'

'Blue for a boy, I'll see you later.'

'The others are coming back . . .'

Leo spluttered as some of his beer went down the wrong way.

'Cough up, chicken,' said Carrie.

'He's no chicken that one,' said Bob, returning refreshed from his visit to the small room, 'he's a cock. Get the beer in, Leo.'

It was midnight before Carrie slipped into Leo's room and he was already in bed. She was wearing a silk shift affair of midnight blue with a design of entwined serpents. It was sleeveless and belted at the waist. She was a beautiful lady.

Leo sat up and patted a space for her on the bed.

'Sit, oh lady of universal beauty,' he said, straight-faced.

'The Bardic Chair is not for you,' she replied. She sat.

'What did you make of her?'

'Janie Orton? She's very beautiful.'

'That I know. Did she talk?'

'Yes.'

'Carrie, for God's sake we haven't got all night.'

'Oh, I thought we had.' Her eyes teased him. 'Sorry, no more fooling. Down to business. You were right about Janie, she's a neophyte. Her father is Master of the Temple.'

'That makes him a big gun, doesn't it?'

'It should do.'

'I don't understand.'

'Anyone can call themselves a Magister Templi. It doesn't necessarily mean they have the power to go with it. Janie Orton is a neophyte which means she should be working to acquire perfect control of the Astral Plane. The fact is, she knows damn all she couldn't read in a Sunday paper.'

'That doesn't put her father in the same boat.'

'Yes it does. As Master he must have initiated her and he must have known her status. No Magister Templi would allow her to advance without achieving the requisite knowledge. It's just too bloody dangerous.'

'He initiated his own daughter . . . that means he must have committed incest . . .'

Carrie gave a grim smile. 'So much the better. That would be the least of it. Perversion is the name of the game.'

'You're talking about a Temple. This isn't a witchcraft coven then? I mean the dancing in the dark type?'

She shrugged. 'What's in a name? It makes no difference how they are organized, the basic aims and principles are the same. This lot call themselves the Second Order of the Silver Star.'

'Ah!'

'That means something to you?'

'Aleister Crowley!'

'Leo, you know more than you pretend.'

'No. I've read books that's all. I know next to nothing, that's why I came to you. A smattering of knowledge isn't enough. It looks as though they've based their group on Crowley's work though?'

'Quite likely.' She shifted her position and sat on her hands. 'They wouldn't be the first. I can't be sure until I've seen Orton but I'd say he's got hold of a few books, including Crowley, and just . . .'

'Turned fantasy into reality.' Leo finished for her.

'It isn't just fantasy. He can't have any idea how dangerous it is. If they've been performing any rituals at all, and they have, it's a miracle they're all still sane.'

'I'm not sure they are.'

'They've got no protection. If they called up even the most insignificant demon they'd never be able to control it.'

Leo grinned. 'There we part company. That the rituals, practices and drugs they indulge in induce madness . . . yes, that I'll go along with but demons appearing out of thin air . . . no thanks.'

Carrie shrugged. 'As you like. It makes no difference, the end result is the same. You said you were going to smash this group. Okay, I'll help you because they are wayward children playing with fire, literally, and sooner or later they'll get burnt.'

'D'you know who else is in the group?'

'Not yet. I'm meeting Janie and her father in Ipswich tomorrow for lunch. I'll see what I can arrange.'

'Carrie, remember something . . . one of these people may be a murderer.'

'I'm a very careful lady. I'm a great believer in insurance.'

'There are things you can't insure against.'

'Relax, Leo. They can't harm me, they don't know enough.'

'I'm not talking about frogs' eyes and toads' tongues, I'm talking about a murderer's hands round that pretty little throat.'

Carrie shivered. 'I'll be careful,' she said.

'I want you to give me your opinion . . .' Leo opened a drawer in the bedside cabinet and took out the notepaper that Mrs Prentiss had thrust upon Commander Orton. 'What d'you make of that?'

Carrie took the paper. Her face paled and fear had clouded her eyes when she looked up at him.

'Where did you get this?'

He told her. 'Since she's the dead girl's mother it seemed possible she was identifying Orton as the killer.'

'Maybe.'

'Or perhaps she's in the group and it's a power struggle.'

'No.'

'Why not?'

'There would be no struggle. She's in a different league. They'd stand no chance against her.'

'You telling me Mrs Prentiss is the real thing?'

'Could be.'

'You all right, Carrie? You look a little pale.'

'I'm all right. I wasn't expecting this, that's all.'

'Carrie, it's a page of Woolworth's writing paper, that's all.'

'A bullet is a piece of metal, that's all.'

'It's the black spot isn't it?'

Carrie found a faint smile. 'Quaint expression. Yes, how did you know?'

'I didn't, but the way she delivered it suggested it wasn't a love letter.'

'He's as good as dead.'

'Come on now!'

'I mean it. How did he react?'

'Scared out of his wits I gather.'

'He's entitled to be.'

'But if he's a fake he wouldn't know what it was.'

'Why not, you did and you're no Master of the Temple.'

'All right, why's he still alive then?'

'She's letting him sweat. When she completes the ritual he will die.'

'So the paper is just the first instalment. What's the second?'

'I don't know.'

'Carrie . . .'

'I don't know, I tell you. It's over my head.'

Leo leaned back against the pillows and scratched his ear. 'Have you been initiated?' he asked.

She hesitated. 'No . . . I pulled out just before . . . sort of diablo interruptus you could say.' She tried a smile but it didn't work. 'It was too enclosed . . . I wanted to study the wider field of the occult . . . besides which I had learnt enough to know how dangerous it is. I came out of it . . . changed.'

'How?'

She shook her head. 'Not important.'

Leo regarded her thoughtfully. 'I've met Mrs Prentiss,' he said, 'she's not by any means doolally tat but she is also not a great mind. She's just a very ordinary country woman of middle age. I can't see her as the organizing genius of a coven of real power.'

'If you're right that's even worse.'

'Why?'

'If she's on her own and lacks the intelligence to have studied and acquired knowledge it means she was born with this power and this sort of thing,' she threw the paper back to him, 'has been passed down through her family.'

'Is that worse than doing it the hard way?'

'Yes. It's like letting a child loose in Piccadilly Circus during the rush hour with a loaded shotgun and telling it to go play.'

'We'd better find out a bit more about Mrs Prentiss, then.'

'Not me.'

'It could be important.'

'We have a deal. Orton and his crowd in return for an exclusive. That doesn't include Mrs Prentiss.'

'Carrie, this is murder . . .'

'Damn right it is.'

'She's got nothing against you.'

'And she's not going to have. I know when I'm outgunned. I know you don't believe it but the fact is she's dynamite. She probably doesn't know herself how good she is and I don't intend to enlighten her. She and I don't meet. That's it, period.'

'What if you'd found that Orton had that kind of power, what about the deal then?'

'There'd have been no deal.'

'Look, Carrie. The woman is normal. Painfully ordinary. I just don't believe it.'

'Have another look at that.' Carrie pointed at the paper lying in Leo's lap. 'The drawing is bad but it's clearly a hexagram from the Clavicle of Solomon. Look at the writing. It's ancient Hebrew script. Where the hell do you think your ordinary country woman got that kind of knowledge? Most of the reference books she'd need are in private collections or locked up for ever in the Vatican library. I'll bet she's never been further than a day trip to Trafalgar Square in her life. It must have been passed on by word of mouth.'

'You think it's Hebrew Script? You can't translate it?'

'No. Maybe it doesn't translate. Maybe it's just a written incantation. It doesn't really matter. The fact is that if she can produce that, she can complete the ritual. He's as good as dead.'

'Suppose I accept every word you say. Demons and all. It means that Orton isn't the murderer, doesn't it?'

'Why?'

'If he'd killed and raped her daughter and she had the kind of power you say she's got, surely she'd have given him the chop long before now.'

'I hadn't thought of that. Yes, I'd think so.'

'So why is she after him?'

'I don't know. What's more I don't intend to find out . . .' she hesitated '. . . unless . . .'

'What?'

'Suppose she knew he was Master of the Second Order of the Silver Star. She'd know they'd held a meeting the night of the murder so she could have guessed that they lied to you. She'd know they were hampering your work, preventing you getting to the murderer.'

'She only has to come and tell us what Orton was up to. Why go for him?'

'I don't know. Unwilling to expose the craft perhaps.'

'She didn't have to, he's a fake you say . . . and if she's that hot stuff why didn't she put the black spot on the real murderer?'

'She may not have the sight.'

'So you think she's on our side then, working for us?'

'May be.'

'She'd never make the C.I.D.' Leo reached across and set the paper up beside the bedside lamp.

'Okay be flip,' said Carrie, 'you asked the questions, I answered them. I didn't come here to act as your straight man . . .' she stopped suddenly, staring at the paper propped against the lamp. 'Leo,' she said quietly, 'hold that paper up against the light.'

She moved up the bed to get a better look. A drawing covered the whole page, lightly indented into the paper with a sharp instrument. A grotesque face with bulbous eyes, grooved forehead, enlarged bovine snout, huge gaping mouth and a single horn-like growth protruding from the top of the head. Huge wings sprouting from the back, spindly arms attached, ending in three talons. A deformed penis between the legs. Skeletal body. A bulky growth beneath the knees ending in cloven hooves.

Throughout this conversation Leo had concentrated his mind on the murder investigation, prodding and questioning Carrie to elicit as much information as he could. He had closed his mind to any serious consideration of the implications behind what she had said. The sight of this representation of evil set icy fingers on his spine. He shivered.

'Poor bastard,' said Carrie.

Leo put the paper in the drawer and closed it, 'Orton?'

'He's going to get a visit from that. Any time she presses the button.'

'Nasty looking piece of work,' said Leo, thoughtfully.

'Pazuzu.'

'Eh?'

'A devil. Mesopotamia, I think.'

'Charming company he'd make I'm sure.'

Carrie stood up. 'Leo, I've had enough. I'm tired. Bloody tired. I'm going to bed.'

Leo looked at her. 'You'll see Orton then?'

'Yes, I said so.'

'Look, if he knows friend Pazuzu is on his tail he'll be wetting his pants. When he learns that you're an adept he might ask your help. We could use that as a lever to persuade him to co-operate.'

Carrie sighed. 'I'm not an adept. I doubt if he'll cry on my shoulder on our first meeting. If he does my advice will be to incarcerate himself in the nearest Catholic monastery and start praying. I'll put him on a plate for you, don't worry. Let's hope your Mrs Prentiss doesn't run out of patience before we get him.'

She turned to go. Leo slipped naked out of bed and put his arms round her from behind. He felt the curve of her breasts in his hand, sheathed in a skin of silk.

'Stay.'

'No, Leo.' She turned in his arms and faced him, a sad smile on her face.

'I'm out, am I?' Leo returned her smile. 'I don't blame you.'

She shook her head. 'Not that. It's nothing to do with you personally. I'm very fond of you.'

'Wrong time of the month?'

She giggled. 'No, dear.'

'What then?'

'There's no easy way to tell you . . .'

Leo held her at arms' length, unconscious of his nakedness. 'Just tell it straight.'

'I said I'd changed . . . after . . . it was probably latent anyway. I expect I'd just repressed it, I can't remember . . .'

'Carrie . . .?'

She stood away from him, looked him in the eye, defiance, guilt, determination.

'Leo, dear, for the last two years I've been a practising lesbian.'

She moved forward, kissed him lightly on the lips and was gone.

The murderer stood beside an oak tree. He had been there for over an hour. Waiting. She must come tonight. She always did. She would be working tomorrow. He looked at his watch, glowing luminous in the dark of the wood. She'd be on the last bus. Let her be on that last bus!

He moved a fraction and a dry twig cracked under his foot. A bird screamed an alarm. He looked anxiously around. Silence. Then he heard it. The distant drone of a diesel engine. The sound dying as the bus pulled into the stop. The harsh clatter as it pulled away. Not long now. His heart beat faster. Mouth open, breathing quickly. Sweat on his forehead and the palms of his hands.

The quick, insistent click of heels. He moved nearer the road, eased his bulk behind a bush, peered out. She was walking close to the bushes on his side of the road. Hands clutching a handbag in front of her Walking quickly. Straight towards him. His subconscious registered a faint annoying sound in the distance.

Thirty yards perhaps. It was her. He could see her clearly now. Recognized her swinging walk. He played the scene over in his mind. Legs splayed apart for him. The smell of her fear. Then defenceless, unable to deny him. Ready for him to prove his manhood. Twenty yards. He pushed his hand down between his legs, felt the flood of lust begin to flow. No erection yet. Soon. Very soon.

The sound was louder now. It finally penetrated his consciousness. The staccato bark of a powerful motorcycle on the main road. Wait, Be cautious. Let it pass first. Fifteen yards. He could see her face now. She was looking around her, watching the shadows. Nervous. The noise of the motorcycle engine abated under deceleration. Not this way. Not this bloody way! Keep going you bastard!

Ten yards. He could almost smell her. The deep growl as the rider opened the throttle. Louder, much louder. Heading for the village. The bastard!

She was opposite him now. Now he should jump out on her. Now he should smash her to the ground. A powerful headlamp cut through the darkness, lit up the road. She turned to look, anxious, fearful.

The rider pulled up beside her, the machine snarling beneath him.

'Hello, Anne, want a lift?'

'Paul,' voice tremulous, 'wondered whoever it was.'

'Hop on then.'

Paul Spender. The bastard. The bloody, bloody bastard.

She hoisted up her skirt, swung her leg across the pillion seat. The flash of white thighs. They thundered off into the night.

He cried. The tears rolled down his face, into his mouth hanging open in despair. Warm, salty. It wasn't fair. It wasn't bloody well fair.

Later he went back to his car and drove home. The house was silent. His wife was sitting up in bed reading.

'Hello.'

'Hello,' she replied, disinterested.

She took off her glasses, put down the book and got out of bed heading for the toilet. He undressed, was naked when she returned. She bent over, straightening the covers. He moved behind her, hands on her breasts, crotch cuddled into her buttocks. She straightened up and faced him. Her hand reached between his legs, took hold of his penis. It was small and limp.

'What are you going to do?' she asked. 'Put a splint on it?'

ELEVEN

Leo picked at his breakfast but Bob tucked in with gusto. During the meal Leo gave an edited version of Carrie's comments.

He said nothing of the difficulty he was having in plastering over the cracks she had made in his disbelief nor the shock he had felt when she had told him that she was no longer heterosexual. He was certain it wasn't latent in her. She'd had a warm insistent hunger for men. Had. What was it that could cause such a radical change? She'd had a need of men as strong as his for women.

To his surprise Bob Staunton did not ridicule Carrie's views. He listened carefully, asked a few pertinent questions and was then silent for the rest of the meal.

A place had been laid for Carrie at an adjacent table but she had not appeared by the time they left.

They had only got as far as the main office in the village hall when the Chief Constable arrived.

'Sorry about the other thing, old chap,' he said.

'What's that, sir?' asked Bob.

'Kenneth Barker.'

'Oh him.' Bob had already put the episode from his mind.

'I had a sharp word with the Duty Sergeant about that.'

Bob looked pained.

'I expect my officers to be able to recognize and sift out the likes of him. You should not have been bothered.'

'No sweat,' said Bob. 'You can't tell straight away with some of them. It was a few minutes before I twigged him.'

'Nonetheless . . .' the Chief Constable wagged a finger, 'keeps them on their toes. Now, how are you managing?'

'We're getting on,' Bob shrugged. 'There's a lead or two we're following up.'

'Local?'

'Yes, local. I said all along we wouldn't have to look far afield.'

'Well, that's fine . . . and you, young man?'

'No problems thank you, sir,' said Leo.

'Accommodation suitable? We can arrange something else . . .'

'We're happy where we are,' said Bob.

An awkward silence. Colonel Boulton looked round the room. 'Cut down on manpower, I see.'

'We don't want waste, do we, sir?' said Bob.

'No. Oh no, quite . . . well that's fine . . .'

'We'll let you know, sir.' Bob sounded like a casting director making it easy on a ham actor.

'Right,' the pipe appeared in his hand as if by magic. 'I'll leave you to it then.' He lit up and when the cloud of smoke dispersed, he had gone.

Sergeant Cobbold came in with Superintendent Day and they were just in time to acknowledge their departing chief.

Bob collected Sergeant Worthington and ushered the three of them into his office. He then gave them their first indication of the esoteric line the inquiry had now developed. Day and Worthington were astonished and more than a little sceptical. Sergeant Cobbold contributed nothing. Even when Bob told them of Commander Orton's involvement in occult activities he showed neither surprise nor concern.

They tossed words around between them for a while. Day and Worthington had not as yet come to any conclusions as a result of their further perusal of the statements. After half an hour Bob reminded them to keep their own counsel and brought the conference to a close.

When they were alone, Bob put his feet up on the desk and looked at Leo.

'The barmaid gone off you, has she?' he asked.

Leo made a face. 'We had a difference of opinion.'

'Pity that, nice girl.'

'Yes, she is.'

'Not mixed up with these witches and warlocks, I suppose?'

'Good God no ... well I don't think so ... no, I've no reason to think that. Why?'

'Just checking.'

Bob pulled his tie down a couple of inches and undid his top button. Leo watched him. Bob had been strangely introspective all morning. He suspected that an idea had been cooked and it was about to be served.

'Let's have a serious talk.'

'What about?'

'About the bold Orton and his team. I've been thinking ... you say he's Master of the Temple, right?'

'Yes.'

'What Temple?'

'Well, the Temple of the Second Silver ...'

'No, I mean where is it?'

'I don't quite ...'

'Look, you say they aren't campfire jumpers these people, they're sort of one up on that ...'

'Yes.'

'So they've probably got a headquarters somewhere. A place they meet regular ... all done up ready for the orgies and that ... yes?'

Leo sat upright. 'Of course. Why didn't I think of that?'

'Just now and then the old man earns his crust. So like I said, where is it? Look at this ...' he pointed to P.C. Trew's masterpiece on the wall behind him, 'everything down to the last pigshed ... but where do we start? What sort of place would they look for?'

'Well, somewhere quiet, out of the way. A disused church would be ideal of course ...'

'A church?'

'Yes ... or any holy place ... they parody established religions so ... just a minute, it's on Orton's estate.'

'Yeah?'

'Perfect.'

'There's no church on his estate.'

'I was down by the river one day, I saw an old stone building in the grounds. Overgrown, you probably couldn't see it except from the river.'

'Show me.'

Leo's finger moved over the map. 'It's not here.'

'If P.C. Trew had known about it it'd be there and if he didn't know about it chances are not many others would.'

Bob sucked his teeth and screwed up his face in thought. 'You sure it's there?'

'Absolutely. Let's take a look.'

'Tell you what I'll do,' said Bob with a sly grin, 'if it's the right place, I won't ask you what you were doing down by the river.'

The tide was out, leaving vast stretches of mud exposed along with rusty bicycle frames, blocks of concrete, broken bottles and the slimy fingers of broken branches. A lone cloud obscured the sun. Leo had an acute sense of loss. The magic had gone.

He led the way along the river bank, up the side of the wheatfield and through a hedge into the wooded area. They pushed their way through thick brambles and clinging undergrowth. Bob's temper was getting noticeably shorter and he had used most of his extensive vocabulary of less acceptable expletives by the time they had fought their way to the building.

'Bloody Eureka!' said Bob as they emerged in the clear area in front of the massive wooden doors.

A well-trodden path wound away from the spot where they stood, into the woods in the general direction of Bacton Hall. The building itself was almost completely overgrown and the windows had been bricked up.

'What the hell is it?' asked Bob. 'An air raid shelter?'

'A little too old for that,' said Leo, who was inspecting the substantial padlock that secured the metal bar across the doors. 'Could be a mausoleum . . . or a church.'

'Don't look like no church I've ever seen.'

'Some of the old wealthy families had their own small churches in the grounds of their estates. Had their own priests as well.'

'Rent a priest, eh? Buy your salvation here.'

'Patronage was the word they used, I think.'

'Well we're not getting in there very, easy, are we?' Bob pushed at the door's defences.

'No. Someone's gone to a lot of trouble to keep out unwanted visitors. This padlock is almost new.'

'Right, tell you what we'll do. I'll sit here and have a rest. You go back to the office, pick up Sergeant Cobbold and see what you can get in the way of housebreaking implements.'

Leo looked dubious, 'Are you sure . . .?'

Bob grinned but his voice was determined. 'In this job you need a break now and then.'

Leo returned three-quarters of an hour later with Sergeant Cobbold who was carrying a sack marked 'GRAINGER AND CO. SELECTED SEEDS'. When he dropped it there was the dull clang of heavy metal against metal.

'What you got?' asked Bob.

Cobbold tipped up the sack and showed him. 'Didn't have much time, sir,' he said, inspecting the padlock.

He selected a huge pair of bolt cutters and advanced on the door.

'Good grief!' said Bob. 'Where'd you get them?'

'Garage, sir.'

'Didn't he ask why you wanted them?'

Cobbold was turning bright red as he strained to cut through the padlock. He stopped for a rest.

'He's all right, Roy Salmon. Keeps himself to himself, don't ask too many questions like.' He resumed his assault on the padlock.

As it dropped away Leo moved forward to remove the iron bar. They pulled open the wooden doors and stepped inside.

The stench assailed them and at first they could see nothing. Bob sniffed, wrinkled his nose in disgust.

'Pot,' he said, 'the bastards have been smoking pot, I can smell it a mile off. Keeping rotten fish too by the smell of it.'

Leo pushed back the doors to let in more light and took a torch from his pocket. They moved further into the room and all three stood in stunned silence as they looked around them.

The walls were draped from ceiling to floor with alternating strips of black and red velvet. The ceiling itself was low over their heads. It had been painted in haphazard daubs of colour, black, yellow, orange and purple.

The floor was carpeted wall to wall in black, except for an area of about six square feet in the centre at the farthest end. Here two concentric circles had been painted in red on the stone floor. Between them, a zig-zag pattern had been drawn and the spaces between the pattern were filled with hieroglyphics.

They stood in an aisle formed by rows of low, cushioned seats upholstered in black hide which filled the whole of the space on either side of them between the door and the uncarpeted area at the far end of the room.

Eyes now adjusted to the dark, they moved further up the aisle and stopped at the painted circle. They could now see that in the centre of the circle stood a black draped, oblong altar and at the head of it a small table covered by a pure white cloth. A number of objects were displayed on the table: a short-bladed dagger with intricate designs on the bone handle, two superb silver cups, three black candles in ornate silver candlesticks, a length of knotted rope, two femur bones arranged in an inverted cross, two silver salvers, a carved bone stick about twelve inches long heavily inscribed and a human skull that acted as a centrepiece.

Above the altar hung a five-pointed chandelier with five black candles and beside it, also suspended from the ceiling, hung two censers. The only object on the altar itself was a huge phallus in white bone set in an obsidian base.

In the limited space between the rear of the aisle and the end wall was a throne-like, high backed chair of intricately carved wood. On the chair, upside down, was a wooden cross on which a black cat had been crucified and disembowelled. Its teeth leered at them in the rictus of death.

On the wall behind the chair hung a painting that was at once the most artistically exquisite and the most horrifying of all the objects in the room. A cowled and robed monk stared down at the intruders. The face distorted in a grin of satanic ferocity. Eyes that denied hope, commanded obedience and shone with the pure impurity of lust and evil. The white robe open from the thighs revealed a hugely distorted penis. In the left hand, held negligently at one side a female child, throat cut, the blood staining the white robe beneath.

Sergeant Cobbold felt suddenly sick. He clapped a hand to his mouth, turned and ran for the door. The others ignored his departure.

'Why did they have to kill that poor bloody cat?' said Bob eventually.

'To guard the Temple,' said Leo automatically.

'Do what?'

'They crucify the animal, kill it and conjure a demon to occupy the body to guard the Temple in their absence.'

'Didn't bloody work, did it?'

'It's symbolic,' said Leo.

'Bastards,' said Bob viciously. 'What's that in the corner?'

Leo swung his torch to reveal a tall and substantial cupboard with double doors. Its black drapes had made it almost invisible in the half light of the room.

Bob picked up the bone-handled dagger from the table and levered opened the doors. A number of colourful robes hung in splendid array, the richest and most outstanding being a black cape embroidered with serpents and other satanic symbols.

On a shelf near the floor were a number of bottles containing a variety of dried herbs and others whose contents were unidentifiable. They opened some, detected vinegar, pure alcohol, cloves, honey, vervain, water, sacramental wafers, aniseed, pepper, sulphur, nail parings, rosemary, sandalwood and dried blood.

There were also more silver cups, copper trays, a mirror, candlesticks, a chalice, an ebony wand and a crystal. Bob rooted among the objects, came up with an earthenware pot with a heavy lid. In it he found a sanitary towel soaked in blood. It was the last straw. He hurled the pot against the wall and it smashed into a thousand pieces.

'Right, Leo, we're going to put a stop to this bloody lot. Sort out all the stuff that looks as if it might have come from a church.'

They removed the censers, the chalice, silver candlesticks, cups and plates and carried them to the door. The morning air was suddenly a heady wine, the sun now more understandably an object of worship.

Sergeant Cobbold was shamefaced.

'I'm sorry, sir ... I just felt sick ...'

'Forget it,' said Bob. 'Stuff this lot in the sack.'

Cobbold, anxious to please, moved quickly to do his bidding. Leo bent down to help him. Bob gave his instructions.

'You stay here, Roger, you don't have to go inside. I'll send a team down to clean the place out. We'll put these bastards out of business once and for all. Leo ...'

'Yes, sir?'

'Pick up the sack, mate, we're going to call on the vicar and show him the loot.'

As Leo drove back down the narrow track leading away from the river the contents of the sack jangled on the back seat. Bob was deep in thought.

'Office first, sir?' asked Leo.

'Eh? Oh, yes. I'll send Superintendent Day down to relieve Cobbold and sort out the inventory.'

'Dirty business, isn't it?' said Leo.

'Yeah. I don't blame young Roger, I felt sick myself ... trouble is, finding that place don't help us all that much.'

'Well, obviously Orton will deny all knowledge. We might try sending the fingerprint boys in.'

'So what if we prove he was in there? So he says he discovered the place the other day and bolted it up while he considered what to do. What chance have we got of a conviction? . . . and what for, killing the cat, smoking pot . . . a good defence counsel would crucify us.'

'I thought you said . . .'

'I said we'd put a stop to it. We will. But as to nicking anybody, that's something else.'

'There must be a prima facie case of handling stolen property against anybody we can prove was in there. Even if they aren't convicted, the publicity will floor them.'

'You may be right but that's not our affair, that's up to the local law. We're here to catch a murderer not hunt down locals with dirty hobbies.'

'Yes, you're quite right. It just seems very important to put them out of business.'

'It is. Don't fret, that bunch won't be crucifying any more cats for a while. Thing is, we've got to separate that from what we're really after.'

Leo slowed down as they entered the village. 'So then use that as a bargaining point when we go to see friend Orton.'

'But at best all he can tell us is the names of the rest of his Order and Carrie Fuller will tell us that.'

'Knowing the names is all very well but we want to make sure they tell us the truth. You've got a lot of faith in Carrie Fuller. Maybe you're right, but me, I like a second string to the bow and that's exactly what we've got, mate.'

Leo looked at his watch as he pulled up outside the village hall. It was 11 a.m. 'He won't be at home until later this afternoon, he's having lunch in Ipswich with Carrie.'

'That's all right, we'll catch him later on this afternoon. There's nowhere he can run is there?'

When they entered the main office Superintendent Day and Sergeant Worthington were huddled over a trestle table at one side of the hall, surrounded by piles of statements. Day looked up as they entered.

'Ah. If you have a moment . . .'

Bob and Leo joined them.

'Got something?' asked Bob.

'I'm not sure, it's not a positive thing . . . more a worrying negative you might say . . .'

'Well?'

'It's to do with Gatwood . . . the grocer in the village here . . . you remember?'

'Well, vaguely . . .'

'He had a breakdown in his car on the night of the murder . . .'

'Oh yes, I remember, what about him?'

'Roy Salmon from the garage went out to him and got him started . . .'

'That's right, so?'

'Well, that was their alibi, both of them. The fact that they were together at the car about the time she was killed.'

'You're thinking they should have seen the girl walking home or the murderer perhaps?'

'That was my first thought because they were on the main road, on her route home, but then I realized that they would have been there too late, after she and the murderer passed probably.'

'Exactly. So?'

'Like I said, it's a negative thing. Not one of the drivers stopped in the road block, those that were on the road that night, not one of them mentions seeing the breakdown.'

Bob screwed up his face and looked thoughtful. 'That's a good point, mate.'

'I mean, two vehicles stopped on the road, one a breakdown truck . . . I should have thought someone would mention it, wouldn't you?'

'I'd have thought so . . .'

'So either they saw it and didn't mention it, which seems unlikely since Inspector Grace and his chaps are too experienced to let a thing like that slip by . . . or they weren't there at the time they said.'

'What about the job card?' Leo put in. 'Salmon must have a record of the work he did on the car, that'll tell us the date and the time.'

'We don't seem to have inspected it,' said Day, rather apologetically.

'It could be something, it could be nothing but we'll have to clear it up,' said Bob, 'but not yet, put the statements to one side and we'll look at it later.'

'I could go and have a look at the job card myself, sir,' Day offered.

'Look, one of them or both of them could be in this Coven or Order or whatever they call themselves. If they are, it could be the reason they're lying. We'll have a list of the names later today, so we'll wait for that before we see them again. Anyway there's something else I want you to do in the meantime.'

Bob explained quickly about the discovery of the Temple and its contents. He made it clear to Day that this aspect was to be a local matter but that he wanted no arrests until all the persons responsible had been cleared from the murder inquiry.

A rather bemused Superintendent Day collected together some men and left for the Temple. Bob and Leo returned to their car and headed for the church.

They found Ray Colville attacking an overgrown hedge in the churchyard with a small hand scythe. He greeted them with a cheery smile.

'Only exercise I get . . . wielding a bagging hook,' he said. 'What can I do for you?'

'We might be able to do something for you, vicar,' said Bob.

Leo emptied the sack and arranged the contents on it.

'Any of this stuff yours?' asked Bob.

Colville bent down and inspected the pieces. He put some to one side. 'These are,' he said, 'although I'd say it was all church property.' He straightened up. 'I'm delighted to see them back. Might I ask where you found them?' He sounded as though he feared the answer.

'In a minute,' said Bob.

'How can you identify these pieces positively as yours, Mr Colville?' Leo asked.

'Ray.'

'Okay, Ray,' said Bob. 'We don't doubt you, but we have to be sure.'

'I marked them,' said Colville. He picked up a silver cup and reversed it, showing that the letters B.F.P.C. had been scratched on the underneath. 'Bacton Ford Parish Church. I marked everything when we first started losing items.'

'Just the job,' said Bob approvingly.

'Is someone to be charged?' Colville asked as he watched Leo pack the items back in the sack.

'Don't know yet,' said Bob. 'We have to keep your stuff for the time being, just in case. You'll get it back eventually. I'll send a local officer up to take a statement from you to formally identify the things that're yours.'

'Can I ask now where you found these things?'

'We discovered a building in the grounds of Commander Orton's house,' said Leo. 'It has been in use as a Satanic Temple. Judging from what we found there I'd say there had been some pretty nasty goings-on.'

'Surely Commander Orton . . .'

'We don't know yet,' Bob put in quickly, 'and I'd appreciate your confidence for the moment.'

'Yes, of course. You know . . .' he hesitated, 'I can't believe the Orton family knew anything about this. They have supported the church for generations . . . they have their own family pew.'

'I dare say. Well, thanks for your help. We've got to be on our way.'

'Mr Staunton.'

'Yes?'

'I may find myself in some difficulty over this.'

'Why?'

'The people responsible are obviously local.'

'I'd say so, yes.'

'Then they are my parishoners. I would be reluctant to appear in court and give evidence against them.'

'You may not have to. Anyway they're not your flock, they've joined the opposition.'

Colville picked up the scythe and fingered the sharp edge with gentle fingers. 'Our Lord in his wisdom teaches the forgiveness of sinners. He makes no distinction as between those who have committed minor sins and those who have sinned greatly,' he looked at Leo, 'so there is time for all to return to his grace.'

'Well,' Bob shifted his feet uncomfortably, 'if it comes to it you'll have to abide by the law, mate . . . but maybe it won't come to that, eh?'

He nodded in friendly fashion and he and Leo returned to the car.

Ray Colville watched them go. He felt a deep sadness and a mounting surge of anger at his impotence and failure. He swung the bagging hook viciously at the hedge. It snagged on a stout branch and jarred his arm.

'Jesus!' he said loudly. Then as an afterthought, '. . . help me.'

A shuttle service was already in action between the Temple and the village hall. Articles taken from the Temple were being piled up on the small stage. In this setting they lost much of their horror. They looked more like props from a play set in the dark ages. Even the painting of the monk seemed less horrific, less artistically mature, more the work of a mentally deranged art student.

They had some sandwiches sent over from the Haywain and sat in Bob's office as they made a makeshift meal. They mulled over the events of the morning but came to no new conclusions. They had to break Orton before their way would become clear.

When they had finished Bob wandered out into the main office leaving Leo alone. It would be a couple of hours before they could visit

Orton with a reasonable chance of finding him in and they had no intention of making an appointment this time, they wanted him off guard.

Leo stared out of the window. The village was quiet and peaceful in the afternoon sun. He turned away and sat at Bob's desk, restless, anxious to be doing something positive.

His eyes fell on the two statements Superintendent Day had left on the desk. Salmon and Gatwood. He read them through again but they told him nothing he did not already know. Something stirred in his memory.

'I got something you want . . .' Mrs Salmon. Drunk. What did she mean? Anything at all, or was she just drunk? Did she know her husband had lied to cover for Gatwood? Fat piggy-eyed Gatwood. She didn't fit in here. She was a city girl. Did she just fancy a quick tumble? Or did she know something? She worked in the garage office. Had she seen an altered job card? If she had, why should she put her husband in jeopardy? What else had she said? He couldn't remember. Why should Salmon cover for Gatwood? Both in Orton's gang? Was it worth seeing her, testing her out?

'No,' said the voice, 'it bloody well isn't.'

He got up and walked into the main office. Bob was up on the stage, looking through the mounting pile of esoteric impedimenta. Leo wandered across the room and out into the open air.

'You're just looking for a quick poke,' the voice reproved, 'a couple of days without and you've got withdrawal symptoms.'

Leo walked slowly through the village in the direction of the Salmons' house.

'You haven't told anyone where you're going. If she blows the whistle on you, you're a dead duck. She's neurotic and a lush to boot. Turn back.'

Leo walked on.

'You know her type. She'll scream rape even if you don't perform. Try and talk your way out of that! You'll be out of a job.'

Leo walked on.

'You're mad,' said the voice desperately, 'you don't even fancy her. She's probably been in the pub all lunchtime getting tanked up. If you must go to see her at least take out some insurance. Go back to the office and get someone to go with you. Leo . . .'

It was hot and there were few people about. He hesitated outside the house.

'Take yourself in hand if you're that hard up,' the voice was getting nasty now, 'she'll stink of booze anyway.'

Leo turned away from the gate.

'There's a good boy.'

She had walked up behind him unheard, from the direction of the village.

'So you came then. Better late than never.'

'Oh, Mrs Salmon . . .'

'Get the hell out of here, Leo.'

'The name is Margaret. Come in.'

She led the way up the neat path with its multi-coloured border. Leo followed. She ushered him into the lounge. It was immaculately clean, neat and tidy, reflecting the woman.

'Like a drink?'

'No, thanks.'

She was not as drunk as when she had accosted him in the Haywain but she hadn't been abstaining either. This time she had it under control. She was wearing a tight skirt and a cream blouse tucked in at the waist. She looked cool and brittle.

'I don't make a habit of this,' she said.

'Of what?' said Leo.

She pulled the pins out of her hair and it cascaded down round her shoulders. It changed her completely, took the rigidity from her face, softened her.

'Propositioning men,' she said.

'Oh.' Leo forced a smile. 'You said you had something for me.'

'Haven't I?' She pirouetted in front of him.

'Make an excuse, Leo. Get out quick.'

'Something to tell me, you said.'

She laughed, soft and feminine. 'You didn't come here to talk business. I saw you looking at me when you came to the garage, remember? You practically stripped me in front of my husband.'

'Now you've brought the matter up, where is he?'

'Working,' she slipped in close to him and put her arms round his neck. 'He's always working. He won't disturb us.'

Leo put his hands uncertainly on her waist. 'He might just drop in.'

'No he won't. Forget about him.'

'Keep her talking, Leo. She might go off the idea.'

'You're a very beautiful woman.'

'Don't weaken, Leo. Just explain you haven't got time.'

159

'I haven't got much time.'

'Then you'd better take me upstairs now.'

'She's a bitch!'

'Come on . . .'

She took him by the hand, led him out of the room and upstairs, pushed him gently into a bedroom. It was a very feminine room, soft furnishings, pastel colours and a subtle scent of perfume. It was as though Leo had been hypnotized. He seemed incapable of free action. He stood unresisting as she undressed him, moving only to facilitate her actions. She placed his clothing carefully on a chair, piece by piece.

He shivered, naked and limp before her. Her hands caressed him for a moment, then she stood back.

'Take my clothes off,' she said.

He moved slowly to obey. Observing the ritual she had performed he placed her clothing beside his on the chair. She swayed and moved her body to assist his efforts until she finally stood naked before him.

Her mouth opened in a smile of anticipation. She moved into him, pulling him to her. Her head came level with his chin, his rising hardness pressed into her stomach.

Leo reached for her, the familiar flood of lust overflowing in him. She twisted out of his grasp, ducked under his arm and stood behind him. He tried to turn to face her but she wrapped her arms round him from behind, holding him tight against her. He reached behind him to touch her as she pushed her hand down his stomach, between his legs and gripped him tightly, hand moving in gentle, firm rhythm.

He twisted in her grasp, desperate to take her, but she clung on, hand moving faster and faster, a breathless laugh escaping her as she sensed his rising desperation. Suddenly she released him and jumped on to the bed, flat on her back, legs open, arms reaching for him.

'Come on,' she said, 'come on.'

Afterwards she lay half across him for a while, stroking him gently in contentment. Leo lay in a stupor, fingers playing idly across her back.

She sat up. 'I really don't make a habit of it,' she said.

'Slut,' said the voice.

'Nobody said you did.'

'But dear God, I did need that.' She slid off the bed, found a dressing gown in a cupboard and slipped it on. She was stone cold sober now. 'I'm no nympho . . . we all need the real thing sometimes, don't we?'

'A whore making excuses, what next?'

'I can't believe your husband doesn't . . . want you.'

'Oh he does . . . but he's always working, always tired . . . he has trouble making it.'

'Oh.'

'Lying cow, she's anybody's.'

'You'd better get dressed,' she said and giggled, 'I don't want to make a pig of myself.'

'Why not?' Leo smiled lazily.

'That would be indulgence.' She disappeared into the hallway and he heard the bathroom door close.

'Indulgence,' said the voice, mocking, 'dear God Almighty.'

Leo dressed slowly. Something nagged at the back of his mind. Something Bob had said. The thought wavered about, just out of reach. He was dressed when she returned. He made an excuse and went into the bathroom.

It smelt of her. He tried to relieve himself but was unable to, so he did up his trousers. On an impulse he took a handkerchief from his pocket, bent quickly down and raked some hairs out of the plughole in the bath with his finger. He placed them carefully in the handkerchief and tucked it away.

He hesitated by the door, then pushed the plunger and waited for the lavatory to flush before leaving. He wandered down to the lounge and waited for her.

When she reappeared a few minutes later, her hair was back up in a severe bun. The tight skirt and cream blouse showed not a crease. Her face wore a polite but distant smile. She had determinedly put away the lusting woman of the last half hour.

'Well, they say nobody misses a slice off a cut loaf,' said the voice acidly.

'Would you care for a coffee?' she asked.

'No thank you, Margaret. I must be going.'

'Nothing happened this afternoon.'

'Nothing?'

'Nothing,' she said firmly.

'Fine, but tell me something. Why me?'

She led him to the door. 'My husband was born and bred here. If I went near any man in the village they'd soon all know . . . I found you attractive . . . and I felt sure that since you were a police officer I could rely on your discretion.' There was a faint edge to the last words.

'And I can rely on yours?'

'You can.'

'Come what may?'

'Come what may,' she said, and closed the door firmly behind him. He believed her. It took a load off his mind.

There was no sign of Bob when he returned to the village hall. Sergeant Cobbold was assisting Superintendent Day in making an inventory of the items taken from the Temple. Leo took him aside and gave him the sample of hair he had taken from the Salmons' bath, instructing him to take it straight to the laboratory with the request that they expedite a comparison with the hair found on the dead girl's clothes.

Roger Cobbold was glad of an excuse to leave others to continue the work on the inventory and disappeared with considerable rapidity. Leo did not enlighten Superintendent Day as to the reason for his subordinate's rapid exit, not wishing to make explanations at this stage. He retired to Bob's office to avoid this necessity and found a message for him. Carrie Fuller was at the Haywain and wanted to see him.

He consulted his watch and calculated that he just about had time to see her before Bob was likely to want to leave to interrogate Orton.

Carrie was looking wan and tired when Leo entered her room. She flopped back on her bed and waved him to a chair.

'Take a pew . . . if you'll forgive the expression.'

'How'd it go?' Leo inquired.

'Sweet as a nut. He's a lamb to the slaughter.'

'You have the names?'

'No. Better than that. I've left him considering my suggestion.'

'Which was?'

'That they should meet you. All of them . . . that's better for you isn't it?'

'Yes, fine, but surely he won't declare himself?'

'No. You would meet the Bacton Ford Historical Association. It so happened they had a meeting on the night of the murder and some of them didn't tell wives and husbands so they told a few white lies to the police . . . easy, isn't it?'

'Will he buy it?'

'He will. He's pooping his pants what with one thing and another.'

'Did he mention Mrs Prentiss?'

'Not by name.'

'Did he ask for help?'

'No.'

'Why not, didn't he accept you?'

'Yes, of course. He wouldn't have talked to me at all if he didn't. I'm going to the house tomorrow, he'll probably ask me then.'

'What will you do?'

'Nothing. I'll put him off, tell him I need to prepare myself. I know what to say.'

'Yes, I suppose that's all right.'

'Leo, what's up with you? The man is on a plate. I'm about to deliver him but you don't seem very interested all of a sudden. All you're worried about is Ma Prentiss.'

'Carrie, something happened this morning . . . I'd better tell you about it . . .'

Carrie sat up sharply on one elbow. 'Don't you go back on the deal, Leo . . .'

'No. I'm not . . .'

'What is it then?'

'We found the Temple . . .'

'The hell you did. Where?'

'On Orton's estate. An old church . . .'

'Does he know?'

'Not yet. We're going to talk to him this afternoon. I came to see you first.'

Carrie sat up quickly and rummaged in her bedside cabinet, emerging with a Rolex. 'Let's go, Leo, of this I must have pictures.'

'Well . . . I didn't think you'd want pictures of the Temple.'

'Why ever not?'

'Because you're . . . well involved.'

'So what? These people are blown. It's going to get into the papers one way or another. If anybody's going to have pictures from the inside, that body is me. I've earned them.'

'Yes, you have . . . you see the problem is that our chaps have cleaned the place out. There isn't a lot left to photograph, I don't think.'

Carrie held her head in her hands. 'He doesn't think. Damn right he doesn't think. Leo, photographs of the whole set-up intact would have been worth a fortune. I could have syndicated them all over the world. Thanks a million.'

'I'm sorry, Carrie, but I had other things on my mind. I'm not a journalist, I don't think the way you do.'

'Oh well, I suppose I can redeem something out of it. I imagine you're prepared to tell me where it is?'

'Certainly. Give me a piece of paper, I'll draw you a map. If there are still officers there, tell them to contact me if they are not keen on letting you in.'

She handed him a scrap of paper and he drew quickly.

'Is Orton going to be charged?' she asked.

'That's up to the local police. We found some articles stolen from the village church but there may be a problem of tying individuals to the actual theft. We're not really interested in that side of it, we just want the truth from Orton and his crowd so that we can get on with the job of catching the murderer.'

He handed over the sketch. 'Tell me something . . . did Orton say why Mrs Prentiss was after him? I know he didn't mention her name, but did he say why he was in trouble?'

'Not really. He just said it was a personal matter.'

'Personal?'

'Yes. What's going on in that tiny mind of yours, dear?'

'I was just wondering . . . how personal is personal?'

They were shown into the same room by the same sour-faced housekeeper. Orton kept them waiting for fully five minutes. Leo became impatient.

'Bloody bad manners, this.'

'Probably changing his underpants,' said Bob, unperturbed.

'Do you want me to talk to him?'

'No thanks, Leo. There's no need for kid gloves now, we've got him by the short and curlies. I'm going to make this quick, then leave him to sweat.'

When Orton appeared he apologized profusely for his tardy arrival and pleaded that he had felt unwell and had retired to rest. It may well have been true. He looked pale and drawn, seemed to have lost weight, and the arrogance and confidence that had been so much in evidence during their first meeting. Bob Staunton did not waste time with preliminaries.

'You're in bother,' he said.

'I don't think so.' The words were right but the tone revealed uncertainty.

'I do. This morning we searched a building on your estate. The old church or mausoleum or whatever it was . . . it overlooks the river. You know what we found, of course.'

'A lot of dirt and a lot of spiders I imagine.'

Bob ignored him and ploughed on. 'The place has been kitted out at considerable expense as a black magic temple. We found drugs there and stuff stolen from local churches.'

'How terrible. I had no idea.' But Orton was clearly shaken.

'Balls,' said Bob emphatically.

'Are you suggesting that I knew of it? You have no proof.'

'Fingerprints,' said Leo quietly.

Orton considered. 'I'm not saying I've never been in there.'

'On a sacrificial dagger,' said Leo, the lie springing easily to his lips.

Orton's face twitched. 'You have come here to arrest me? That might be an error.'

'Strange as it may seem to you, mate,' said Bob, 'we're not here because you're a mentally deranged pervert, we're here because you're a bloody liar.'

'Mr Staunton, whatever your opinion of me, even if it were true, there is no call for gratuitous insults and gutter language.'

'I thought Chief Superintendent Staunton's language perfectly proper,' said Leo blandly.

'I see,' said Orton bitterly, 'support for the team right or wrong.'

'How perceptive of you,' said Leo, with a cold smile.

'Let's get a few things straight,' said Bob. 'We're only interested in finding out who killed Joy Prentiss. It's up to the local police what they do about your other activities. I want to see you and the rest of your boy scouts and I want another statement about your movements on the night of the murder and this time I want the truth. Right?'

Bob stood up. Leo and Orton followed suit as if pulled up on the same string.

'And time ain't on your side or ours,' said Bob.

Orton made a tiny gesture of submission with one hand. 'I may be able to help you,' he said. 'Perhaps I could contact you later?'

'You know where to find us,' said Bob, 'we'll show ourselves out.'

Orton hesitated only momentarily after the door had closed behind them then picked up the telephone.

On the way back in the car Bob was in good humour. He punched Leo amiably on the shoulder.

'I bloody enjoyed putting that dirty bastard in his place,' he said, rubbing his hands together with a usurer's pleasure.

Leo grinned. 'Working class lad puts down the local squire,' he said.

'I don't go along with that class stuff,' said Bob. 'After all, I put up with you, don't I? No, that Orton is a nasty piece of work. If he wore a cloth cap and clogs I'd still hate his guts.'

'Well, if Carrie is right, Mrs Prentiss is going to deal him some rough justice.'

'I'll grant you and Miss Fuller have been right about this business up to now but visiting demons I won't buy.' He shook his head in emphasis.

'Not quite that perhaps but there have been authenticated cases reported in Africa of witch doctors causing the death of people they put spells on.'

'That's different. The witch doctors make bloody sure the victim knows what's coming and the victim has to believe in it or it doesn't work. I read that somewhere.'

'Orton does believe in it. That's what worries me. If he dies, how do we go about proving that Mrs Prentiss killed him?'

When they arrived back at the village hall, Bob wandered off to see Superintendent Day. Leo joined Sergeant Cobbold who was back at his desk. Cobbold held up a small plastic sachet.

'The lab have examined the sample, sir.'

'Already.'

'They did it while I waited. I said you were in a hurry like.'

'What's the verdict?'

Cobbold shook his head. 'They won't commit themselves, sir. The sample we found on the dead girl's clothes was male pubic hair. There was only two strands of male pubic hair in what you gave me. They say the colour is the same and the texture is right but they'd need a larger sample to provide enough evidence to stand up in court as a positive identification.'

'Well I can't get any more. What did they think though, did they give an off-the-record guess?'

'You know what they're like, sir. He said that if he were asked in court he'd have to say that he couldn't identify those hairs as coming from the same man as the control sample.'

Leo sighed. 'Well, it was just a thought. Put it in the exhibit book and forget it.'

'I have to know where you got that sample, sir.'

'Leave the column blank for now. I'll fill it in myself later.'

'If you say so, sir,' said Cobbold dubiously.

The library at Bacton Hall was not a large room. The number of people gathered there that evening filled it to capacity. Fear and doubt clouded their faces. Commander Orton called the meeting together and addressed them.

'I have asked you here to inform you of certain developments regarding the future of the Temple. The situation has become progressively worse and a decision now has to be made. We became aware a few days ago, through my daughter, that the police suspected the existence of our group. This was confirmed later by one of our brothers. At that time, however, they were clearly speculating and had no proof. It seemed, therefore, that if we kept our counsel we would be safe.

'Some of you will know that I have been, and still am, under personal attack by another magician. It had been my intention to ask you to join me in a ritual with the object of warding off this attack. Regrettably that will no longer be possible. This afternoon the police discovered our Temple and I have no doubt that by now they have ransacked it.'

Murmurs of apprehension swelled in the room. Orton raised a hand for silence.

'There are however two rays of hope. It was my good fortune to meet recently a lady freelance journalist. Some of you will have seen her in the village, a Miss Fuller. She occupies an exalted position in the craft, in fact I think she may well have crossed the abyss. I took the decision to acquaint her with our problem and she made a suggestion which I have since decided to act upon. She feels, as I do, that we must separate the craft from the involvement with the murder inquiry. This means that we must tell the police the truth, or at least the fact that we were met together on the night of the murder. We do not have to reveal our involvement with the craft.

'The police visited me today to inform me of the discovery of the Temple and I have reason to believe that once they have taken fresh statements from us, we have little more to fear from them. I now invite comment.'

Orton sat down. The buzz of conversation mounted. Eventually a member stood.

'I can't believe the police will do nothing about the Temple. They must have found the things that were there.'

'They did,' Orton replied, 'but the officers from London are interested only in the murder. They are not fools. They know that none of us could have committed the murder because we were elsewhere at the time. Therefore they have no interest in the Temple and will leave that aspect to the local police. As you will be aware, I am not without influence. I think we have little to fear from a local investigation.'

Another stood.

'If the Temple is destroyed we will have to disband. So now each of us must decide on our own whether to talk to the police or not.'

'I have power over each of you until the day you die and beyond.' Orton's eyes blazed. 'The Temple can be rebuilt in time. I invited comment not dissent. You will obey me in this. Every one of you will return here tomorrow morning when I shall entertain the police officers. I shall now tell you how you will conduct yourselves at that interview.'

The chastened member dissolved into the group, eyes averted.

The Haywain seemed strangely deserted that evening. Bob and Leo occupied a corner table with Superintendent Day and Sergeant Cobbold. The conversation was disjointed and difficult. They all felt the end was near but speculation as to the identity of the murderer was still dangerous. None of them wanted to name a name and be proved wrong.

Carrie joined them at half past eight and the conversation brightened up. At nine o'clock Cobbold made his excuses and left. Shortly afterwards, Sergeant Worthington entered the bar with a message for Bob from Commander Orton. Bob read it.

'Ten o'clock tomorrow morning,' he told them.

When Sergeant Cobbold left the others, he drove straight through the village towards the river. He entered the Orton estate by an almost hidden farm gate and drove slowly along the rough track which ended at the Temple.

He took a carrier bag from the rear seat and approached the front doors. He took a key from his pocket and used it to unlock the padlock with which he himself had secured the Temple earlier in the day.

The hinges creaked. Pale moonlight filtered through the trees around him but failed to penetrate the gaping black hole left by the doors. Gentle night sounds surrounded him. He shivered and felt the cold sweat in the palms of his hands.

From the carrier bag he took a hammer, nails and two horse shoes. He worked quickly, nailing the horse shoes firmly into position above the doors.

That task completed, he took the rest of his implements from the carrier bag; a torch, a carton of salt, several cloves of garlic and a small crucifix.

He entered the blackness of the Temple holding the crucifix before him. Just inside the door he stopped and declaimed in a loud voice.

'Avaunt thee Satan. Jesus Christ, Lord of Light, aid thy servant Roger Cobbold to banish the powers of evil.'

He split open the carton of salt and walked up the aisle, spraying it around him, the torchlight cutting holes in the darkness as he went. He placed the cloves of garlic on the now empty altar, then reversed his route, discarding the empty carton by the entrance.

Once outside, he re-locked the doors and his last act before he drove away was to pin the crucifix above the lintel.

Roger Cobbold had a tidy mind. He did not believe in leaving a job half done.

TWELVE

Bob and Leo parked their car in the drive outside the Orton home just after ten o'clock the following morning and noted with satisfaction that a selection of vehicles had preceded them.

Superintendent Day pulled up behind in a second car with three other officers and behind him came Sergeant Cobbold and three more detectives. Bob Staunton had felt that a show of force would not come amiss.

Orton was disturbed at the size of the deputation but Bob was in no mood for compromise and in the end they were shown into the morning room. A few moments later Orton led his wife and daughter and a rather sheepish group of ten other people into the room.

Leo recognized some of them. Piggy-eyed Gatwood from the village store, his wife, and rather surprisingly, Dave Bull, the local reporter. The rest were just faces but he could see Sergeant Cobbold counting heads with a grim look on his face. He caught Janie Orton's eye but she stared straight through him.

Orton ushered in the last of his flock and closed the doors behind them. He then moved to a position in the centre of the floor and went into an obviously rehearsed speech, addressing the detectives.

'You see before you the ladies and gentlemen of the Bacton Ford Historical Association. On the night of the murder of Joy Prentiss, all of us were present at a meeting of the Association, here in the . . .

grounds of Bacton Hall. We live in a county in which the laws of the Christian Church are held dear but it happens that part of our studies lie in areas which would not find approval within the Church. For this reason we withheld part of the truth in the statements we made to you concerning our movements on the night of the murder. We now realize this was extremely foolish and very wrong. We hope you will accept our apologies and we now place ourselves at your disposal to rectify our omissions.'

Bob Staunton had become increasingly restive during this oration and he was somewhat abrupt when he spoke.

'Right. That's enough speeches. We all know why we're here, let's get on with it.' He turned to Superintendent Day. 'Your lads take one apiece, and I'll stand no nonsense from these people. They tell the truth first time or they go down the nick.'

The room was a bustle of activity as the detectives sorted themselves out partners and started to take their statements.

Bob and Leo stood by the french windows, looking out on to the sunbathed grounds of the house. It was a scene of peace and tranquillity that did not match the officers' mood. They were both edgy and impatient.

Superintendent Day had taken Commander Orton's statement himself. When he had finished he brought him across to the french windows.

'The Commander says he has something to tell us privately that he doesn't want included in his statement.'

'You tell me what it is. I'll decide if it's private or not,' said Bob sternly.

Orton dithered. 'Well . . . it's something that on the face of it might seem incriminating but in fact . . . that is, it actually has nothing to do with her death but . . . well, you might find out anyway and it might look even worse then . . .'

'Spit it out man.'

'Well . . . the fact is . . . I had a brief affair with the girl.'

'Joy Prentiss?' Bob's shock and horror was evident in his tone.

'Yes. It finished over a year ago . . . a very short-lived thing actually.'

'You and Joy Prentiss?' It was more than Bob could comprehend.

Orton shrugged delicately. 'She found me attractive . . . she said she didn't want her first time to be with some inexperienced yokel behind a haystack . . . as for me, well, she was very pretty . . . but one gets tired of having to teach every move.'

Bob was speechless.

'Go back with the others for now,' Leo ordered.

Orton inclined his head and moved away. It was several seconds before Bob recovered the power of speech.

'The bastard,' he said. 'Whatever persuaded her to give herself to him?'

'He has a certain animal magnetism I suppose,' said Leo. 'I could well imagine him being attractive to women and the young girl-older man syndrome is well documented.'

'But a lovely girl like that . . .'

'Maybe she wasn't all she seemed.'

Sergeant Cobbold appeared beside them with grocer Gatwood in tow.

'Can I have a word, sir?'

'Yes?'

'Mr Gatwood here seems to be the exception like.'

Bob looked at the grocer. Gatwood stared back fearfully, beads of sweat standing out on his bald pate.

'Why's that then?'

'Well, all the others gave alibis for each other but he got someone outside the group to alibi for him.'

'Yeah . . . Salmon, bloke from the garage . . .'

'Yes, sir. But the breakdown took place the night before the murder. Salmon mistook the day and Mr Gatwood here took advantage of it.'

'Have you got his statement?'

'Yes, sir.' Cobbold waved it.

'Right, put him in your car and take him to the office.'

'Yes, sir.' Cobbold took a determined grip of Gatwood's elbow and led him away.

'But I didn't do it,' Gatwood pleaded over his shoulder. 'Really, you've made a mistake.'

Cobbold bundled him unceremoniously out of the door. Bob turned to Superintendent Day.

'Finish up here, Bruce, then join us back at the office. Come on, Leo.'

Leo spun the car out of the drive and headed back towards the village.

'Got the bastard,' said Bob with deep satisfaction.

'It's a nice feeling.'

'It is that. I'll tell you now, I got a bit worried about this one a few days ago.'

'So did I. Office?'

'Yes. We'll have just a few more words with fatty Gatwood before we exercise our powers of arrest.'

He relaxed back into his seat and looked around at the passing countryside with appreciation. 'Bloody lovely country round here, you know,' he said.

They sat Gatwood in the interrogation chair facing the desk in Bob's office. Sergeant Cobbold stood beside him, Bob and Leo behind the desk.

Gatwood was sweating profusely. Partly the heat, partly his evident fear. Bob kept him waiting as he read through the statement Cobbold had just taken from him. When he looked up his face was stony. He tapped the statement.

'According to this, you went into Salmon's garage for petrol four days after the murder . . .'

'Yes, sir.' Gatwood rubbed his hands anxiously together.

'. . . and you got into conversation with him about the murder?'

'Everyone was talking about it . . .'

'. . . and he casually mentioned that on the night of the murder you and he were together because that was the night of your breakdown on the Ipswich-Felixstowe road.'

'That's right, sir.'

'You knew he'd made a mistake about the day but you encouraged him because you realized that would give you a perfect alibi?'

'Yes, sir.'

'You're saying you didn't plan this. In fact it was he who brought the subject up and you just went along with it.'

'Well, yes, sir . . . I didn't see anything wrong with it at the time . . . I couldn't say where I really was so . . .'

'Gatwood, you're a bloody liar.'

'No, sir . . .' Gatwood shivered, his tongue flickered round his lips.

'I'll tell you what happened,' said Bob, 'you went to the meeting at the Temple but you slipped out before the end. You picked up Joy Prentiss on the road and you killed her. After that you went home as if nothing had happened. A few days later you were at the garage and suddenly realized that if you could confuse Salmon as to the date of your breakdown he would give you a perfect alibi. He fell for it and sometime later you went into his office and stole the job card showing the correct date. No doubt you've burnt it since. What about that for a theory, Gatwood?'

Gatwood's mouth hung open. He made motions of speech but it was several seconds before he became audible. The officers waited.

'It's not true. I didn't kill her. I told you the truth . . . honestly I did . . .'

'Honestly?' Bob grinned with his mouth. 'You don't know the meaning of the word, mate. Take him outside, Sergeant Cobbold, and keep an eye on him.'

When they had left Bob loosened his tie an inch and relaxed. 'Beautiful,' he said, 'bloody beautiful.'

'You were a bit hard on him, weren't you?' Leo asked.

'No more than he'll likely get in court. I had to be sure what he'd say.'

Superintendent Day knocked and entered. 'All tidied up, sir?' he said.

'Very nearly,' Bob replied. 'All we've got to do now is make an arrest.'

'Sir?'

'Yes, Leo?'

'Do we keep our promise to Carrie Fuller?'

Bob hesitated. 'Yes.' he said finally.

Leo telephoned her before they left the office.

A few moments later they pulled up on the forecourt of the garage. Salmon was working on a car in the service bay. There was no sign of Mrs Salmon or Paul Spender.

'Leo, go and get the last three months' job cards from the office,' said Bob, as he got out of the car.

Leo disappeared into the office as Salmon came out on to the forecourt to greet them.

Carrie Fuller pulled up in her car on the opposite side of the road and poked a discreet telephoto lens at them.

'Where's Paul Spender?' asked Bob, as Salmon walked slowly towards them a monkey wrench in one hand and an oily rag in the other.

Salmon cocked an ear to the wind. 'That's him coming now,' he said. The harsh sound of the powerful motorcycle was obviously close.

Bob pointed to another machine leaning against the side of the service bay. 'Isn't that his?'

Salmon looked. 'Oh, yes. He just repaired one, he's giving it a test run. You want to see him again then?'

'Both of you,' said Bob, as Paul Spender rode on to the forecourt and sat astride the coughing machine, staring at them, 'but specially you, mate.'

'Oh?' Salmon looked wary. Day moved in beside him.

'Roy Salmon, I am arresting you for the murder of Joy Louise Prentiss. You need not say anything . . .'

Salmon swung the monkey wrench upwards and caught Day on the face. He went down backwards, blood gushing from his nose.

Bob jumped forward but Salmon brought his knee up into his stomach with sickening force and pushed him aside. Across the road Carrie hit her horn.

Leo ran out of the office just in time to see Salmon smash Paul Spender off the motorcycle with a single backward blow of his hand. He dropped the pile of job cards he was carrying and ran towards him.

Salmon leapt astride the machine and gunned it forward at Leo who dived to one side to avoid being hit, rolling sideways across the concrete. He got to his feet and ran across to the service bay where Spender's cycle was lying.

Carrie ripped her car across the road to the forecourt where Bob was staggering to his feet. Leo screamed past them on Spender's machine, following Salmon who was heading through the village towards the river.

Bob staggered into the passenger seat of Carrie's car and they shot off after the two motorcycles.

Salmon drove out of the village at a wild speed and set the machine at a suicide angle as he negotiated the first long bend.

Ray Colville, stuttering along towards the village, just had time to wrench his steering wheel to the left and push the nose of his ancient saloon into the hedge before Salmon was upon him. He heard the screech of metal as the motorcycle glanced off his rear wing. Somehow Salmon kept control and had no sooner passed than Leo, riding only a fraction more steadily, screamed past. Colville crossed himself and started to open the door to get out of his car. He rapidly closed it again as Carrie, tyres squealing on the bend, bore down on him.

Salmon scarcely reduced speed as he turned left at the end of the road and headed past the Orton estate towards the river.

When he reached the rutted track that led to the foreshore he was forced to slow and Leo, on a lighter machine, began to close the gap. Behind them, Carrie, driving fast and with style, ignored the ruts in the rough track and, indifferent to the effect on her car's suspension, managed to close on both of them.

Bob, already sick from the blow to the stomach, clung grimly to his seat as the car bucketed and jolted in high-speed pursuit.

Salmon turned left along the foreshore and, taking advantage of the firm sand, opened a gap on Leo. They raced for four miles beside the river with Salmon always pulling ahead. By the time the first partly constructed buildings of the outer limits of the Felixstowe Dock area were in sight he had a lead of nearly a mile.

Then he made a mistake. He chose the river side of a huge baulk of rotting timber and ran into thin mud. His machine slid from under him and skittered across the mud flat; he followed in a whirl of arms and legs. He pushed himself to his feet almost before he had stopped sliding and manhandled the heavy machine back on to the firm sand, but by the time he had kicked it back into life and set off again Leo was within a hundred yards of him with Carrie not far behind.

Ahead of him a lorry was tipping rubbish, filling up the mud flats for further development. He carved his way up through the piles of rubble and down the rough slope on the far side.

He was facing a concrete road in the course of construction. To his left a huge pre-mix concrete lorry was disgorging its load into the next prepared section of the road, surrounded by a bevy of workmen. They looked up as he turned right and accelerated hard along the already completed road, through an area of partly built warehouses.

Leo had trouble crossing the rubbish tip and had lost another fifty yards by the time he emerged on to the concrete road. Ahead of him Salmon rounded a bend to see a huge articulated lorry loaded with bricks completely blocking his path as the driver manoeuvred to reverse on to a building site. He braked hard and swung right, straight through the open front of a warehouse. Carpenters and electricians jumped for their life as the two motorcycles roared through, scattering tools and boxes in their path.

As they emerged from the building Salmon found that both ahead of him and to the left his way was blocked by a wire fence. He turned right, up the side of the warehouse and back to the concrete road. To the right, the road was still blocked by the articulated lorry, so he turned back the way he had come and opened up the throttle.

Carrie had been unable to negotiate the rubble pile in her car and had skidded to a stop in front of it. She and Bob scrambled up through the rubbish and ran to the ramp down to the concrete road. They could already see the motorcycles screaming towards them in the distance.

Behind them, the driver of the dumper truck, having completed his task, drove towards the road. Seeing the oncoming motorcycles he stopped in confusion, blocking the ramp.

Salmon, travelling fast, was only fifty yards from the ramp when the truck blocked it. He decelerated and braked hard but the speed was too great to control. Forced to go straight on, his front wheel hit the wet concrete at more than sixty miles an hour and stuck.

His body was shot forward off the machine, it turned in the air and his back struck the lip of the huge rotating bucket of the pre-mix concrete lorry. The body seemed to hang on the lip of the bucket for a moment, then fell in slow motion, face down into the wet concrete.

Leo, with the advantage of an extra hundred yards to stop in, pulled up beside Bob and Carrie. All three stared as the workmen pulled Salmon's body out of the concrete. Leo took his hands from the handlebars and rubbed them together. He was shaking badly. He looked at Bob.

'Thought it was a nice day for a ride,' he said, his voice cracking slightly.

Bob didn't sound too steady either. 'Got a licence to ride that thing, son?' he asked.

Carrie laid down her camera and cuddled Leo's head against her shoulder.

'Wouldn't like to do a re-run would you, dear,' she asked, 'in case the pictures don't come out?'

THIRTEEN

'Sweet or dry?'

'Whatever you got. I'm not fussy.'

'Very well then.' The Chief Constable poured sherry into minuscule glasses and handed one to Bob who was sitting at ease in a leather armchair. 'To a job well done,' he said.

'Thanks,' said Bob, and drained his glass at one gulp.

Colonel Boulton sat at his expansive desk and lit up his pipe. He cast a benign eye on Bob through the resulting smoke cloud.

'How are you feeling now?' he asked.

'Fine. Bruce Day got the worst of it, a poke on the nose can be bloody . . . pretty painful.'

'Nothing broken though, I'm told?'

'No, he'll survive. He was back at work this morning.'

The Chief Constable chewed the stem of his pipe and relaxed into his chair. 'His attempt at flight condemned him of course but . . . I suppose there can be no doubt that Salmon was the murderer?'

Bob jiggled the empty glass between his fingers. 'No. We can prove he did it. See, he knew the girl had a row with Paul Spender because Spender worked for him, so it didn't take much to work out that she'd be coming home alone when she was on late shift. He had a bit of luck bumping into Gatwood who was also looking for an alibi and having set that up he destroyed the job card. His wife's statement fitted as well because she thought he was working on the night of the murder.'

'Mmmm.' Colonel Boulton consulted the ceiling. 'Circumstantial though, isn't it?'

Bob leaned forward and placed his empty glass rather pointedly on the desk. 'You'll be getting a copy of the full report of course, as soon as we have it ready. You'll see that the lab found fibres from the dead girl's clothing in his car. Also the type of oil and the bootmark found on her clothes matches his boot size and oil deposit on the boots he was wearing when he died. Apart from that the seminal and pubic hair samples match and of course he fits the description of the other unsolved sexual assaults in the area in the last year or so. I'd say we had enough evidence to sink a battleship even before we start thinking about the fact that he lied his head off to us, then had it on his toes when we tried to arrest him.'

'Ah, yes, of course. I wasn't aware of those details. Well, a very satisfactory conclusion.'

'A bit messy at the end. I prefer to take my prisoners alive.'

'That was regrettable of course. I suppose the cynical would say that justice was done and we were saved the cost of a trial.'

'Yeah.' Bob squinted across at the sherry bottles standing on top of a dearwood cabinet. 'Was that sweet or dry I had?' he asked innocently.

'Dry . . . would you care for another?'

'Well,' said Bob, 'since you've asked . . .'

Whilst Bob paid his courtesy call on the Chief Constable, Leo held the fort at the village hall, supervising the run-down of the inquiry office. Since Salmon would not be coming to trial there remained only the chore of the final report which they could complete with the assistance of Day, Cobbold and Worthington in a couple of weeks.

Leo had a strong feeling of anticlimax following the hectic events of the previous day and found his attention wandering somewhat. He was looking forward to the weekend. They planned to return to London on the Friday night and take the weekend off before tackling the report.

He settled himself in Bob's chair and began to sort out statements for use in the report. A few minutes later Sergeant Cobbold brought in Mrs Salmon. She seemed calm and cool, cold acceptance masked her face. She handed him a plain postcard with an address printed on it.

'I thought you'd want this,' she said.

'You're leaving?'

'Wouldn't you?'

'Yes.'

'I shall be staying with my mother.'

'Will you come back eventually?'

'No.'

'What about the business?'

'I'll leave young Paul to manage it for me. That way I keep the freehold and provide myself with an income.'

'I see,' Leo felt ill at ease. There was a practical streak in this woman that was almost inhuman.

'I almost told you, you know,' she said, as she stood to leave, 'that day when I met you in the Haywain. I was almost drunk enough to tell you. We all have our weaknesses. I suppose an occasional drink is mine.'

'You knew then?'

'No. I knew that he was impotent. I knew he hated himself for it and I knew he was capable of violence. I knew a job card was missing for the day before the murder and that he used that job as an alibi. I knew he had lied to you . . .' She shook her head, 'but I could not believe that I'd made such a mistake as to marry a man capable of murder.'

'Mrs Salmon, it is my belief that given the right circumstances we're all capable of murder. You have nothing to reproach yourself about.'

She hesitated briefly at the door. 'I don't feel guilty,' she said, 'it's just that this whole thing is an untidy mess . . . it offends me.'

She was gone. Leo stared at the door. He wondered how he could ever have brought himself to make love to her.

They held the party on the Thursday night, having commandeered the saloon bar of the Haywain for the purpose. They had used over fifty officers in the course of the inquiry and all were present, crowding the room, drinking hard, talking fast and loud. Tobacco smoke hung in a grey cloud between the tallest heads and the low-beamed ceiling.

Tom and Rita Stack and Anne Partridge were all serving behind the bar non-stop, shouting to make themselves heard above the noise. The Chief Constable and his wife were holding court in one corner with Bob Staunton. In another Leo was with Carrie Fuller, the tumult around them giving privacy in the crowd.

'I discovered something you might be intersted in,' Leo shouted in her ear.

'Another scoop?'

'No. The reason Mrs Prentiss has her hooks into Orton.'

'Yes?'

'He told us he'd laid Joy. She was a virgin apparently, didn't want to be mauled about by one of the local lads on her first time . . . at least that's his story. Her mother must have found out somehow after the murder.'

'Oh hell!'

'That a good enough reason?'

'I'd say so. How'd you like to discover that your daughter had been seduced by a middle-aged fake magician?'

Leo shrugged, 'Seems a bit drastic.'

'These are pretty basic people. Pride carries a high price.'

'Talking of high prices, how's business?'

'Fabulous. I'm a rich lady.'

'You know what they say . . . the devil looks after his own!'

She stuck her tongue out at him. 'Watch it,' she said laughing, 'I might hex you.'

Roger Cobbold forced his way through the throng and appeared beside them. 'Can I have a word, sir?' he asked.

Carrie touched Leo lightly on the arm. 'See you around, dear,' she said, and eased herself away towards the bar.

'Yes, Roger?'

'Well, I'm sorry to bring it up . . . it's those samples you took, the hairs, the entry in the exhibit book is still blank, where they came from, you know.' Cobbold seemed anxious.

Leo laughed. 'Forget it. I'll delete the entry tomorrow. We don't need it now, do we?'

'Well no . . .'

'So don't worry. I'll square it up.'

'The Chief Constable finds things like that, you see . . .'

'Maybe he won't this time but if he does, blame it on me.'

The Chief Constable and his wife left at half past nine and thereafter the celebrations picked up momentum. A noisy scuffle in a corner ended when an embarrassed Crime Squad officer was pushed up on to a chair and, having obtained a modicum of quiet, sang a gentle love song in a passably good baritone voice.

He was cheered down and another took his place. After a while and a few more rounds of drinks Superintendent Day was coerced up on to the chair and recited a faintly bawdy monologue which was received with rapturous applause. They turned their attention to Bob Staunton and he obliged with several rousing cockney songs that set the floor bouncing.

They then came for Leo. 'I can't sing,' he protested.

The chant went up.

'Sing, sing or show your ring!'

'I would lads, honestly, but . . .'

'Sing, sing or show your ring!'

'Look . . .'

'Grab his pants . . .'

'Get 'em off . . .'

Leo struggled furiously, 'All right, all right.' They pushed him up on to the chair. 'A few jokes.' They groaned.

'I hear that Sir Ivor Cutt, the famous spare parts surgeon, is giving a ball tonight.'

Groans and boos. 'Get 'em off.'

'Right then. Notes from our court reporter, 'police raided a shop today and charged the proprietor with selling dirty books. Giving evidence Inspector Wilf Filth said, "In places the dust was an inch thick".'

'Get him off . . .'

'Don't call us, we'll call you. . . .'

'Patience, lads, I'm just warming up. A man appeared in court today charged with stealing a potted chrysanthemum. He pleaded not guilty and said, "It's a plant, and the pot's not mine either".'

Laughter mixed with boos and catcalls.

'Okay . . . you don't want that . . . what *do* you want?'

'Give us the dirty ones . . .'

'So that's it, you want the blue jokes do you? Right, you lucky people, here we go . . .'

He escaped twenty minutes later with his trousers intact, and the party settled down to some steady drinking. Leo circulated among them, soaking up the friendship and brotherhood in success. He noticed Carrie leaning over the bar counter, holding Anne in close conversation, her hand resting on Anne's arm, apparently by accident.

By three in the morning there were only about a dozen left, surrounding Bob and listening with owlish seriousness as he recounted the story of one of his earlier murder inquiries. Bob was holding his drink well, enunciating clearly and holding the thread of his story. Leo felt very drunk.

Tom Stack joined the group around Bob. There was no sign of Rita or of Carrie and Anne. Leo felt suddenly very tired. He pulled himself to his feet with difficulty and headed uncertainly towards his bedroom. He had trouble negotiating his bedroom door. Once inside, the room started to spin. He crashed face down on to the bed.

The following afternoon the train sped them towards London. Bob seemed none the worse for his late night but Leo felt badly hung over.

'You know something that puzzles me?' asked Bob.

'No?'

'Why Salmon took it into his head to run . . . I mean he couldn't hope to get clean away for ever, could he? Married man, business and all that. No passport . . .'

'He was mentally unstable.'

'You don't look good.'

'A bit fragile today.'

'You did a good job, mate.'

'Thanks.'

'Want to come with me next time?'

'If you're asking.'

'That's it, then.'

Silence as they stared out at the summer countryside flashing past.

'I was glad to get this one under my belt . . . my thirteenth, you know.'

Leo screwed up his eyes to focus on Bob.

'Are you superstitious then?' he asked.

'Of course,' said Bob, grinning. 'Aren't we all?'

A car was waiting for them at Liverpool Street Station and it took them to New Scotland Yard where they arrived just after six. Most of the offices were already empty. The Deputy Commander had waited for them and they joined him and some of the other senior officers in his room.

Leo had to listen as Bob recounted the story of the inquiry to this new and appreciative audience. After a while the Deputy Commander produced a bottle of whisky and it did Leo a lot of good.

At half past eight they went their separate ways. Leo hailed a taxi in Victoria Street. He intended to go straight home but the Deputy Commander's whisky had done its work. Leo had the taste.

Ten minutes later he was at Paula's Place. Paula was glad to see him. She had a double waiting by the time he reached the bar.

Mrs Prentiss was alone in her bedroom. Her movements were slow, careful. She took a small bottle from a bedside table and emptied its meagre contents into the palm of her hand. Skin and blood gouged from her victim's face, carefully scraped from beneath her fingernails and preserved.

She sat in front of her dressing table, the scrapings clutched in her hand, staring at her own reflection in the mirror. She rocked gently, side to side, mumbling words that were not of her native tongue.

As the tempo of the words increased, her whole body became taut with self-induced tension. Her pupils dilated and bitter hatred scarred her face. Her lips pulled back as if afeared of the gnashing teeth.

As she stared into the mirror she saw her image blur and another take its place. Powerful, ugly, naked, an obscene parody of the human form set on wings black as night.

Commander Orton was on his hands and knees on the floor of his study. On his desk were a number of books, open at different pages. He consulted them frequently as he chalked markings between the concentric circles he had drawn on the wood block floor. He finished his work and stepped out of the circle with a sigh of relief, reaching for the garland of entwined garlic on his desk.

At that moment he felt the compulsion. Instead of the garland he picked up the sharp, bone-handled knife. For a moment his face contorted as he fought to regain control, then he moved to the door with leaden, puppet-like steps, the knife clutched in his hand.

He walked slowly across the deserted hallway and up the wide staircase. The portraits of his ancestors long in their graves glared down at him, blind eyes tracing his path upwards. He walked to the end of the corridor, up a smaller flight of stairs into the servant's quarters.

His progress was unobserved in the empty house as he climbed the turret steps and emerged on to the roof. The moon was partially obscured by a wispy cloud. He moved forward inside the parapet at the front of the house until he was immediately above the circular drive.

He stared out across the moon-shadowed grounds of his estate. He saw but did not comprehend. A faint breeze ruffled his hair as he climbed up and stood swaying on the parapet. High though he was, the conifer tree that faced him across the drive was taller, reaching bulky arms out to its sides, head bowing acknowledgement to the wind.

As he stared, it seemed to him that the tree grew larger, blotting out the moon. It seemed a head formed, bulbous eyes, grooved forehead,